The
OWL,
the
RIVER
and the
VALLEY

The
OWL,
the
RIVER
and the
VALLEY

ARUPA PATANGIA KALITA

Translated by **MITRA PHUKAN**

PENGUIN BOOKS
An imprint of Penguin Random House

PENGUIN BOOKS

Penguin Books is an imprint of the Penguin Random House group of companies
whose addresses can be found at global.penguinrandomhouse.com

Published by Penguin Random House India Pvt. Ltd
4th Floor, Capital Tower 1, MG Road,
Gurugram 122 002, Haryana, India

First published in Penguin Books by Penguin Random House India 2025

ISBN 9780143466109

Typeset in Adobe Caslon Pro by Manipal Technologies Limited, Manipal
Printed at Thomson Press India Ltd, New Delhi

www.penguin.co.in

To
My son, Ayanmoni (Rajarshi)
(Arupa Patangia Kalita)

For
Meenaxi Phukan, thank you for all the encouragement
over the years.
(Mitra Phukan)

Contents

Translator's Note

A brief background of the history of Assam, and the language in which these stories were originally written, would perhaps be in order here. Our past and our understanding of it shape our present in so many different ways. Assam, the land of blue hills and a Red River, the Brahmaputra, is situated in India's north-east region. In a land of multiple ethnicities and tongues, Assamese is the language within the north-eastern region of India. It has some of the highest number of native speakers and a script that dates back many centuries.

Among the early known writings were the Charyapadas—Buddhist songs composed between the eighth and tenth centuries. There are also poets such as Hema Saraswati (late thirteenth century) and Madhab Kandali (fourteenth century). And there was Srimanta Sankardev (1449–1568), the saint poet of Assam, whose luminous compositions in praise of the Almighty are considered beautiful works in varied genres. There are the effulgent lyrics, the *borgeets*, or great songs, set to music in praise of the lord. There is the Kirtan Ghosa, which is recited and chanted before home shrines even today. There are prose writings, and there are the *bhaonas*—the plays—which were mainly written to propagate the Vaishnavite faith known as Ek Saran Naam Dharma, of which Srimanta Sankardev was the founder. These writings, a part of the Bhakti Movement, took religion to the people through literature, music and dance.

Several of these *naams* and other hymns find their way into the works of contemporary writers, so ingrained are they in the minds of the people of the valley. In this collection, too, there are occasional references to these beautiful hymns at appropriate times.

As with most other literature, the appearance of prose in general, and fiction in particular, in the form of brief stories and novels, was a progression.

Among the first influences on Assamese fiction was *Orunodoi* (1846), the journal of the Baptist missionaries, who also set up the first printing press in Sibsagar, eastern Assam. Initial stories were mostly Christian parables, fables and moral tales from Indian and Greek stories in a rudimentary short story format, sowing the seeds for more secular writings later. It was during what is known today as the Jonaki Era that fiction in Assamese began to flower. *Jonaki* was a very popular and influential literary journal that flourished between 1889 and 1903. Many writers thrived during the decades of its existence and brought in a richness of content in the genres of poetry, lyrics, drama, novels, short stories and essays. It brought in romanticism as well, across genres.

Lakhminath Bezbaroa (1864–1938) first collated folk tales in the volume *Burhi Air Xadhu*, or *Grandmother's Tales*. He was also a fiction writer of distinction and is often referred to as the Father of the Assamese Short Story.

Early fiction writers included Sarat Chandra Goswami, Dandinath Kalita, Mitradev Mahanta and the well-known historian Suryya Kumar Bhuyan. Others made their mark on different genres, notable among them being Jyoti Prasad Agarwala (1903–51), the dramatist, lyricist, essayist and pathbreaking film-maker. The writers of the Romantic Era had, in their stories, a combination of romantic love as well as a reformative mission, to correct the wrongs that they perceived in the social set-up of the time.

The next important era concerning Assamese fiction is the Awahon Age (founded in 1932), once again named after a very popular literary magazine. Along with romanticism, the seeds of realism were sown at this time. The writers and thinkers of the time were now exposed to the works of world literature as never before, as well as the literature of various Indian languages, especially Bangla. Foreign education mingled with a strong sense of rootedness in their culture and created a syncretic and unique Assamese literary tradition.

The mores and traditions of their birthplace and motherland, which often formed the backdrop to these stories and the motivation, often, for characters behaving in particular ways, gave a depth and uniqueness to them. It remained strongly universal in appeal.

Just as the Second World War itself changed the world, Assamese fiction, both long and short, after 1940s, changed irrevocably in theme, mood, style, use of language and many other aspects. The ferment of war, of the freedom movement, brought new ideas and new ways of looking at things. People moved out of the villages, travelled the country and also, to an extent, the world, either as students or professionals. Gradually the area itself became more urbanized. All of this was naturally reflected in the writings of the time. Gradually, various journals came up which reflected the changing themes and styles of fiction, which began to be seen as a wonderful vehicle for putting across ideas through the medium of a story and fiction. The genre now went beyond romanticism, to realism. During the fifties of the twentieth century, Marxism and Socialism were among the streams that influenced writers such as Saurav Kumar Chaliha. However, any good writer everywhere rises above '-isms'. The imperatives of plot and character that are employed to illustrate, unobtrusively, the theme inevitably create a world of their own. For at the core of all great literature is the '-ism' of humanism.

Fiction flourished through the decades with writers such as Mamoni Raisom Goswami, Birendra Kumar Bhattacharya, Homen Borgohain and Bhabendranath Saikia enriching the genre greatly. Historical events such as Partition and the creation of Bangladesh, and the war that took place in the neighbourhood of what was undivided Assam at the time, had a huge effect on the region. These events also echoed in the fiction of the times.

Assam went through a period of great turmoil and unrest during the years of the Assam Movement (1979–85), which degenerated into violence. Fear stalked the land, extortions, killings and kidnappings were common. Inevitably, many powerful, hard-hitting stories emerged at the time. Short stories and novels both, showed the effects of violence on the people and society, highlighting their sufferings. This violence is the backdrop in several of Arupa Patangia Kalita's stories, as well as in this selection.

Years ago, when I started my journey as a translator, one of my several worries was whether a translator had to be completely in sync with the mindset of the author she is translating in order to do justice to the work. Does everything, from the overall vision to the settings, from the characters to the style, from the political stance to the writer's take on gender relationships, for instance, have to mesh before the translation can be called at least a competent work?

Actually, over the years, I have found that all this does not really matter, thankfully! Since I translate fiction, both long and short, I find that as long as the story itself is engaging, and the characters are lifelike and believable, other things don't matter. Whether it is language or an understanding of character, as long as the story 'flows', the translator should have no problems. A completely distinctive skillset, different from that which is required for creative writing, is needed to be an empathetic translator. If the translator is also a writer herself, the first thing she has to do is set aside her own style, her own point of view, and enter the writer's mind.

It helps the translator to have at her disposal, rich and engrossing stories, such as those written by Arupa. She is a writer at the peak of her abilities, a writer whose imagination, command over language and power of observation are of a very high order. I have been a reader of Arupa's stories for decades now, and her thought-provoking fiction about the contemporary world around us today, in all its complexity, beauty and ugliness has never failed to move me. Her works have been translated into other languages, but the twelve stories in this collection have never been translated into English before. This effort was long overdue, because of the years we have spent reading each other's works. Her works are dense, richly layered, and very rooted to the land.

When discussing the project, both Arupa and I decided that she should pick out recently published stories where a woman should be a central character. This was to be a joint project between two women friends, one a writer and the other, a translator.

Arupa Patangia Kalita's works are realistic. Couched in a lyrical style, they read very well in the original and yet convey many thoughts and ideas within a single delineation of character and setting. The characters and incidents can very well be placed in the settings she describes. The characters are based on truth, even if they are imaginary. Their motivations, their emotions, and the chain of consequences that their actions bring about are all detailed with a clear vision, set in empathy.

Gender is an important construct in Arupa's stories, and I feel women would find themselves in many of the themes discussed—such as those of surrogacy or access to medical facilities for reproductive health services. *Rajmao: The Queen Mother* is just such a story. The story *Pani Gabhini Hol (The Water Is with Child)* was without doubt the most difficult to translate, as I knew it would be from my very first reading of it. It is a dense story, full of allusions which would be easily understood by people who read in Assamese and live in Assam. This allusiveness made it difficult to translate without going into footnotes and breaking the flow of the story. But even this was not the most difficult part of translating this story. It is the atmosphere, the evocativeness of the language, the vocabulary, the imagery. The title itself, the gentle, nuanced *Paani Gabhini Hol* translates badly into *The Water Is with Child*, which seems like quite a bald statement to make. These losses are what make translations always a kind of 'work in progress', even after the work is published after multiple revisions and sensitive edits.

Most of all, the difficulty arose in this story with the language itself, as it is extremely specific to its locale. The word *xattra*, for instance, is immediately understood by the Assamese, yet the concept, the richness of what it denotes' is difficult to put into another language. There is the sound of the *khol*, again specific to worship and there are the beautiful songs of worship penned by Srimanta Sankardev himself, which defy translation. For this story, I have given a few lines in the original, and the gist in English as a device to convey the meaning without meddling that the original.

Another difficulty in this particular story came from the fact that Assam, a land of huge rivers and many waterbodies, has numerous ways of describing both the water and the activities that abound on it. The story begins and ends with a journey across the river on a stormy night. On board is a girl going through the pangs of childbirth. The many ways in which the waters of the river are described, as well as the phrases and idioms that describe the boat journeying across it, are common in conversation, music and writings. They are easily understood in this land where water is present throughout the year, often submerging the land to such an extent that only water is visible to the human eye. But to bring these words across to another language proved a challenge. Yes, English is one of the most flexible languages, with the largest vocabulary. But when it comes to cultural, topographical and geographical phenomena specific to a particular land and its people, it becomes a challenge to put it across without interrupting the flow of the story.

When it comes to translating fiction, one of the most important things is the 'movement' of the story. Storytelling should not be interrupted by explanations. Ways must be found to incorporate explanations into the story without stopping its movement. It must seem natural, yet it must add to the meaning. This is always a challenge for any translator, and it was no less for this collection since the stories are so rooted in the culture and lifestyles of the people living in these valleys of Assam.

Besides, the author's vocabulary in these stories is sprinkled with colloquialisms and words which cannot be found in any dictionary, but which are, in the original, very apt. She uses a range of words that are culled from dialects of Assamese, or the spoken language. As the translator, it was not possible for me to find the exact word in English that would be appropriate there. I often had to put in the approximate meaning through a phrase, or even a couple of sentences.

There are the usual complexities of syntax and style. The syntax of Assamese sentences is very different from that of English, and as a translator, one has to be constantly aware of this. Multiple revisions are mandatory to catch the stiltedness that sometimes escapes on to the page. As for style, I always try, when translating, to forget my own style of writing, and try to follow, as closely as possible, the writer's own. Not always successfully, perhaps, but the attempt is always there.

Every one of the stories in this collection is firmly set, each in its own time and surroundings. Arupa Patangia Kalita's fictions are all vividly imagined. The settings for each story are relevant to the unfolding of the narrative, and often they are integral to the development of character. In *Xonxar Jatrat Anita (Anita's Journey Through Life)*, for instance, the protagonist, after numerous disappointments throughout her life, finds meaning and solace in the inanimate objects that surround her.

The characters in these stories are firmly set in real-life situations, mostly in contemporary Assam. They come from different socio-economic backgrounds. The common denominator of each of these women is that through all the hammering they receive at the hands of society and other individuals, they refuse to be cowed down. They rise again, choosing a path for themselves that brings them the most solace and peace.

In *Bhorduporor Aita* (*The Afternoon Grandmother*), for instance, the woman whose life revolves around her little family, especially her grandson, is suddenly elevated to the status of a Goddess.

And in *Malotir Xopon* (*Maloti's Dream*), the plot plays out incidents that actually do happen, in many ways, in urban centres across Assam.

In many of these stories, there is betrayal, of different kinds. Through force of circumstance and also sometimes through the weakness of the primary male character in their lives, the women are forced to change. Several have to become the sole breadwinner. At other times, in stories such as *Baghjori* (*The Reins*) the woman herself undergoes a transformation, so that she becomes the person she feared.

In *Koli Memor Jiyek* (*Daughter of the Dark Memsahib*), we see a story that sometimes played out in the tea gardens of Assam during the times of the British tea planters, and just after. Several well-known fictions and movies have been written and made in Assamese about those times. The culture in the vast tea estates of Assam and the ways of life of the different ethnicities are glimpsed in this beautifully etched story. The human cost of an unequal power equation, socially and economically, is sensitively delineated.

On occasion, the British planter would take a 'wife', a woman among the workers at the plantation itself, especially if his European wife and children were back in England.

Jot (*Tangle*) is the story of a woman who was so beautiful that anybody who saw her declared that she was fit to be the queen of a rich household. However, she was from a poor family; but she clung to this belief that she would be a rich man's wife—a person who would be smitten by her beauty.

These twelve stories show how relationships and circumstances can shape lives, for better or worse. The author explores situations and interactions to bring these changes to their logical conclusion. They may be satisfying or horrifying in different cases, but they are always coherent in the way they play out in the stories themselves.

Several of these stories have very intriguing titles. As a translator, I wished to keep their creativity and ability to grab the reader's attention intact, but it was difficult to put across the uniqueness of these titles. They are not, in the original Assamese, straightforward. They have an evocativeness that often brings to mind other sayings in the language or hints of other stories.

Manuhjoni Phesa Hol (*The Woman Who Became an Owl*), an attention-grabbing title, is about a woman abandoned by her husband, and left to bring up her children alone. Indeed, in life as in Arupa Patangia Kalita's stories, this theme of abandonment, either physically or through the husband becoming an addict of some kind, is a leitmotif. The 'truth' of the story lies in the way each woman deals with this, how she fends for herself and manages to care for her children.

Economics and the powerful way in which it plays out between human relationships are an undercurrent in many of these stories. Arupa Patangia Kalita is deeply humanist, and understandably, the theme of humanism runs as a dominant current through all her works. In *Halodhiya Hawai Sandal* (*The Yellow Flip-Flops*), this is shown very well. A wedding in a well-to-do family shows the regard that people who have good incomes get from others. Even their wives and children are accorded respect. However, the youngest brother and his wife do not have the same financial clout as the others and are treated with scorn and contempt.

Ghori-Koka Aita is the Assamese title of a story about the wife of a man who was extremely punctual. That this could become a burden on others, especially his wife, is depicted beautifully here. I have translated the title as *By the Clock*, and indeed, throughout the story, we seem to hear the ticking and the sonorous call of the large grandfather clock that dominates the wife's existence.

The title of the story, *Ausi Othoba Hausi* itself posed a challenge. I translated the title as it is, *Ausi or Hausi*, but within the story, I have explained the meaning and appropriateness of the words in a few sentences that I have tried to weave into the story itself.

Reading Arupa Patangia Kalita is always rewarding, as her numerous admirers will agree. It is hoped that a selection of her stories, in this translated volume, will bring the same satisfaction to readers through the medium of another language, English.

RAJMAO:
THE QUEEN MOTHER

(Originally published as 'Rajmao')

Certainly, their parents must have given these women a name. Those names were lost in the river of time. What indeed did they have that would allow them to hold their names firmly in their grasp? After extracting as much domestic toil from them, these girls were then sent off to the custody of some random person. The illusory bonds of a few children, the torture from husbands, and till the last journey on to the funeral pyre, this was all a familiar struggle. And through all this, was it possible to recollect their own names, their own identities? An unlikely thing.

The parents of this girl, too, had given her a name. Komola. She, too, was heavily burdened with domestic responsibilities in her parental home. Komola tended to the cows, looked after the ducks and hens, cooked the meals. She would take everybody's clothes and soak them with washing soda in boiling water. She would then take them to the river and clean them till they were sparkling white. At night, she would make paper bags.

Toiling unceasingly in a household that barely survived through numerous crises, Komola reached the age of twenty-three. Almost all her friends were already married. It was because of her mother's ill health that nobody had brought up the subject of Komola's marriage. After giving birth to five children, Komola's mother had become bedridden because of problems in her uterus. It was after her brother brought home a girl that Komola was given in marriage to Pobon Das.

The wedding celebrations were nothing much. Somehow, after the guests were served tea and biscuits once the wedding ceremony got over, she was sent off with a bed and a pair of clothes. She also carried with her a set of glass bowls that a wedding invitee had gifted her, a brass pitcher and, along with a bucket, a few other domestic necessities.

Pobon was a tree cutter. There were four others in his group. The five of them would take up contracts to cut down trees. There was no dearth of work. Every day, there were reasons for trees to be felled. If at one place the road had to be widened, in another, the yard needed to be cleared in order to raise a new house. And during the season of storms, the five of them, the Ponso Pandob as they were ironically called after the heroes of the Mahabharata, were on a different plane altogether.

Certainly, their income was adequate. If nothing else, they could meet their domestic expenses and get along. But then, what could one say? The Ponso Pandob were alcoholics addicted to country liquor. They gathered at a liquor den every night. Gradually, they were all becoming sick. They took no notice of what others said. The five of them chopped down trees, received their money and drank.

It was to this cohort of the five cronies that Komola came as a wife. Upon her arrival, she noticed that everything was a complete mess. The so-called dwelling that she came into could hardly be called a house. There was a large heap of earthworm castings inside the house. There were large gaps in the flimsy walls, caused by his staggering steps. In a corner of the yard was a heap of bottles.

In just about six weeks, Komola completely transformed that house which even spirits would have shunned earlier. She threw herself and her work-hardened body into shaping Pobon's bit of land, about a *kotha*-and-a-half of it. She would wield her tools, machete and knife, broom and brush even under a light at night. When the Ponso Pandobs came and sipped tea served by Komola, they commented, 'This woman has completely changed the look of the house, *dei*.'

The 'completely changed house', the intoxication from the newness of physical intimacy, the constant proximity of a hardworking woman, the promises and pledges that Komola extracted from Pobon kept him away from the liquor den for a while. He would give his share of the group's total income to Komola.

Komola's domestic setup was now quite satisfactory.

But how long could this continue? Pobon began to frequent the liquor den again. He and Komola had in the meantime become parents to a girl. Komola began to work as a helper in other peoples' homes, carrying the baby with her.

And then, Pobon fell very seriously ill. His body swelled up. All that liquor had affected his liver. The doctor declared that unless he gave up this habit, he would die.

But after staying away from liquor for a while, he started again.

Even then, things continued somehow. The little girl, too, was growing up. When her period started, Komola managed to borrow money from others and celebrated it ritually. Komola had had her admitted into a school. She was moving ahead in her studies, clearing her exams annually. Next year, she would move on to wearing the school uniform of mekhela sador that senior girl students wore, leaving behind the junior school uniform of skirts.

In the meanwhile, Pobon had somewhat controlled his drinking, but had not fully given it up. He had once been a very fit person . . . that was probably why he hadn't yet become an invalid. Even now, it was he who had to lop off those branches from the trees which had no foothold. The income from these was now coming home.

Like her mother, the daughter was capable of hard work. Even at that young age, she could serve up a full meal of rice, duck, chicken and other items. Komola could now breathe somewhat easy. When she returned home after work, she would find the water buckets filled up, food cooked and the washed clothes brought in after drying and folded neatly away. After seeing to these domestic chores, her daughter would sit to study. Komola's heart would fill with emotion when she saw her daughter with her books and papers. No matter what, Komola would see to it that her daughter would pursue her studies. One day, Komola's daughter would be a teacher. Mastorni Baideo—she would be addressed as an elder sister, as an honorific added to Mastorni, teacher. Stroking her daughter's head, Komola would ask her daughter, 'You have all your books and stuff, don't you?'

Without looking up from the books she was studying, Komola's daughter Purobi would say, 'Yes Mai, I have them. I have them all. Have you had any food yet?'

Gradually, Komola's name began to die out. She was now Purobi's mother.

Pobon had developed a bit of a tremor in his hands. It was all due to the liquor. Of the group of five, the Ponso Pandobs, two had already departed for the other world. Purobi's mother decided that she would not let him go to fell trees anymore. Pobon was getting weaker in front of her very eyes. She would get him a job that would allow him to sit and work. If she sold their goats and added the amount she had saved, she would have some money in hand. She would be able to manage something. Her heart would quake when she saw the way his hand trembled even when he took a tumbler of water. These very hands would once climb those huge trees that seemed to touch the skies. She could barely think straight. Seeing the man she loved in this condition, she was shaken. His only fault was his addiction to liquor. Besides this, he had no other flaw. Even when he was intoxicated, he would simply come home and go to sleep. Not once had he raised his hand on her. Unlike so many other men, he did not have an eye for other women either. He was a quiet, peaceful man.

Enough, she decided. There had been enough tree cutting. No more. She would find a way. If nothing else, she would hawk chickpeas and other snacks near the school. She went secretly to the holy man, the Babaji who sat under the banyan tree and paid obeisance after proffering him a ritual offering of tamol paan, areca nuts and betel leaf. She told the Babaji everything, openly. Babaji screamed out loud, and informed her that Saturn, the evil Shani himself, was casting his malevolent eye on her husband. He had displeased the forest deity. After all he had massacred so many living trees. He had sinned, he had committed a very grave sin.

On her way back from the Babaji, she bought a bucket to soak the chickpeas, which she would use for the snacks she planned to sell.

The evil eye of Shani that Babaji had told her about crashed on her as though a tree had been felled on her head. The weight of it bore down on her in such a way that there was no way any roots, branches or leaves could sprout.

On the same day, Purobi's father set forth with his two friends. In his hands were a machete and a rope. After the five-member gang lost two of its members, their spirits too were low. On top of that, here was this news about Pobon leaving this job for good. They were now completely dejected. Besides, they could not fell trees with just two pairs of hands. The other two began to think about going off to Kerala or Delhi in search of work. People were migrating to other places in droves. One just had to tell them, and the people from the agencies would come and fetch them from their homes. The train and bus fares were borne by them. Some people had got together and without going through the middlemen and contractors, had taken the help of those who were already working there, and had gone off. In short, people were leaving, and their families were provided for.

Before leaving for work, Pobon and the remaining men from the group of five were sitting in Purobi's mother's courtyard and discussing all this. Purobi had served them tea with malpuas, fritters made with flour, in the courtyard itself. They enjoyed their sugary milky tea and the soft malpuas sweetened with molasses, which had puffed up very temptingly. The three of them then left.

They walked out of the house, true. But when Pobon finally returned, he had to be carried back. They had gone to Dr Saikia's house. He was one of those people who had been in this town for a long time. His spacious house was on a large plot of two *bigha*s. There were several coconut trees in front of the house. The doctor had planted them when he had bought this land. The plants flourished and were now very tall. At that point, the bridge was a wooden one and the road was a dirt track. A concrete bridge replaced the wooden one, the road was widened accordingly, and the electricity wires approached nearer. Dr Saikia's coconut trees touched the electric wires. When it was windy or rainy, the green fronds of the coconut trees would touch the wires and emit sparks. The doctor had been trying to get Pobon and his friends to come to trim the trees. There were ten of them. He would give a thousand rupees for each one. His neighbours were constantly complaining. One said of them said that the TV had broken down beyond repair. Another complained that their fridge had gone.

It was decided to cut the trees taking all safety measures, Pobon would take on the main task, the other two would remain on the ground and operate the ropes. The doctor had already got the authorities to suspend electric supply to their area for a while.

Eight coconut trees were felled without incident. Something happened to Pobon while chopping the ninth one. Maybe he grew dizzy, maybe his hands shook, perhaps his foot slipped, or maybe his vision grew foggy. He tumbled to the ground.

One of Pobon's legs got multiple fractures. The doctor arranged for treatment at the government hospital, besides helping out himself. It was because of this treatment that he could at least hobble again. This man, who had once been striding around, was now a cripple. He got a new name. Pobon Lengera. Pobon the Lame. Pobon the Cripple.

How could Purobi's mother watch the man lying in bed all the time? Day or night, through the drone of mosquitoes, in the murky nocturnal darkness? It would actually be better if he sat outside and showered abuses on her. She would be at peace then. It was as though she was sharing a home with a silent corpse. She somehow managed to keep the home going. Her job at Professor Baideo's house was keeping her afloat. She paid her more than the going rate. Even so, she was finding it increasingly difficult to make ends meet.

One day, Purobi came to her and informed her that she would not study any more. She would work instead. Komola sat in the corner of the verandah and wailed uncontrollably. What could she do? How could she look on at the silent man's agony? It wasn't just his lame leg. Numerous other illnesses had taken a huge toll on his health. Every now and then, he would swell up from his eyelids to his ankles. All her earnings were being spent on his medicines. The other day, Purobi had had a dizzy spell in school. How could a young girl remain standing after a frugal meal of puffed rice and tea? Her daughter would have to be educated, her man too would have to have proper medical treatment.

She was pondering on all this when some of her friends prepared to go to Delhi. They would work as domestic helps there. Barun, who had already had the experience of working there, would arrange everything. After his wife died, Barun had placed his two daughters in the care of his wife's brother and begun working in a factory in Delhi. He came home annually. His appearance was much better. His two daughters were studying. She saw them going to their English-medium school on a battery-operated e-ricksha, wearing the school uniform of skirt and blouse.

The pay was twelve thousand a month, and it was the usual domestic work. She would receive ten thousand in hand. The agency would get their cut of two thousand.

Komola prepared to leave. She had expected her husband to say, 'Don't go.' She thought Purobi would weep. None of this happened. The father and daughter told her to go instead.

The woman who would always be seen hurrying from one place to another with such speed that the pebbles on her path would scatter here and there, suddenly disappeared. People saw a lame man leaning on his daughter's shoulders and hobbling to the crossroads in the evenings. By the light of a tiny earthen oil lamp, he would set up his stall and sell chickpeas. People would sometimes ask the girl about her mother. Gradually, they stopped enquiring. If somebody persisted with their questions, she would tell them about the money that her mother was sending home. However, she did not divulge a certain matter.

There had been no news of her mother for a year. The money, too, had stopped coming in. The last time she had sent home money, it had been quite a large sum. After that, there had been nothing.

It became known that the woman named Komola had gone to Delhi to work and was now lost. The money that the father made from his fried chickpea and boiled egg stall somehow kept him and his daughter from starving. Purobi spent the large amount her mother had sent them very frugally. Who could tell what would happen to her father? That corpus was her source of strength. It gave her courage. Certainly, the quantity was dwindling, but it hadn't yet been used up completely.

Gradually, though, the last of the money was spent.

Purobi began to work as a domestic helper after returning from school. Just as the corpus had diminished, Purobi's memories of her mother, too, were beginning to fade away. She sometimes forgot that she had had a mother at all. Her weeping on her bed at night, too, began to subside over time.

But then one day Komola returned.

There was a lot of talk about this woman who had returned after such a long time.

. . . She's brought back a huge amount of money it seems!

. . . Haven't you seen her looks?

. . . Have you seen the clothes she wears?

. . . As soon as she returned, she hired a taxi and took her husband to the Medical College in Guwahati.

. . . She's making a concrete house. The roofing material has already been brought into the compound.

. . . She's going to put up a shop for her husband in front of the house. The daughter will be sent to college. She herself will open a tailoring shop, it seems. She's already bought sewing machines. Not one, but two. If her husband is not cured with the Medical College treatment, she'll take him outside the state.

All of this was said in the open, under the light of the sun in broad daylight. The rest of it was said in secretive whispers, in groups that gathered under the trees, and in front of their bamboo gates in furtive undertones.

. . . It appears that things are not what they seem. She was the mistress of a Punjabi man. I've heard that he is very wealthy. She was practically buried in riches. She lived in the red-light area. It seems she got ten thousand rupees each time.

. . . Ten thousand? What's so special about what she has to offer? Ours are no different, are they?

Saying this, those women would stuff the ends of their saris and mekhela sadors into their mouths and giggle.

Purobi's mother, Pobon's wife was completely buried by words spoken out loud in the broad light of day, in the middle of different kinds of conversation. People would also like to visit and watch Pobon's dilapidated house take on a new look. Half brick walls topped with plastered reed replaced the old walls of split bamboo matting. Several carpenters and masons would always be at work every day. The house was coming up quickly. Two rooms were being built near the road in front as well: Pobon's shop and Purobi's mother's sewing school. People calculated that the cost of all this was not in the hundreds, it was all running into thousands. The men who were working there said that they got their wages at the end of each day.

These days, Komola stood in line and withdrew money from the ATM. Sometimes, she would go to the bank. It was true that many people had left home to work elsewhere. But nobody returned this wealthy. Leave alone hawking fried chickpeas under the silk cotton tree at the crossroads, her husband Pobon hardly left the house. As soon as he went out, he had to listen to many comments and was asked questions. Purobi was still going to school. She would be accosted on the way. Fed up, she would screw up her face and say, 'Go and ask Mai, why don't you?'

After all, what else could she say? Gradually, the woman named Komola became an enigma. Purobi's mother, Pobon Lengera's wife, was now the topic of idle gossip in the town.

She, Purobi's mother, came to visit me. She stood at the entrance of my home on a holiday, a Sunday. She knew that I usually finished my household chores by around eleven o' clock. I had begun on this day off tackling these chores at the crack of dawn and had just then relaxed enough to sit and take a breath in the verandah when she opened the gate and entered.

I could barely recognize her. She had changed completely! Her looks, the way she carried herself, her walk, even the way she talked, everything had changed. There was no way one could recognize her. Her hair was clipped back in a ponytail. It was quite obvious that an expert beautician had given her hair a U cut. Her eyebrows had been shaped. Her colouring had always been on the fairer side. She now had a peaches-and-cream complexion, having become much fairer. Her cheeks were the colour of people who had good nutrition. She was wearing an expensive green handloom tant saree with a yellow border. She hadn't pinned up the *aasol* pleats on her shoulder. Rather, she had let it flow loose down her arm. Her breasts were noticeably full.

I glanced at the sandals she had left outside. The doctor had advised me to wear special footwear from the brand known as Dr Scholl. She was wearing the same expensive brand! When I had handed over the money at the Bata shop after buying my pair, the expense had made me cringe. In this last leg of my career, I was getting a good salary. And yet I was not used to spending so much on my feet. And Purobi's mother was now wearing the same brand of sandals!

All the rumours about her came to my mind.

Purobi's mother offered me a packet of sweetmeats she had brought for me from Delhi. I recognized the expensive sweets. These were long-lasting ones, made with thickened flavoured milk and khoya. The woman before me had really come into money. I looked once more at her. Something . . . a kind of rawness seemed to be clinging to her. She appeared to be very tired. Her eyes had sunk in their sockets. But what was much more noticeable at first glance was the lustrous appearance of this person who had now filled out and become so fair-skinned. It was only after one looked closely at her for some time that her tiredness became apparent.

'You've brought me some really good mithais,' I commented.

'It's not I who have bought this, they bought it for me.'

'They?'

'Bhaiyya and Bhabhi. *Bahut achha aadmi*,' she said in Hindi. 'Very good people.'

Purobi's mother narrated the story of these very good people. A Punjabi couple. The man owned a huge factory manufacturing those rubber flip-flops known as Hawai sandals. Besides, he owned textile mills, too. They lived in a palatial mansion in a very posh locality in Delhi. The topmost floor remained vacant. The Bhaiyya and Bhabhi lived on the middle floor, and the elderly parents on the ground floor. The seniors had a large amount of farming land back in Punjab. They had been well established for generations. With his white beard and turban, it was easily apparent that the senior man must have had a powerful physique in his youth. He was quite strong even now. He would sun himself on a string cot in the courtyard in the mornings, while having a pile of rotis, along with black tarka lentils as well as a bowl of clotted cream. He also had a masala chai made with full cream milk and spiced with ginger and bay leaves, with this was a four-egg omelette.

At first, Purobi's mother had been astonished. The man would die after downing all this every morning. But nothing happened. He would digest it all. It was his wife, the old lady, who was in really bad shape. She had put on so much weight that she now resembled a sack of salt. On top of that, she had pains in her knees. She remained splayed out on the bed like a huge tortoise. She would constantly feel the pain all over her body.

Purobi's mother's main duty was to look after the old lady. She hardly allowed Purobi's mother out of her sight. If she went out of her line of vision for even a little while, she began to shout, 'Gulabi! Ei, Gulabi!'

Pobon's wife, Purobi's mother, Komola was now Gulabi. Gulabi of the Gill family. She needed to lightly massage the piles of flesh in hopes that there would be some respite from the constant pain.

Barun had brought her to an agency run by an Assamese couple in Delhi. She had entered the Gill family as Gulabi through them. She realized that several people had received money from this circuit through which Barun brought Assamese people to the distant city. After bringing them here, he made them stay with an Assamese couple, who ran the employment agency, for a week, after which they were placed in different homes. Komola was sent to the Gill mansion. Barun received his cut. It was because of this that his daughters rode e-rickshas and went to English-medium schools. The couple who ran the agency got a large amount of money. They would get it every month for sure. She, too, began to receive a good amount every month. There was no way she could have earned this amount if she had remained in her hometown.

She told me, 'In this place, even the "Miss" in an English-medium school doesn't get so much money. A new teacher in a college doesn't get so much, either. After all, the Baideo I had worked for brings the rice and vegetables from her home.' Before leaving for Delhi, Purobi's mother had worked for a while in Mala's home. Mala had recently joined college as a temporary teacher in the history department of the college.

Komola had repaired her home a little and left a small amount for her daughter's expenses. The doctor who was treating Pobon, had informed her that the medication that he would need would be expensive. Otherwise, he would remain confined to bed, shitting and pissing without any control.

She had not returned from Delhi after that visit. She lost all contact with her husband and daughter. The woman who bore the name Komola was completely lost. And here she was now in front of me, having returned, regaling me with tales of '*bare dilwale*' Bhaiyya and Bhabhi, and Dada and Dadi . . . about their large heartedness.

Minoti's mother brought me a cup of tea and a cup for Purobi's mother, too. Minoti's mother did not really want to go back to the house after handing over the teacups. With the excuse of dusting this, straightening that, she kept hovering around us. I realized that she wanted to take part in the conversation. Sitting in front of me was this woman shrouded in mystery, Purobi's mother. How could Minoti's mother go back to her chores inside?

I had to send her away from there. 'I had put the clothes in the washer, they must be done by now. Go and switch off the machine, will you?'

Unwillingly, Minoti's mother went inside.

After having her tea, Purobi's mother brought up the subject of her large-hearted employers again. Bhaiyya and Bhabhi were deeply religious. They would touch their parents' feet in the morning and step out barefoot in the car. Purobi's mother would prepare a bag of sliced fruits and leftover rotis from the previous night along with other food items. They would both go to a dairy farm some distance away and would return after feeding the cows there. On the way back, they would stop near the park and feed Hanumanji's progeny, the monkeys. The elder couple would feed the birds in the courtyard and give them water. They were truly very religious. They cared so much for animals and birds, they spent so much money on feeding cows, monkeys and birds! That was probably why God had blessed them with prosperity. For their petty domestic expenses, they brought in and took out satchels of currency notes. This, for them, was small change. They spent lakhs through their cards for their larger expenses.

Purobi's mother pronounced the word 'card' with great pride.

They had four luxury cars, long and fancy. At times, they would throw huge parties at their Mehrauli farmhouse. A huge variety of foods was arranged then. All those who worked in the Gill Manzil went there. There was so much work to be done at these parties. Only the two security men remained behind glumly. Parcels of food would be brought back for them. One of the security men was from Assam. She informed me that his home was not too far away from here, only about twenty kilometres or so. His name was Mohon Boro. His home, too, ran on his income from this job.

Perhaps I was staring too much at Purobi's mother. A rich, animal-loving family, huge parties, a large variety of food preparations and cuisines, luxury cars, the entertainment, the songs and dances at the farmhouse parties, payments being made in lakhs through cards, bags filled with cash for petty expenses, a vigorous old man who ate a four-egg omelette with a pile of rotis, an enormous old woman with vast rolls of flesh whose body would ache constantly, an energetic, hard-working couple, an entire floor kept vacant in a city such as Delhi, a palatial house that was built with plans for three generations to live together. And in all this splendour, a woman was constantly massaging the old woman's body, arranging food for the cow worship for a fit young couple, bringing back food from the party for the security men. The people in the house constantly calling out to her . . . Gulabi! Ei Gulabi!

She was indeed a royal attendant in a fairy tale.

A royal attendant in a fairy tale, Gulabi, Pobon's wife, Purobi's mother, Komola—this woman was sitting before me, tugging at her yellow-bordered green sari. Why was she pulling at it in this way? She was constantly pulling the end of the sari, the aansol, around her shoulders, and trying to hide her body. What was wrong with her? The thin material above her full breasts was wet. The green blouse was completely wet and was sticking to the sari. Through the damp material, her nipples were quite apparent. These nipples, which always become firmer and larger during particular times in a woman's life were now pushing against the wet sari and blouse. And that familiar sour aroma was all around. Every woman who had experienced motherhood was familiar with this sourish smell. These full breasts, these erect nipples? This abundance of milk that was completely wetting her clothes? Gushing out from her full breasts was a stream meant for the eager, flower-like lips of a babe, for whom it was nothing less than nectar. This was the familiar experience of every woman who had given birth. It was the cry of breast milk for the baby.

I was sure I was not mistaken. Purobi's mother was tugging at her aansol to hide her chest. The cloth at the edge of the sari had a delicate orange-coloured design. The orange floral design became wet in front of my eyes. Only the breasts of well-nourished new mothers could lactate in this way. It was only when no baby's lips touched the breasts that the milk flowed, weeping, in this manner. Certainly, the streams of milk from Komola's breasts were crying out for a baby that had recently come into this world from Komola's womb.

Hastily, she got up to leave.

I abruptly took hold of her hand.

'Purobi's mother, your baby . . . where is your baby . . . and his father?'

Purobi's mother began to sob out loud. She collapsed on me. With that sour smell enveloping her, she wept, broken-hearted.

I heard footsteps inside. Minoti's mother had sent word across to others. 'Purobi's mother has come all decked up and is now talking with our Baideo!'

The seller of puffed rice, Aroti's mother; the vendor of banana flowers and edible ferns, Kajol's mother; Minoti's mother's mother-in-law; Roton's mother from Jonali's household—they were all peeping and peering at us. Inquisitiveness prevailed all around. This woman who, like them, would once worry about where the next meal would come from, had disappeared, and then reappeared. And she had come back as a queen. Such clothes, such a get up! Such arrogance of money and the power that came with it, it was as though her feet wouldn't touch the ground even. They had surely heard Purobi's mother sobbing. Their curiosity had burst all bounds and was uncontrollable. They had come in and surrounded Purobi's mother. They passed all kinds of slurs and innuendoes quite freely. Roton's mother was known among these women as the news channel NewsLive. This tale would sail out from her mouth and fly around like the floss from the ximolu, the silk cotton tree. All of them were now climbing up the steps to the verandah.

'Purobi's mother, let's go to my study. It's become very hot outside.'

Her sobs had lessened in intensity somewhat.

'What's the matter, Minoti's Ma? Go and fetch a bottle of water from the fridge. Purobi's mother is feeling dizzy.'

I helped Purobi's mother into the study, and switched on the AC. She composed herself, a little. I shut the door.

This woman, a lactating mother, with breasts full of milk, bared her naked heart to me as completely as one would split open an areca nut. One couldn't reach out to touch it . . . it was full of great gushing gobs of blood.

Purobi's mother had gone back to Delhi with a heavy heart after her last visit. If things continued the way they had, it was doubtful that she would see her husband alive next time she came. Purobi would be clearing her matriculation examinations in a while. The father and daughter had survived on the money she had sent them every month. Purobi's mother only saw darkness on the path ahead. At some point, everything would come to a stop. How long could she work away from home, in a different place, like this?

When she returned to Gill Manzil, she received a proposal from the young master and mistress. In return for a substantial sum of money, they wanted her womb. They would hire her uterus for ten months and ten days. The doctor had opined that Komola's employer, the mistress, would never be able to give birth. She had become pregnant several times through artificial means. But always, within a short while, she had developed a raging fever and bled huge blood clots as she miscarried.

They had searched far and wide, across the globe for a solution. In the end, they had come to Purobi's mother with their begging bowl. The senior Gills had five daughters and just one son. The Bade Dil Bhaiyya, Komola's large-hearted employer, was the one lamp of the Gill family. The lamp of the lineage was flickering and about to be extinguished. Who would inherit all this property! Would a new generation never live in the empty top floor? Or would it remain vacant like this forever?

Purobi's mother readied herself. She signed all the necessary papers. Before embarking on the whole mission, she sent a large amount of money to her daughter.

And then, Komola disappeared. She did not keep in touch with anybody. Gradually, her body took on a glow. She proposed to her employers that she would not stay on at the Gill Manzil anymore as there were many people here from her side of the country. If the security man from near her place came to know about it, the news would spread back home. She feared stepping out into the light as her belly grew. She began to remain inside her room. Her feet swelled up. But she completely stopped going even to the park in front of the house. She had her meals in her room and would lie in bed with her badly swollen feet. She remained stuck in the small, dark airless room in the servant's quarters.

There was great exhilaration in the Gill family. The heir of Gill Manzil was in her womb. She was no longer the maid Gulabi. The family had a house in Shimla, where she was sent. Everything had been set up there; she just had to go and stay. The cool hilly weather, nutritious food . . . the serving maid called Komola became the Queen Mother, Rajmao, the Ahom title for the mother of the ruling King. Yes indeed. The child growing within her would become a prince as soon as he was born. She was indeed Rajmao.

Her cheeks took on colour, her skin took on a delicate smoothness which she had never had before. She was bursting with good health. She filled out noticeably. The doctor examined her thinking that she was bearing twins. When she had been carrying Purobi, her pregnancy had become apparent only in the last month. Till then, she had rushed about from one end of the town to the other, raising the dust on the roads as she hurried to work. If she had draped her clothes with care, her condition would be covered even in the last month. Purobi had been extremely underweight at birth.

I gave Purobi's mother another cup of tea. Minoti's mother was in the kitchen, pretending to work while straining to hear what was going on inside the study. I told her that Purobi's mother was feeling dizzy. She sat down for a while. Looking at her gloomy face, I understood that she was not at all happy that I had taken Purobi's mother to sit in the study. There was so much gossip about this woman, why bring her inside, give her tea and sit her down? All this would result in a loss of 'respect'.

I asked Purobi's mother, 'Your life in the hills was really good, wasn't it?'

'How could I have a good life there, Baideo? I was fearful all the time.'

'What were you afraid of, Purobi's mother? What were your fears?'

'I had many fears. If the baby turned out to be lame, crippled? They wouldn't keep the child. And where would I go with a crippled child, what would I do? The child in my womb was not a gift of God. It was man-made.'

Purobi's mother's eyes grew damp again. 'I was very careful those days. If I fell and miscarried, I would not get paid. After all, if they didn't get a child, why would they pay me?'

'You had many worries?'

'I would see a lame child in my dreams. One of his hands, and a leg were missing. I would weep every day; I missed Purobi and her father so much! I could not send away the armless, legless child from my mind. I lived like a madwoman in that house in the hills.'

I looked once more at her wet breasts. 'And your baby?'

'I went straight to the hospital from the hills. It was a boy. I heard them say that it was a beautiful baby who weighed four kilos, with long limbs. I had closed my eyes. I heard his cry. It was such a loud cry! Deafening.'

Purobi's mother smiled slightly.

'They paid you what was promised? Did you suckle your child?'

'The nurses took out milk from my breasts and gave it in a bottle to the baby. I came back home, here, straight from the hospital.'

'Does Purobi's father know?'

'Yes, he does. But what can he do? He's half dead. But he's realized that nobody laid a finger on my body.'

Purobi's mother rose to leave. She went to the washroom and turned her sari around, to hide the damp portions. 'I'm having medicines to dry up the milk,' she told me after she came out.

She started to leave but returned from the door again.

'I didn't get to look at the child Baideo. Not once.'

Saying this, Komola, Pobon Lengera's wife, Purobi's mother, Gulabi, went out without looking back.

DAUGHTER OF THE
DARK MEMSAHIB

(Originally published as 'Koli Memor Jiyek')

Before I begin to talk about Koli Mem's daughter, I shall have to tell you about my father, I shall also have to speak of that beautiful century-old Mission School in that small town in Eastern Assam. I must also tell you about the aristocratic home in that town, of Arnob, the young son of that house. I shall have to bring in a bit about myself too. I shall also have to talk about the Irishman, the Saheb Edwin Smith, who lived in Ireland; about the Xontoli tea garden, where he worked for forty years before returning to Ireland, about Sabitri of the tea garden; and about how Sabitri became 'Koli Mem', the Dark Memsahib. I shall have to talk about Koli Mem's daughter Rosie and her son Charles. Indeed, I shall even have to talk about the person who married Rosie and about Charles' wife Chameli. In short, before coming to the subject of my story, that is the story of Helen, Koli Mem's daughter, I shall have to talk about all these people and their interconnected relationships.

Deuta, my father, had a connection with the school. He had an association too with Edwin Saheb's Sabitri. I had a relationship with Helen, and also with my father's ancestral home. Before I start to speak of Helen, I need to talk about all these associations and connections too.

We'll have to start by talking about my father. Deuta was the son of the well known, highly respected Barua family. It wasn't that the family was wealthy. They were known for their intelligence. Even though they were not astoundingly rich, they were comfortably off. My grandfather had been an employee of the Steamer Company and was employed by the British. White men and women, sahebs and mems would travel in the Company's huge vessels. My grandfather, Kokadeuta, was stationed at the port known as Nimati Ghat. By the time I was born, Kokadeuta had retired to a town near Nimati Ghat, where he had bought land and built a house.

I remember Kokadeuta's appearance very clearly. He was light fawn in colour, very much like the colour of a ripe guava. A tall man, he would always clasp his hands behind his back and bend forward a bit when he walked. He was always dressed in a coat and trousers. When he went out, he wore a felt hat. He carried a walking stick, the handle of which was a silver-headed lion. Kokadeuta drove a Ford car. Of course, he did not take out the car too much after he retired. He was commonly known as Barua Saheb owing to his education at the Dhaka University, and his fluency in spoken and written English.

Kokadeuta had educated his three sons to the best of his ability. Even when he was marrying off his daughters, he looked for educational levels rather than looks, lineage or economic status in the potential groom.

My grandmother, Aita, would talk about the eldest daughter's wedding, my Pehi's. The union of Pehi and her husband, my Peha, was known as the marriage of white rice and black lentils. Pehi had Kokadeuta's colouring. She was known to glow even in the dark. And Peha did not look the slightest bit fair even in the black-and-white photographs. It is customary at our weddings for women to sing simple ditties, often with lines made up on the spot. There are two groups, either belonging to the bride's or bridegroom's side. These *biya naams*, as the ditties are called, often tease people on the other side. At my Pehi's wedding ceremony, the women from the bride's side sang with gusto about the bridegroom: 'Bopai, son, you are as dark as the therju fruit.' Before sitting for the ceremony, Pehi had peeped out to have a look at the bridegroom. She had fallen back on her bed and remained there. Aita had clasped her eldest daughter and bawled uncontrollably until Koka came in and scolded them. 'I've chosen this intelligent, highly educated boy after searching high and low. And here are the mother and daughter, looking at something like skin colour,' he shouted.

Peha was a graduate from Calcutta University and also held a degree in law—a BA and BL. Koka had lived to see his son-in-law sit on the judge's chair. All his sons-in-law were educated. His eldest son was a lawyer. Koka had the greatest hopes from my father. Deuta was a gold medallist in mathematics from Calcutta University. Koka had many dreams about Deuta's future. But Deuta left it all behind and jumped into the freedom movement. Deuta went around with all the freedom fighters in his town.

Koka had grabbed at everything he wanted in life. He did not get to see Deuta entering the civil services and becoming a magistrate. Instead, he saw him go to jail. After Independence, when his father passed away, Deuta became a mathematics teacher in the Mission School. Before his death, Koka had divided all his property equally between his three sons. For reasons unknown, Deuta did not touch any bit of his father's property. The Mission School Trust gave him a bit of land near the school. Deuta first made a hut of bamboo and straw. Later, he upgraded it to a small house. Till halfway up, the walls were brick, and the rest was reed and clay. The ceilings were made of bamboo matting. I remember that first hut of straw and bamboo very clearly. The new house was constructed not too long ago, and the old one was demolished.

Another picture is linked clearly to the memories of that house made of bamboo and straw. My other grandfather, my mother's father, was a famous freedom fighter. Deuta had married my mother and brought her straightaway to the bamboo and straw hut. The family did not live an ostentatious life. We had all grown up in that house. I used to love flowers. When Deuta brought home a flowering plant or the seeds and cuttings, my young face too would bloom like a flower. No matter where he was returning from, Deuta would always bring home a flower sapling for Ma. There was a small path leading in from the road to our front room, the sitting area. The path was surfaced with stones. Lining the path on both sides were small shrubs. During the rainy season, the small shrubs would be covered with white and pink blossoms.

The first room in the bamboo and straw house was a kind of office room for Deuta. Many people would come for work and wait for him. Ma would send tea and tamol, areca nuts, through us there. Among these people, there was only one woman who would come and sit in Deuta's office room regularly. She was Koli Mem herself. The Dark Mem, Edwin Smith's Memsahib, Helen's mother. She would come straight to the house and wait near Deuta's office room. She would always come precisely at five in the afternoon. She would come about twice a month, sometimes three. Koli Mem was an Adivasi, possibly from Orissa. She was a little bit taller and fairer than most Adivasi women. Her face had a tranquil expression and a kind of charm. Even at first glance, there was something very attractive about her. Her hair was always neatly combed. She would fashion a bun around a donut-like ring, with never a strand of hair out of place. The parting of her hair and her forehead would be bare. Koli Mem would wear beautiful pastel-coloured saris. I would always want to touch the fabric, which looked really soft. We had never seen such fabric before. Our clothes were made of rough fabric. Ma would weave the cloth on her loom and then dye it. She would stitch our clothes with this material. Indeed, we had never had the opportunity to even feel fabric of the kind that Koli Mem wore. Her feet were shod in high pencil heels, which would pierce holes into our mud floor. Each time, after Koli Mem left, a beautiful fragrance hung in the air. She always carried a pink umbrella. We had never seen an umbrella of that colour. The umbrellas we carried were round and black. I wanted to touch the umbrella and also her hair, fixed firmly around a ring, as well.

Koli Mem would always come to our home with a letter in her hand. It was the letter that Smith Saheb sent from Ireland. She was illiterate. All her children studied in a school in Darjeeling. As soon as she entered, she would give the letter to Deuta, who would put on his glasses and read it out loud to her. Whenever she came over, the room next to Deuta's office room would fill up with people who would jostle and push to get a better view of what was going on inside as they peeped into the room. She would sit on a low stool. We would stare at Koli Mem's face. She would listen to the contents of the letter very intently. The letters would always begin with 'Dear Elizabeth'.

The letters would be quite short, dealing with just two subjects. Finances and the children. After the letter was read out, she would fold it and keep it in her bag again. After which Deuta would come inside. Quite often, it was I who carried the tea and tamol paan to her. She would have her tea sitting in the office room itself, though it was Deuta who had the tamol. Leaving behind a fragrance in her wake, Koli Mem would depart. We would stare at her till she disappeared.

*

Koli Mem's eldest daughter was Helen. Of all her three children, it was Helen who had perhaps taken the greatest share of Smith Saheb's genes. Her sister Rosie had less, and the boy, Charles, inherited the least of all. Helen had blonde hair, her skin colour was that of gleaming pearls. However, she had her mother's dark eyes, which glowed like two brilliant stones. Rosie's eyes were brown like those of her father's. She was only a few shades fairer than her mother. Charles' colouring was the same as Rosie's. He too, had got his father's eyes and hair colour.

It wasn't just the fact that a white man's blood ran through her veins. Anybody who saw Helen would get the impression that some sculptor had crossed the seven seas to gather, one by one, the choicest items from some magical land to create her. When she smiled, in that face which gleamed like a pearl, surrounded by golden hair, her dark eyes would dazzle like stars. Her lips, as red as the *latumoni* seeds, her teeth like pomegranate seeds, her beautiful fingers and toes, her proportionate build . . . with these features, anything she wore looked good on her. Indeed, even if she tied up her hair in a towel after her bath, she looked as though she had come out after beautifying herself for hours.

Koli Mem's home was known as Koli Mem's Bungalow; it was just behind ours. It was built on a spacious compound in the format of the tea garden bungalows. It had quite a few rooms. The front porch was encircled with mosquito-proof netting. The entire area in front was a lawn with varieties of flowers. We had heard that after retiring from his job in the tea garden, Smith Saheb had lived in Koli Mem's Bungalow. Even at that age, Smith Saheb had been as active as a young man.

Helen and I were almost the same age. When I was younger, I would often go through the bamboo gates across our compounds to Koli Mem's Bungalow. There was an age gap of twenty to twenty-three years between Koli Mem and Smith Saheb. When Koli Mem was yet to become Elizabeth, she would go with her mother every day to Smith Saheb's enormous bungalow. She was Sabitri at that time. There was a Mem in the Saheb's bungalow. Not a dark Koli Mem, but a *real* one, a Memsaheb from Ireland. The Saheb had two sons. Some years before Smith Saheb retired, the Mem went to England for her son's marriage. She never returned. Possibly she stayed behind with her son and daughter-in-law. It seemed she had inherited a large vineyard and also a huge ivy-covered twenty-roomed house from her father. Helen had shown me pictures of it. The windowsills were full of pots of geraniums. The picture of the house, with its green ivy-covered walls, looked like a painting. I was a schoolteacher's daughter. On top of that, Deuta had taken part in the Independence struggle. Our parents had kept us away from any kind of luxury. We wore rubber flip-flops, Hawai sandals, to school. That uniform, provided by the school, was our best outfit. Our other clothes were rough in comparison—dyed at home and handwoven, too.

I wanted to touch each and every item in Helen's home. There were carpets in every room. The dark dining table gleamed. We would always visit on the children's birthdays. We saw them every day.

Our father did not go by the rules laid out by society. He kept our home free from these restrictions. But our neighbours did not accept Koli Mem and gossiped endlessly about her. It was from them that we learnt the tale of how Sabitri became Koli Mem.

Sabitri's mother used to work in Smith Saheb's home. She did personal chores for the master and his wife. Sabitri would follow her mother around everywhere. Gradually, Sabitri too learnt to take care of some of the Saheb's needs and requirements and as she grew up, she learnt to do a lot of the chores around the bungalow. After his wife went to stay with their son, Sabitri took over the tasks of serving the Saheb his tea, arranging for his towel and soap before he took his bath, giving him a basin of hot water to wash his feet, bringing him his hat, coat, tie . . . gradually, Sabitri took on all these tasks.

Once, the Saheb fell ill. By then, Sabitri's parents had passed away. Her brothers, too, had married and set up their own homes. At that time, she was living in the servants' quarters of the bungalow. After he fell ill, she began to stay in the bungalow. The Saheb recovered, but Sabitri remained in the bungalow. She became Elizabeth. She remained in the bungalow as Elizabeth for seven years. She gave birth to three children. After he retired, before returning for good to his own country, the Saheb bought two *bighas* of land in the nearby town, near the Mission School, for Elizabeth and the children. He arranged for everything during the six months he stayed after retirement. People said that Saheb had deposited a large sum of money in the bank. Koli Mem could live quite well on the interest from that money.

Although Elizabeth became Koli Mem, she could not become a part of the town's social community. To us, she was a marvel, and her bungalow was an object of wonder and curiosity.

We were the only children present at the birthdays of Koli Mem's children. These occasions would be celebrated very joyfully. Other parents would not allow their children to come to the bungalow. The birthday girl or boy would wear beautiful clothes. Koli Mem would bake a cake and place it on the attractively decorated table. There would be candles, flowers and gifts packed in shiny paper. Those gifts were not brought by us. They were meant for us. We would bring a gamosa woven by our mother, a hand-embroidered handkerchief and a bunch of flowers from our garden. It was always Deuta who tied up the flowers in a bunch. We would bring back cake and sweetmeats for Ma and Deuta. Our hands would be full of all kinds of toys, dolls, chocolates and balloons of different colours. Everything was from abroad. The Saheb would send them. We would look forward to their birthdays. All of us were studying at the Mission School at that time. It was only after they reached class four that Helen and her siblings went to Darjeeling and Shillong to study.

But from nursery to class four, Helen and I studied together and sat next to each other in class. Just as I wished to touch the objects in Koli Mem's home, I wished to touch Helen, too. When we would mark sections on the ground and play games with the large seeds, the *ghila*, of a particular plant, or with potsherds, I would stare at

Helen's legs when she hopped on one and pushed the ghila forward. It looked as though a crimson rose, the colour of blood, was lying in the dust. It was so rosy that it seemed as though the blood would come bursting out. The twig of the rose was being propelled forward by the breeze. I would forget everything when she sang, accompanying herself on the piano. She had a very sweet voice. When she painted, I loved to see the way her rosy hands moved over the canvas.

Like all my siblings, I too excelled in mathematics and science. In fact, our prowess in these subjects was well known in our town. I was good only in these two subjects. My elder siblings would get excellent marks in all subjects, around eighty per cent or so. In our time, it was not difficult to get a job if one passed the examinations with good marks. The six of us siblings established ourselves well.

Helen excelled in English language and literature. She would explain the poems we had to study for our English paper, while I tutored her in math. She would write poetry, too. I remember when she left after class four to study in Darjeeling. I fell on her shoulders and wailed and wept uncontrollably. I really loved her. I could not imagine a life without Helen. I would really look forward to Helen returning home for the holidays. Her letters would fill up my mailbox.

Time passed. We cleared our matriculation examinations. Helen passed with a simple first division, while I got three letters, that is over eighty per cent marks. Like my elder siblings, I too got myself admitted to a local college. We would study here for a year, then move out to another college outside our town. In my case, too, Deuta did what had become the norm in this matter. At that time, Helen too had come back and enrolled in the same local college in which I was to study. Charles, Rosie too came back and began to attend local schools.

It was apparent from just looking at Koli Mem why her children had to return. There she is, Koli Mem, coming this way. She's coming to our house. She never came through the backyards. She always took the front path. When Smith Saheb had stayed in Koli Mem's bungalow for those six months, he would visit Deuta quite often. He would always come by the main pathway.

Koli Mem has her umbrella in her hand. The umbrella is no longer that bright rose pink. It is faded, like a wilted rose, and turning patchy. There she is, Koli Mem. She's closed her umbrella and placed her hand on the gate. She is standing near Deuta's office room. Koli Mem wants to meet Deuta.

*

'Is Mastor Babu in?'

'Yes, I'm in. Come in. Have a seat.'

'Thank you.'

'Anju, go and tell your mother that we have a visitor. Tea and tamol . . .'

'It's okay, Mastor Babu.'

'Let's have a look at the letter.'

'This isn't a letter from Saheb.'

'Who is it from? Where has it come from?'

'It's come from England, like the others, but it's not in Saheb's handwriting. It's a printed letter.'

'A printed letter? Let me have a look.'

Anju's father pauses. A sob comes from his kind face. Anju comes into the room with the tea. She stops, staring at her father's face. She has never seen this expression before.

Today, the usual greeting in the first line, 'Dear Elizabeth', is missing. Instead, it starts, 'To whom it may concern.' It's a typed letter. The first line itself gives the news that Smith Saheb has passed away. The 'maidservant' in Assam would no longer be receiving the regular payments.

Koli Mem got up hastily and went out after opening the gate. For the first time, Koli Mem did not unfurl her umbrella while leaving. Today, she did not nod and wish the Mastor while leaving. She did not even close the gate after her.

After this news, Koli Mem cut down on her household and other expenses. She brought her children from Darjeeling and admitted them into our local educational institutions. The beautiful birthday celebrations stopped. She wiped away the colours of the bright seasonal flowers of every winter and dug up the lawns to grow potatoes. She planted chillies, cauliflowers, cabbages and watered them herself. She cast away many things. She dispensed with the perfume she wore, that same perfume whose fragrance would fill our home when she visited earlier. She stopped taking a ricksha when she went out, she did not take along her pink umbrella either. Now, everybody could see Koli Mem walking through the streets come rain, come shine.

It's from this point that Helen's story begins.

I've met up with Helen again today after thirty years. She has come after learning of my father's death.

All around us, the people were talking about my father's death. He was eighty-five that day. On this day, his birthday, he had had his bath in the morning and had tea and a sweetmeat given to him by his daughter-in-law. Ma had passed away quite some time ago. We had all called and spoken to him. That very night, Deuta had mentioned that he was feeling uneasy, and gone to bed a bit early. That was it. He never woke up again.

We got the news in the morning and rushed to the old house. It seemed as though the whole town came to pay their respects to Deuta's departed soul. We had not had any idea that Deuta had been so highly respected. Perhaps Deuta himself had not thought this. Among the crowd was Helen.

I hugged Helen and sobbed uncontrollably. I was wild with grief just as I had been when she had left for her school in Darjeeling. There was just one difference. That day, Helen too, had wept along with me but today, she was silent and still. When I saw the stony expression on her face, I became even more agitated. Other people came forward to support me. They all told each other, 'Her father loved this child the most. She is the youngest in the family, after all.'

I was quite unaware of all that was happening around me at the time. I pushed away those people who had come forward to help by supporting me physically. Helen placed her hand on my head and seemed to murmur a blessing. I became even more frantic. I was a well-known, established pediatrician. Seeing me like this, my two sons, my husband Rupam, even my elder siblings were very surprised. In all that commotion, Helen left. Nobody noticed. Her eyes, Helen's bright, gem-like eyes! Let it be for now. We'll talk about that later. Let's go back to Helen from thirty years ago, and her eyes.

Here she is, then, thirty years ago.

Helen's eyes, set in her pearl-like face, glistened with a strange joy. This glow comes to a woman's life quite naturally when she thinks of herself as a queen. She soars, and in her pride, her feet hardly touch the ground. Then there is no person as happy and satisfied as she in the whole wide world. She forgets the world, and all the people in it. For like a deer netted and caught, she is trapped by a man. The man becomes her sun. She faces the sun and follows him around like a sunflower. She gazes at the man she loves and keeps going around him from east to west, and west to east. She moves around, constantly. She believes that her whole life will pass in adoration, in worship of this sun. Her life will be a honeyed dream. Her body is youthful. She is tender, like a sunflower. Her body is addicted, obsessed with this man. Her beloved becomes the ultimate truth in her life. She gathers a golden–orange colour, the joyous hues from him. Drop by drop, seeds gather within it. She believes that this *basanti* colour, which has gilded her with a golden hue, is hers alone. This sun has given only her the brightness of the sun-washed petals. She bathes in the light of the sun and blossoms as she shines in that glow. She does not remember that the light of the sun can scatter all around the world. She looks on with eyes that are smeared with the kohl of illusion. There is just one sun. And she is a sunflower always facing him, singing praises to the sun. She sobs throughout the night but starts to move around the sun as soon as it appears at dawn.

When their flesh is as velvety soft as the petals of a flower, almost all women become sunflowers. At this point, Helen was a sunflower, immersed in chanting hymns to the sun. She thought the sun was hers alone and would remain hers for all eternity. She would bring the gold from the sun and would colour her world. Her life would be golden hued, always. Her sun was a man.

Of course, he was no Adonis, but this strong, intelligent man from a respectable family was still a good match for the beautiful Helen. He became Helen's sun.

Gradually, this man entered Helen's heart.

At that time, Helen and I were inseparable. Like the rest of my family, I had middling brown-coloured skin. I was short, as well. However, people commented that my personality was very attractive. But at that point in time, none of it mattered. I just wished to be Helen's friend. I knew how the young man from that very respectable family wooed her, how Helen became a sunflower. We were like white rice and dark lentils, but we two friends were inseparable.

*

See those two girls sitting under a tree? One of them is Helen, the radiant one, like the full moon. Sitting next to her with two plaits wearing handwoven, home-dyed clothes is the Mastor's daughter, Anju. Both are engrossed in conversation. Helen is saying something to Anju. She blushes every now and then. Even a glance at Helen can reveal that this is a woman who is gazing at a man, singing hymns of adoration to the sun. She is now a proud queen; the world is at her feet. She is a bit of clay in the potter's hand. Just a sprinkle of water will soften it. And then, she will be shaped by the hands of that sun. A mango, a banana, a Goddess, a cat. She loses her all, her very identity, as the sun keeps giving shape to her. She is that part of clay, which keeps moving up and down, down and up, under the potter's hands.

She shows Anju a letter. Her God has gone to the big city for work. He has sent her a letter from there. Anju reaches out for the letter. She takes it very delicately, as though the letter is a fully bloomed white rose. If she handles it carelessly, the petals will fall.

'My baby,' Anju reads and laughs. The blood of Smith Saheb runs in Helen's veins. Her father had been six-feet-three-inches tall, well built with the physique of a person who played lawn tennis regularly. Helen's shoulders and arms are larger than those of most men here. She is five-feet-seven-inches tall. Her sun always greets her with, 'My baby, my little bird, baby mine.'

'Oi, Helen.'

'Hm?'

'Why does Jeetda address you as a baby?' He was my cousin. His name was Jeet, and since he was older, I addressed him as Jeetda. 'Why does he call you his little bird? Such a big girl like you.'

She covers her face with her golden hair and places her head on her knees. Her dark eyes gleam like beads as she looks at Anju and laughs.

'On the other hand, when somebody comes to me to offer his love, I am addressed as "my little dark dorikona fish". No, "my tadpole". That's what they address me as.'

'Like those?' she points to the cemented pool that Smith Saheb had once built. There was a time when waterlilies and lotuses bloomed there. But now it is full of frogs and tadpoles.

Helen has turned into a red rose; she is laughing so much.

'The things you say, Anju!'

'It won't do to laugh like this. I've not understood the matter. You . . . and a little baby, a small bird. *Dhet*. Okay, let him write "my peacock, my pine tree . . ."'

Both of them look at the straight pine tree that Smith Saheb had planted and burst into laughter.

Remembering her father, Helen started to sob. Between her sobs, her face shone like a diamond. Anju wiped away the tears from her face. She begins to tell Helen a story, a fairytale.

'Oi, Helen, listen to this story.'

In the land below the waters there lived a mermaid. She was just like you. Golden hair like yours, and a pair of black eyes like jewels. Her voice, too, was sweet, like yours.

One day, the mermaid came up from the water to look at the sun. She saw a handsome, well-built young man like our Jeetda on a ship. The young man was a prince. The mermaid was gullible. Even though she was unaware of it, her heart became a song that tumbled about on the waves. The waves came and fell near the prince's feet. On their backs, they carried the song. The prince changed the direction of the ship. The mermaid was sitting on an island encircled and shaded by cinnamon trees in the middle of the sea. From her waist up, she was on land, the rest of her was in the water. Her tail was beating on the water.

For many days and many nights, the prince stayed with the mermaid on the island shaded and encircled by cinnamon trees. While leaving, he promised her that he would return and take her back with him. The mermaid became a sunflower, just like you. She waited and searched for the prince. Finally, one day, she went to the old witch. In exchange for her sweet voice, she came back with a pair of human legs. As a human, she went looking for the prince. The day the mute girl finally found her prince was the day he was bringing home his new bride. But she danced through the festivities at the wedding. Her feet felt like they were on live coal, or a thicket of needles. But she danced, nonetheless.

Helen listened to Anju's story and came back with one of her own—the story of Mary Magdelene and Jesus, her God and her sun. They were both important tales.

*

Their lives were as magical as the island on which the prince had lived with the mermaid. The only things missing were the cinnamon trees. The place was surrounded by a forest. There was moonlight. There was a canopy of stars covering the sky. Helen had become a mermaid in the lodge in the middle of Kaziranga's wilderness. She would dive in and come out in this encircling of moonlight and wilderness. That day, Helen had dissolved into her sun. Her sun had promised her that he would return as soon as he had joined his job and marry her. Helen stayed in the wilderness of xaal trees for three nights instead of one.

At that point of time, Koli Mem was in a helpless condition. Charles was neglecting his studies. He had come to know the difficulties that his mother was facing. The money that Smith Saheb would send on a regular basis had stopped a long time ago. The savings were almost gone. Several luxury items in the house had been sold off. Only the piano was left. Helen would sit at this piano and sing every day. She had not progressed much in her studies either. Rosie was not yet of an age to understand what was going on. Helen was, of course, a sunflower. She saw nothing, understood nothing now. She was now a mermaid who was prepared to go to the magic-dispensing old woman and in exchange for her sweet voice, get herself a pair of legs. She was ready to dance on live embers and on needles. She was Mary Magdalene. She was immersed in worshipping her God who had gone to Calcutta to work. She would often sit in front of a mirror, gazing at her own reflection. But she had lost her eyes. She could not see herself. She could only look at herself through the eyes of her man. Within her body, a man's hand roamed. There was magic in that hand. Whichever part of her body the hand touched turned to gold. She became a gold doll. She kept gazing at herself.

The man approaches the nymph in the mirror. She melts into his arms . . . she becomes a little bird. The warmth of security and the sense of having reached a haven lulls the little bird to sleep. Her man was everywhere, he was spread out in all directions. He was the moonlight, he was the rain, he was the wind, the fragrance of the flower. Helen would lie down with her window open at night. She would gaze at the moon and drift into slumber. The moon had appeared in this way in the wilderness of the xaal forest. Like the mermaid who had rested on the cinnamon scented island, Helen was a doe pierced by many arrows. The moonlight was her man's touch. Whichever part of her body it touched, her velvety smooth body resembling rose petals, was scorched. Raindrops scattered on her body; she felt it was her man's damp touch. Her enchanted man drifted to her on the fragrance of flowers. She was always intoxicated. Seeing nothing, hearing nothing, she was oblivious to everything around her in the intoxication of love.

Every woman who makes a man her sun loses, at one point, her ability to realize the truth of what goes on around her. This happened to Helen, too.

She was incapable of understanding her mother's difficulties. How could a girl who had forgotten even herself understand what was happening to others? Her mother had asked for her signature. The only savings that were left now was the amount that Smith Saheb had left in the names of his two daughters. The money in Charles' name had already been taken out before. Charles had wished to start a small enterprise in which he would make metal gates, wire mesh and so on.

Helen lashed out at her mother. Not physically, but certainly through her voice and words. Striking her in a rough voice, she asked her mother how could her marriage take place if this money was used up? People would be arriving from the Barua family. Wouldn't they need to be looked after? Wouldn't she need clothes and other essential items to take along with her to their house? How could her wedding be solemnized if this money was spent now?

Her mother did not say anything. She kept quiet as always. When Sabitri became Elizabeth, when Elizabeth became Koli Mem, she had kept quiet through it all. Now, like before, she kept quiet. Everybody in her life had always seen this expressionless face of hers. Smith Saheb, Helen, Rosie, Anju, Mastor . . . they had seen only this face. She spoke very little, and it was not possible to gauge what she was thinking simply by looking at her face.

Helen, preparing to become the daughter-in-law of the Barua family, was oblivious to everything else. She even forgot about Rosie, the Rosie who remained silent always, like their mother. She stopped wearing skirts and trousers. She bathed early every day and put on a pair of mekhela sador, the traditional two-piece Assamese dress. After shutting the door, she would take a red lipstick and fill the parting of her hair with its colour. She would draw a *phot* on her forehead. Sometimes she would even take an oroni and cover her head with the ansol of her sador, like a married woman. She would look at herself through the gaze of a particular man, as she stared at her reflection—her face bright with the red of the fake xendur, encircled with the oroni. She put up an altar in her room, and on it she placed the sacred book of *kirtans*, devotional songs. Koli Mem and Rosie would look at her secretly, without Helen being aware of it. Sometimes, Charles would grumble to his mother. He had started his enterprise. He was facing a lot of problems while trying to establish this tiny business. He kept nagging his mother to sell off the piano. For some reason, the mother had not been able to broach this subject to her elder daughter. Helen would sit at the piano and sing every morning and evening. She had not been able to say anything to her even when she had returned after three days and three nights, though she was supposed to just go out for a bit with Jeet. Actually, she had spent her entire life with a bowed head, and now, she was unable to lift it and speak up.

In the meantime, Jeet's family got to know of this. There was a huge uproar. Several objections were raised.

Anju's uncle, her father's elder brother who was also Jeet's father, spoke of the importance of a worthy lineage. How could he accept Sabitri, who was from a different religion and caste, as his *biyoni*, his son's mother-in-law? He had had a relative in Smith Saheb's tea garden. The uncle knew everything there was to know about her.

Jeet's elder brothers' wives, *bous*, objected to Helen's lack of educational qualifications. How could a college dropout be deemed suitable for an intelligent, qualified boy?

Jeet's elder brothers objected to Koli Mem's financial position. The whole family would come and sponge off Jeet.

His elder sisters wondered how they could take their husbands to Koli Mem's courtyard when they would have to go to bring the bride home. Koli Mem did not even have the means to offer them a cup of tea.

Jeet listened attentively to it all. He had not yet disclosed to anybody that he had left his job in Calcutta. He felt the job had no future. He had other plans. He had only spoken to his father about it. They had some houses that were rented out in the centre of town. He would get those houses demolished and clear the land. He planned to set up a nursing home there. His father would put in some money, and he would take a loan as well. His eldest brother-in-law was a bank officer; he would surely help in securing the loan. His brothers, too, would help generously when he told them his plan. He had the means, he had the will, he had the ability. He was the youngest in the family and much loved. There had been so much joy, such celebrations in the whole house when he had ranked among the first ten students in the state in his matriculation examination. He was embarrassed even when he thought of it now. A marquee had been put up in the front garden, every visitor was served sweets and tea. His father had been proud of his results.

Now, his family came to him and spoke about Bonani. Dr Bonani Chaliha was a gynaecologist. She was his brother's wife's sister. They were from a good family, moneyed. Bonani was an intelligent girl. Jeet had seen Bonani. Helen had once stood next to Bonani. She was barely five feet tall and of a middling dark complexion. And then there was Helen, whom people would return to see if they saw her glimpsed her on the street. A nondescript, drab *kopou* bird next to a peacock dancing with its feathers unfurled.

But even though one could be intoxicated by the colours of the peacock's feathers, one could not confine it within the four walls of a house. The peacock's colours were only suited to the wilderness of the xaal forest. The common turtle dove, which pecked at the broken rice grains in the courtyard of a home, was best suited for domesticity.

Anju was not present that day. But she had heard about Bonani from Jeet.

Anju did a very strange thing that day. She spat on Jeet's face. Without protesting, he quietly wiped his face. He only said, 'I haven't put her in any trouble.'

Anju wished to reply: It's not her body that is in difficulty, but it is the mind—the heart of that mermaid who exchanged her sweet voice for human legs! The mermaid had lost her voice and danced on a bed of needles now.

*

I had taken Helen on a picnic on the day she got to know of it. It was our annual family picnic. I always proudly took

Helen along with me. I liked to parade her to my friends—this great beauty with a beautiful voice.

Will you be able to forget her ever? If you meet her just once, will you be able to ever forget her? Look how gentle she is. And her mind, her heart? You can't even guess how her mind is, how she can love with her whole being, her heart and soul. She loves me so much. Even if I have a slight fever, she sits by my side, stroking my forehead.

I would swell with pride before all the people gathered there: my sisters-in-law, brothers and sisters, my cousins. If I failed to bring Helen to the picnic, like every year, my relatives would all be disappointed. Jeetda's guitar and Helen's songs would always enliven the picnic greatly. Perhaps it was these melodies that had brought the two of them together.

At first, Helen would not look Jeetda in the face. Perhaps she was aware that there could be a wall between them at any time, and he was distraught by her rejection. He did all kinds of things to get her. Helen had also thought of moving away from there, to put a distance between Jeet and herself. At one point, she was about to leave for a job in a hotel in Mumbai, as a singer. She almost took a job in Air India as well. Jeet became wild with anger. Gradually Jeet, bright with the purity and radiance of youth, became Helen's sun.

As always, the annual picnic was organized. As always too, Helen got ready to accompany the group. In the last two years, she had come to the picnic wearing the two-piece mekhela sador. This year, too, she wore a red pair with a woven yellow floral design. She had grown her golden hair and left it open. It was the fashion in those days. She adorned herself with two light corkscrew curls near her ears. It seemed Jeet loved it when she wore her hair like this. Helen prepared to go to the picnic with her mekhela sador and curled hair. I had not asked her to come along to the picnic, I had only mentioned that it would take place. She came over to our home very early in the morning. When the bus that was to pick me up arrived, she went inside it before me and began to greet my cousins' wives, my bous. She did not notice that none of them were at ease with her. Jeetda scolded me: Why did I have to bring that girl? I did not reply. Even in the cold of December I was sweating. I went with her towards the rear of the bus. I noticed that she seemed a little out of sorts. She had seen Jeet sitting with Bonani on adjacent seats in a two-seater row. Previously, the three of us would always sit together in a three-seater row.

Everything seemed the same to the casual glance. Helen did sing. Just after she had sung three songs, Jeet got up, saying he had to cook the mutton. I took Helen on a walk by the riverbank. I was only looking at Helen. Her face was gradually becoming wan and pallid.

While returning, I told Jeet to tell Helen everything upfront. I could not bear to look at Helen's drawn face. She was still and motionless, like trees and shrubs that became immobile before a storm. If only she could express that storm within her, it would be better . . . if she cried in a frenzy, like a storm-beaten tree, if she could tear to shreds her blood-red clothes, if she wrenched off those golden curls that rested on her cheeks, if the hailstorm swept away the black irises of her eyes. She was a sunflower, now broken and seared by the storm, let the petals fall on to the muddy ground, let her golden colour melt away, let the plant be completely uprooted.

Jeetda did not wish to come with us at first. I grabbed his hand. He looked at my face. I was breathing hard. He said, 'Okay. Let's go.'

It was a misty December night. The bus roared off, leaving in its wake dark fumes that combined with the mist to make it even thicker. In front was a tall girl. Her pearly skin glowed even in the dark. Beside her was a short, thin girl. Bringing up the rear was a man, walking with his head downcast. The short girl repeatedly looked up at the tall girl. Her strides were so long that it seemed as though the pearly skinned girl was being chased. She stood in front of a house and ran in. A dark woman came out and stopped on seeing her. The girl was panting. The woman did not pose a single question. Like a dumb animal, she kept looking. A young girl was standing close to the woman. She, too, did not utter a word. A young boy went striding out. The girl entered a room. The short girl switched on the light. The whole room was filled with the fragrance of tuberoses. On the table was a picture of a young man, smiling. On the side was a bunch of tuberoses, spreading their scent all around. There was an uncovered piano too on the top of which was a photograph. It was the angelic face of a girl with two ringlets dangling on her cheeks. The face seemed cast in gold. She had taken up the chain around her neck between her teeth and was smiling. It looked as though the girl was smiling at her man, her lover.

Anju's skin crawled when she entered the room. Helen had assumed that Jeet would come to her room as soon as they returned from the picnic. He would stay on for a long time before returning home. They would take the narrow lane to see him back towards his home. Anju would stop below the banyan tree. At that time, the pair would be conjoined on a silent melody. Some moments would lapse. Anju would look at the stars in the sky and bless the couple. Her only wish was that Helen's soft heart would remain this way. Let her live her entire life as a sunflower.

The smell of the tuberoses assailed her as if it were the acrid aroma rising from the roasting of dry red chillies. It scorched her chest when she inhaled. Once, Jeet had mentioned that he liked the fragrance of this flower. Immediately, Helen too had started liking tuberoses. She brought in the tuberose bulbs from Anju's mother, and with spade and trowel prepared the ground and planted them herself. Actually, for this mermaid, the fragrance of the flowers and her sun merged and became one.

Anju took up the vase with the flowers and kept it on the ground. She turned around the photograph on the piano, so that it faced away from them. She knew the story behind this photo. Jeet had said that he loved her when she bit the chain around her neck and looked down with her shy smile. Helen had taken Anju with her and gone to a photo studio. Anju had watched the golden-haired mermaid as she sat in the circle of bright light and smiled shyly while she bit her chain. The smile had formed a knot in Anju's heart. Helen had sent the photo through Anju to Jeet. At that time, Anju had gone for admission to the Medical College. Helen was in adoration of her sun and was taking typing lessons. While returning from the typing school, a small knot of young boys, all eager to catch a glimpse of her, would follow. When Jeet got to know of this, he stopped her from going to these classes.

Helen began to ¬dislike going out even for small errands. When she came home for the holidays from her college, Anju scolded her friend soundly. Why did she stop her typing lessons, why did she stop going to her short-hand classes? Helen had replied that Jeet did not like her stepping out to take these classes. On seeing her friend sitting in the room decorated with tuberoses, fashioning her hair into golden vines, Anju became wild with anger. But Helen had only laughed on seeing her so angry.

Helen saw nothing. She did not notice Anju turning the photograph, she did not realize that she had placed the vase of flowers on the floor. She grabbed the front of Jeet's shirt as he entered the room. She seemed crazed. Distraught, she asked Jeet about another girl. Why did he sit with her while going to and returning from the picnic. Why had he been at that girl's side all the time. Why had he said that he needed to cook the mutton and left after only three songs, to go with that girl towards the hills. When she had expressed a wish to have some fried fish, he had brought it to her himself, and then fed her. Why had he held her hand while crossing the stones across the stream? Why had he kept stroking her hair even after he had removed the leaf that had fallen on it? While asking the last question, she looked like a crushed sunflower. She tore Jeet's shirt. Her sador had come undone and was lying on the ground. Her hair had come unbound, loose. A strand of the frenzied sunflower's golden hair blazed with the intensity of fire.

He could not stand the heat of that blaze. He fought too. He, too, shouted. He was a man, wasn't he? Not a woman whose life revolved around the four walls of a house. He had to move around in the world outside; he had to step out. Just because she didn't like it, did it mean he couldn't have a relationship with anybody else? Would he just sit around, staring at her face? They had gone on a picnic; would he not have a little fun with other people? When his elder bou's brother had requested her to sing a particular song, hadn't she laughed and obliged, smilingly? That had been a love song. Hadn't she invited the boys from the typing school and her teacher to their home for Christmas? Hadn't she laughed and had fun with them, hadn't she sung for them?

Defensively, trying to cover up all that had happened, he beat about the bush. He began to shout loudly. His manner made Helen grow wilder. At one point, unable to speak any more, Helen fell on Jeet's chest and wailed loudly. Repeatedly, and exasperatedly, he pushed her away as she clung to him. He kept trying to pry her loose as though she was a swarm of leeches, or a slug.

Looking at her friend weeping piteously and falling on Jeet, Anju got up from where she was sitting. She threw away Helen's photograph. It broke and splintered with a loud crash. She threw the beautiful vase with the tuberoses on the wall; it smashed. The glass from the photo frame and its base shattered. Startled, Helen came away from Jeet. Anju held her hand and spoke.

'Listen to me. Jeetda is going to marry Dr Bonani Chaliha,' she said. 'Next Sunday is the ring ceremony, the engagement. After that, he will get the bank loan that his eldest brother-in-law has arranged and establish a big nursing home on the land given to him by his father. Jeetda's middle brother's wife, his Maju Bou and Bonani are sisters. Their father is a doctor, so is their elder brother. They will all buy shares in the nursing home, and they will put in their own money.'

Jeet hung his head and looked at the floor. Helen halted. Anju prayed that she would get into a frenzy again. Let her pick up the photograph from among the shards of glass, let her pick up the bunch of flowers. Let her cut herself and become bloodied. Let her be the dumb mermaid, dancing on the live coals and needles. Let whatever was supposed to happen, happen.

But nothing happened. Helen became silent. She concentrated on picking up the shards of glass and gathering them together on a piece of paper. Along with the shards, she also put the photo and the flowers on the paper. She went to throw them out. When she returned, she had washed her face and changed her clothes. Only her eyes remained swollen. She brought two cups of tea with her. She gave me a cup and offered the other to Jeet.

He said, 'Look, Helen, I can't go against the wishes of my family. How can I ignore their wishes? How can I ever forget you? Bonani is your . . .'

Jeet wanted to compare Bonani to Helen. He actually wished to make Helen feel better. Holding up a finger, she stopped him from talking.

In a begging tone, Jeet said, 'You had wanted to learn shorthand, you had wanted to learn stenography too. I'll pay the costs. Do whatever you wish to do . . .'

Helen remained calm. Like a dog that dares to lie down on the still warm ashes after a roaring fire has died down, Jeet's courage, too, was growing.

'I'll still have a connection with you,' he said, adding, 'Your mother also had a relationship with Smith Saheb. He, too, was a married man. This would be nothing new in your family.'

'It's very late, please go,' Helen said, using the formal '*apuni*' to address him, rather than the '*tumi*', which she had used all this time. Her voice had the hissing sound that came from pouring water on warm ashes.

She got up and went slowly to her mother. She looked at her mother's face, which was like a dumb animal's. On her mother's eyes was stamped a look of sadness.

'Mummy, bring me the paper, I'll sign it,' she said, without any preamble. She was of course referring to the document that would allow her mother to take out the money that was in Helen's name from the bank.

Her mother's face remained expressionless. Then Helen then did something she had never done before. She abruptly hugged her mother tight, and softly said, 'Ma.'

That night, Anju stayed over at their place and shared Helen's bed. She held her close throughout the night. She massaged her throbbing temples. She combed her golden tresses and put unguents on them. Helen fell asleep holding Anju's hand, which she clasped and placed on her chest. Anju couldn't sleep a wink. Throughout the night, she gazed at the sobbing, pearl-coloured girl of unearthly beauty. She picked up the clothes that had fallen, she wiped the tears that coursed down her cheeks, and she dried the eyes that became damp, repeatedly.

As soon as Helen woke in the morning, she habitually looked towards the place, where the picture and the bunch of flowers had been. Her eyes rested on the empty space. She paused for a bit. It was still dark. Soundlessly, she got up and after washing her face, returned with two cups of tea and two slices of cake. Anju knew very well for whom this cake, decorated with cherries and raisins, was meant. Previously, this cake used to be made very often in Koli Mem's home. Anju was aware that the expensive ingredients for this cake had been bought with the money that Helen earned through taking tuition for children at home.

Sipping her tea, Helen suddenly said, 'Remember, you had said, that mermaid . . .'

'Yes. The story of the Matsyakanya. The Water Spirit.'

'Did the mermaid get her voice back? Or did she die? There's so much water in the sea. She lost her tail, didn't she? She couldn't even return. Her mother, her sisters lived underwater. After the prince went away with the princess, where did she live? Did she stay on that cinnamon-scented island? The island was surrounded by so much water, wasn't she afraid to live there? She fell into the water, and died, didn't she?'

Helen's voice was choking. Anju held her close and began to tell her a new fairy tale.

'This is not a story of a mermaid, but of a princess.'

'The story of the princess who sailed off on a ship with the prince?'

'No. It's the story of an eleven-year-old princess. Do you know what she wanted?'

'A prince?'

'No. The moon.'

'The moon in the sky?'

One day, gazing long at the moon in the sky, the princess grew distraught. She wept and cried piteously. She wanted the moon. She stopped eating food or drinking water. She would starve herself to death if she didn't get the moon. And really, the flower-like princess was wilting. She took to her bed and remained there. She stopped speaking. The royal physician apprehended a crisis. There was a huge outcry all around. What was to be done? The princess was dying.

One day, the king's jester went to the dying princess. She had no strength left to look at his antics. She couldn't even open her eyes. The jester asked her about the moon.

'You want the moon?'

'Yes.'

'Look, here's the moon, here in your hands.' The jester placed a mirror on her lap. The moon was reflected in the mirror. A smile appeared on the princess's pale face. She took up the mirror from her lap. The moon vanished. Tears rolled down the princess's cheeks. She fell on to the pillows again.

On another day, the jester once more came to the princess.

'Tell me, what is the moon made of?'

'Gold, of course.' The princess smiled weakly. Early that morning, the jester had got made a pendant in the shape of the moon. He had attached it to a chain, which he now fastened around the princess's neck.

The princess was very happy. She got up and began to show everybody around her the moon dangling from her neck. She drank some water and then she had some fruit juice. The royal physician ordered that she should be given no solid food for a while. Oil lamps were lit all through the palace. There was joy everywhere, there were celebrations and music.

'But the moon will come out in the sky at night,' said Helen as she looked at Anju's face.

'Yes, it came out. Why shouldn't the moon come out at night?'

'What did the princess do? She threw away the moon of gold? She began to weep and cry again, and took to her bed once more? She died.'

'The princess was not a fool like the mermaid. Neither was she obstinate.'

'What did the princess do?'

'The moon appeared in the sky. The people around began to tremble. The king and the queen looked at the sky tearfully. What would the princess do? They all saw that the princess was staring fixedly at the sky. She then looked at the gold moon around her neck. Nobody dared to come near the princess.

'But the jester approached her. He pointed at the moon in the sky.

'"Isn't that the moon?" he asked.

'"Yes of course it is."

'"And yours?" The jester touched the gold moon on her chest.

'"Mine is the moon, too." There was annoyance in the Princess's tone. She began to explain to the people around who were staring fixedly at them, as one would explain to small children.

'"Don't you know that if you cut your nails, they grow back? If you cut your hair, it grows again? If you lop off the branches of a tree, in time they grow back again? That, in the sky, is the moon. And mine is the moon, too. This is old, that is new."

'Once more, there were celebrations in the royal palace.'

Anju's story was over. Helen pointed outside through the window at the sky. Between the branches of the tall, straight pine tree, the moon was shining brightly.

'See there, the moon, it's new. It's grown back again.'

Both Helen and Anju now laughed out loud at the same time.

MALOTI'S DREAM

(Originally published as 'Malotir Xopon')

Noren's wife Bulbuli's mother lived in the big city. Yes indeed, a big city girl. After all, she did live in Guwahati, the only metro city of Assam. The Ayurvedic College was a short distance from where she lived and a step away from there was the Engineering College. A little distance away, down the bend in the road was the solemn presence of the University. A short walk down the road was the Bhupen Hazarika Samadhi Khshetra and the eye-catching flyovers. At just about arm's length, there was the Saraighat Bridge over the Brahmaputra. And the airport itself was nearby, too.

Our Maloti lived in this kind of an area. Indeed, she was a hundred per cent Big City Girl.

Maloti's neighbours were important people. Since she lived cheek-by-jowl with them, they had to be called neighbours. Maloti lived in a small two-room house behind a strikingly beautiful three-storeyed building. The owners of that striking building were Pratap Chandra Barua and Nomita Barua. Both had retired from high posts in the government. They had studied in the very same Engineering College that Maloti saw every day. Their two sons, too, were respected engineers who had high-paying jobs abroad. People referred to this gorgeous, flower-bedecked house, surrounded with greenery, as the Engineers' Residence.

On the eastern side, adjacent to the wall of the house in which Bulbuli's mother lived was another three-storeyed house. In it lived the eye specialist Barua and his wife Professor Dr Ivy Baruah. To her west was the home of a retired high-ranking police officer, to the north was Maloti's landlord's house. And to the south was the university professor, Dr Girish Chandra Sarma's house. Weren't they all notable personalities? Maloti's neighbours were eminent persons in society. Visitors who came to City Girl Maloti's home would meet these important people. And all the homes and the people who lived there were familiar to Maloti. They all needed Maloti, she was indispensable to them. They also very much needed Noren, a daily wager.

It was next to the huge compounds of these prosperous people that Maloti lived.

The story of how Maloti came from her flood-ravaged village to live among these highly respected people was also interesting. Not just hers alone, it was the story of thousands.

Just as it did every year, that year too, the embankment was breached by the river it was meant to resist. The flood waters drowned the village, and the villagers took refuge in shelters on the main thoroughfare, the main Trunk Road which was at a higher level. This was a fairly normal occurrence. When the flood water receded, the people went back to their homes and tried to repair the broken pieces of their lives.

But that year, the villagers were overwhelmed by the destructive force of the flood water. The swift and powerful currents of the river completely destroyed towns and villages leaving utter devastation in its wake. The people had heard that a dam had burst somewhere up in the hills. Water gushed down, sweeping aside all obstructions. Everything that was in its path was washed away.

The flood waters came and went. But the villagers could not go back to their homes again. Their village was in ruins. Their fields, their homes were all buried in sand. These people did not have the capacity to bring this desert back to life. And they moved out and roamed far and wide in search of even a morsel of food.

This is a story that has been told many times. It has been listened to many times, as well.

Carrying her child on her hip, Maloti had come here with a group of people and become a Big City Girl. There was food to be had if one could but grasp it. There was strength in her body. She grabbed the opportunity with both hands. She managed to get a shed near a marshy wetland to live in. The owner of this hut had a boat. In the dry season, a narrow bridle path would reveal itself. It would go along the edge of the marsh and climb on to the main road. During the rains, when the waters rose, there would be no sign of this path. They had to rely on the boat. The owners of a few fishing families would punt the people across, and earn a bit of money.

Maloti and Noren, too, would use these boats to go to work. Maloti would bundle up Bulbuli on her chest. But the child was terrified of travelling on the boat. Both Noren and Maloti felt this could not continue. They would have to shift from this house. But where could they go? And even if they found another place, how could they afford the rent? Winter would come . . . the rainy season would go. Maloti's domestic life continued in this way.

Noren was a skilled worker. The wealthy people who lived in spacious compounds on the fringes of the main city could not move out of their air-conditioned rooms during summer and so, they needed people like Noren to keep the household running. They were happy with Noren's services and paid for them generously.

This was how Noren came to know of the engineer's family. One day, Maloti too became associated with this family. An elderly couple lived in a large house by themselves. Their children lived abroad. The couple would sometimes go and stay with them for a month or two. Many of their problems were solved when they met Noren and Maloti. Their younger daughter-in-law who lived in Australia would be having her baby soon. They were able to leave their house in their capable hands when they travelled to Australia to help their daughter-in-law with her new baby.

Barua, the engineer, was a practical person. He calculated that if the hut behind the main house—which was full of junk at that moment—was repaired and cleaned out, and some stuff from the main house was sent there, it would be quite habitable. There was already a toilet and bath area behind the house. Electricity and water connections, too, were organized.

Noren and Maloti gathered their few belongings from the shed at the edge of the swamp and began to live in the cottage behind the red-and-green house. The gate mentioned the name of the house—Xewali Nibax or the Home of the White-and-Orange Xewali Flower. A new chapter of their lives started. The dark days of the village that had been buried in the sand, the mosquito-infested hut at the edge of the marsh, the slippery path through sticky mud all became hazy memories. They were surrounded by the safety and security of Xewali Nibax and its eye-catching beauty. Maloti's surroundings were now as beautiful as Xewali Nibax.

When Barua and his wife returned from abroad, they had aged greatly. Baruani, the wife, seemed to have become almost infirm. She alighted from the plane on a wheelchair. Even though Barua himself was in a better state of health than his wife, he was certainly weaker.

Noren and Maloti proved indispensable to them now.

And Xewali Nibax continued functioning more or less as before . . . as did Maloti's home and her domestic arrangements.

Time passed. The Baruas rarely travelled abroad now; long trips by air were becoming too difficult for them. Instead, Baruani spent her time with little Bulbuli, helping her with her studies and playing with her. She even gave her a new name, Mahashweta, after the Goddess of Learning, Saraswati. True to her name, Bulbuli shone in many ways.

The Baruas were very happy with Mahashweta's report cards. And Maloti? A dream had come and alighted in her mind. Her daughter, too, would become an engineer. Just like Baruani Aideo . . . like Aideo's son who lived abroad. The dream grew roots in her mind.

Just as Arjun had seen only the eye of the fish when he was about to shoot his arrow at it, Maloti too now saw only her dream. She had affectionately planted the seed of this dream within her daughter, too. Maloti and her daughter nourished this dream in secrecy, without letting the world know of it. In truth, Maloti only saw the eye of the fish. She was blind to the leaves of the tree, its branches. Indeed, sometimes the entire tree looked hazy. Nothing could change her mind.

But Noren's fate was different. Maloti's mild-mannered, hardworking husband seemed to change before her very eyes. At one point, Noren got typhoid. He became quite weak. He remained at home, unable to work, for almost a month. These days, he could afford to sit like this without working. Besides her work at Xewali Nibax, Maloti had taken on the job of cooking breakfast at the homes of the doctor and the police saheb who lived nearby. Breakfast consisted of rutis and a vegetable stir-fry. Maloti would pronounce the name of this meal slowly and carefully, '*Beyreykphast*'. The soft round flatbreads, the wheat rutis and the different vegetables she cooked were indeed delicious. She was well paid for this. She collected the money painstakingly, bit by bit. Besides, the generosity of the Baruas always helped.

Noren recovered from his illness. With his newly purchased cellphone in his palms, he sat on a chair under the neem tree and hardly ever got up through the day.

Sometimes he had a headache, sometimes he was unwell. Maloti would have to serve him tea and snacks while he sat there. He only left his chair to have his meals; but the cellphone always remained in his hands.

Noren changed in front of Maloti's eyes. The only thing he did was to bring home the free government ration and other items that they were eligible for. The person who had brought Noren the papers that entitled them to get these free items from the government, grew very close to him.

Maloti gradually realized that the two of them often went for a tipple. Like fungus, these liquor shops had proliferated everywhere. How could a soft-spoken person like Maloti prevent Noren from going there? The person who had facilitated the paperwork had introduced him to the liquor. On the days that followed, Noren argued with Maloti without any provocation. He would get angry if she spent some extra money on Bulbuli. Why spend so much on a person who was being raised only to go off to someone's home later? He would frequently express his sadness at not having a son. All of this was actually targeted at Maloti, who hugged her only child close to her heart.

Bulbuli passed her high school examinations with flying colours. Looking at her marksheets, both Maloti and Aideo wept uncontrollably. About four months before Bulbuli's exams, the tall tree that had sheltered Xewali Nibax with its shade, had fallen. Unable to breathe, one day the man of the house had passed away. And then, those very same events that one heard about and saw all the time took place. The elder son came and arranged for the house to be razed and in its place a multi-storeyed building was to be erected as soon as his mother died. He gave Maloti the document in which his father had gifted them that bit of land and the two-room house that stood on it. While handing over the document to Maloti, the son also reminded her of her responsibilities towards his mother.

In the lives of the wealthy, this too is a common occurrence. And now, it happened in Xewali Nibax as well.

These events began to tug at Maloti's dream, trying to uproot it. But the dream did not budge. Bulbuli, too, kept staring at the eye of the fish. And one day, she pierced it with an arrow. From a very young age, she had seen the buildings of the Engineering College a short distance away from their house. And one day, she became a student of this very same institution.

On Bulbuli's first day of college, Xewali Nibax had an air of festivity after a long time. Baruani organized an elaborate prayer gathering of women. Ignoring the sharp pain in her left leg, which had constantly bothered her, she rushed around the house, arranging things. The prayer gathering was a celebratory event.

Six or seven months after that gathering, a white-cloth canopy came up in the compound of Xewali Nibax for the people who gathered for the death obsequies. Maloti's beloved Aideo had left this world forever. A few days after the final shraddha ceremonies, the sons finalized the plans for the multi-storeyed building that would replace Xewali Nibax and left. The small plot of land at the back remained with Maloti and her family.

Maloti's house grew damp and the hearts of the three people who lived in it grew cold. Everything rotted in this dampness. There was mildew inside and slippery green moss outside. Even a chilli plant would etiolate and shoot up, only to droop and die. Grass would become pale and unhealthy looking. Only the colocasia and fiddlehead ferns survived. Noren had turned alcoholic by then, intoxicated day and night. Maloti couldn't keep any money lying around the house. Noren would use it to get drunk.

In the meantime, Bulbuli had already spent three years in college. She had become quieter in those days. How could a dream grow in a cold, damp house where not even a blade of grass grew?

Maloti hired a person to trim the branches of a large bogori tree, an Indian jujube that grew to the east of the house. When Barua and Baruani had been alive, it was Noren who had pruned these trees. A person who was reluctant to pick even a blade of grass now, would he trim a tree for Maloti? She had stopped hoping for anything from him. When the tree was pruned, Maloti's home became somewhat brighter and less damp.

Till Aideu was alive, Maloti had not felt any monetary pinch. She did not have to worry too much about Bulbuli's expenses. Bulbuli, who mostly sat around morosely these days, informed her mother that she would take up running and practice on their college field for some days. Many students came for their running practice there. She would definitely pass the written tests for her finals. She needed to practice running.

Bulbuli bought a pair of running shoes with her own money and prepared to go for her run early one morning. Maloti said, 'You are going to run in the morning, that's good. Your body will get a touch of sunshine and air. How long can you sit with your head buried in books and your laptop? But there's no need to go to the college field. Just run on this road. You're not in the habit of running, don't overdo it on the very first day.'

After this, she handed over the polythene bag with her papers and bank documents to her daughter. Bulbuli calculated the savings they had and withdrew what, for them, was a large sum of money. Bulbuli knew that her mother was planning something. Whenever her mother pursed her lips in a certain way, and took out the polythene bag with these documents, Bulbuli knew that her mother had made up her mind about something.

Maloti had indeed decided on something. Bulbuli looked at the handcart that her mother had bought and realized what her plan was. Noren began to shout angrily when he saw the amount of money spent on it. But he couldn't really shout too much these days and began to cough if he did so.

Maloti told her employers that she would shift the jobs she worked for them from the afternoon to the morning. They had agreed. On returning from work, they had grown accustomed to unlocking their doors and having the phulkas and different vegetables with a variety of chutneys kept warm in their hotcases.

After completing these chores, at around twelve or one o'clock, Maloti would enter her own small kitchen and take out the vegetables and wheat flour. After giving Bulbuli her food, Maloti would push her small handcart down the road to Bulbuli's college itself. She would stop under the large peepul, the huge ahot tree, the ficus at the gate.

At first, people were a bit surprised. But then they got used to having the fluffy rutis and tasty chickpea curries, the boot dails and lentils and chutneys that Maloti made. The boys and girls who stayed in the college hostel would wait for Maloti to arrive with her handcart.

As Maloti's handcart moved on ahead, her dreams too unfurled their branches and leaves. At times, Maloti felt really tired. Sometimes she would get chest pains. She would feel dizzy, there would be a tingling in her hands and feet. Her vision would grow hazy. She would endure it all, grimly. Who could she talk to about this? Like a heron hunched up to catch fish, Noren would sit at a little distance from Maloti's handcart. When the rush of customers was less, he tried to snatch Maloti's money purse. She started hiding her purse and set aside some money for him. As for Bulbuli, this quiet girl barely spoke, but she did what was necessary without fuss. She took her mother to a very well-known doctor in a large hospital.

But it was difficult to follow the medical advice that the famous doctor gave. All right, the bottles of medicines and the tablets could be bought and given to the patient. But how could she stay at home and rest?

Bulbuli took over half her mother's workload. The items on offer on Maloti's handcart, too, changed somewhat. Bulbuli learnt some new recipes from YouTube which

became quite a hit with the students. Bulbuli also did
something else. She arranged for a boy to push her mother's
handcart to its location under the ahot tree. The boy was
Binoy, who ran chores in one of the homes where her
mother worked as a cook. Binoy Das. People called him
Binoy Lengera. Lame Binoy. His left leg was twisted from
birth. He limped a bit when he walked. He studied in Class
ten. He was a quiet boy and a good worker, too. This Binoy
Lengera pushed Maloti's cart to its spot under the ahot tree,
for a small payment every month. He did not come away as
soon as he reached the place with the cart. Though nobody
actually asked him to, he helped out Maloti with a few small
chores of his own free will. Maloti would pack some ruti
and vegetable curry for his dinner, too.

As some time passed, Naren started keeping away
from alcohol. He could not drink any more. He was
now suffering from advanced liver disease. The mother
and daughter bought medicines for him and kept him
alive somehow. One day, however, he passed over to the
other side.

He did not live to see his daughter graduate from
college as an engineer. It was Bulbuli's mother who was
there to witness it.

When she heard about her daughter becoming a
qualified engineer, something happened to Maloti. She
left her small enterprise halfway and took to her bed even
though it was only early evening. She, who never slept
before midnight or even later, after completing her chores,
now slept so heavily that Bulbuli grew frightened. She

slept through the night and awoke only at nine the next morning. Bulbuli stayed up the entire night at her mother's bedside.

Engineer Bulbuli could no longer help her mother regularly. She became busy giving interviews. But she was not successful in being selected in any of the numerous interviews she appeared for. Most of her friends from college went off to study some specialized courses in other cities. The fees for those were very high. Several of them went abroad.

Only Maloti's daughter Mahashweta remained behind.

She grew quieter. Bulbuli, Engineer Mahashweta, was exhausted. These days, when she returned home after appearing for an interview, her mother had stopped asking, 'Is there any hope?' or 'Will something come of it?' Bulbuli, too, did not say anything.

Maloti had grown weaker during those days. Her dizziness was chronic. Sometimes, her regular customers would get tired of waiting for her and leave. Maloti could not vend from her handcart for two or three days every week. The pain in her back bothered her constantly. Like a shadow, Bulbuli was always by her mother's side. The hot water bag, the curry of catfish and skunk vine, the bowl of dail made palatably tangy with freshly squeezed lemon . . .

As soon as she recovered even a bit, she would resume vending from the handcart. Bulbuli took it upon herself to finish all the household chores by herself. Lengera Binoy was there to help with the handcart. He was already being given a monthly remuneration.

The time came when Bulbuli faced a dilemma. What should she do? She had almost decided to take up a job with a company where the pay would be low but the workload huge. But her mother! Who would look after her mother? Who would help her with the work? Her mother was gradually unable to carry on the handcart business.

And then Maloti fell ill with a high fever. In her weakness, she could barely lift her head from her pillow. This time, it was Bulbuli who took out her mother's polythene bag and sat cross-legged on the floor. Inside the faded bag was only emptiness and calamity. Maloti was asleep. Though her fever had abated, she was still very weak. She had had so many medicines in the past few days! Bulbuli put the covers on her mother with care and went to the kitchen. She brought down her mother's containers and packets. There were still a few supplies left there.

That evening, Mahashweta had her bath and wore fresh clothes. She gave her mother a cup of black tea along with a couple of Marie biscuits and went and stood near the handcart. Rutis, chickpea ghoogni, and a chutney of ground curry leaves and sesame. She filled a glass bottle with the popular tamarind and gur relish, the ombol that customers really liked. She cut up some onions too and squeezed a bit of lemon juice on them.

Looking back at her mother, she smiled, then pushed the handcart on to the road. From her bed, Maloti saw that on that day Bulbuli had worn the running shoes she had bought. For some time now, the shoes had been wrapped carefully in a bit of cotton cloth torn from a sador and stored away; but they were still in good condition.

Maloti kept her eyes open for as long as she could see her daughter disappear from sight. Her daughter, Bulbuli, Engineer Mahashweta, who had once wished to run, was now pushing the cart down the road.

BY THE CLOCK

(Originally published as 'Ghori-Koka Aita')

In my childhood, I had a habit of giving nicknames to people. I would bestow a name on any and every object frequently. And as for people, don't even ask. I would address everybody with the name that I had conferred on them.

I had a grandfather. Not my own grandfather, but my father's mother's youngest brother. My granduncle, actually, but we called him Koka, Grandfather. He was even younger than my father. But how could I call that young man Koka? Still, he was after all my *koka*, but 'Powali Koka' or 'Baby Grandfather'. I called him Powali Koka throughout my life.

I called my aunt, my mother's sister, *mahi* . . . Cinderella Mahi. However did that aunt become Cinderella Mahi from Jorhat! Once, I had gone with Mahi to a large gathering in the prayer hall, the Naamghar. When we came out, we discovered that one slipper had gone missing from the pair she had left outside, before entering the sacred space of the Naamghar. A single slipper was lost. Mahi had wondered, why would anyone steal a single sandal? Perhaps a street dog had come and snatched it. I had told Mahi, 'What if some prince has taken the slipper?' Mahi had laughed, and replied, 'A Doggie Prince? Kukur Konwor?'

'Perhaps the dog has a thorn in its ear. Once the thorn is removed, it may become a prince.'

Mahi had laughed uproariously. Watching her laugh, I grew annoyed. What was there to laugh at? It was after losing the slipper that Cinderella married the prince. Maybe the same thing would happen to Mahi.

That is the story behind the name 'Cinderella Mahi.'

And then there was the Double-Fry Jethai. How could we have my Jethai, my mother's elder sister be 'double-fried?' I remember her very well. She was a very affectionate lady. She loved to cook. Her kitchen was enormous. It had a wood-fired hearth, built up and cemented so that one could cook standing up. It seems Jethai had once asked me how I would like my egg, boiled or fried. I had replied, 'Double fry.' Jethai had asked, 'What kind of egg fry is that?' She was not familiar with the term and seemed to have learnt about it from me.

That was the beginning. Whenever I was at Jethai's home, everybody would take me to the kitchen and sit me down near the hearth. 'So,' they would say to me, 'teach us how we should cook a double-fry egg.' I would get fed up. With an annoyed face, I would answer, 'Why do I have to teach you the same thing every time?' And then I would tell them, in a very systematic manner,

'Place the pan on the fire.'

'Pour a little oil.'

'Be careful, don't let the yolk break.'

'Now turn it over.'

'Don't let the yolk break.'

'Sprinkle a bit of salt.'

The double-fry egg was ready. Jethai would then put it on a small bell metal dish and place it before me to eat. I would slurp up the unbroken yolk with great enjoyment. Jethai would regale people with this story, about the egg fry while she was alive and laugh. When I was a little girl, Jethai would often mimic me and say, 'Why do I have to teach you the same thing every time?'

This was my Double-Fry Jethai.

And then there was Rapunzel Pehi. This Pehi was my father's younger sister. She had long hair that reached down to her hips, and that was what gave her the name. I loved her hair when I was a little girl. No doubt the prince had climbed up just such a headful of hair to go up to Rapunzel's bed chamber. While combing her hair, I would often tell Pehi the story of Rapunzel. She loved it. When I went to visit a sickly and feeble Pehi some days ago, she had repeated her request: 'Will you tell me the story of the long-haired princess?' she asked. There was no trace of hair on her head now. When I merely touched Pehi's emaciated hands, her eyes filled up.

Throughout my entire even-paced and happy childhood, there were many people who drenched me with love. But they left one by one—those people whom I had called affectionately by their special names. The fair-as-milk aita was a grandmother, whom I called Gakhir Aita or Milky Aita. Then there was Lusi Borma, who would fry discs of fresh, puffy lusis for us whenever we visited. The rather plump aunt, my *khuri*, who would come up with a story whenever I pestered her for one, was 'Khuri with stories in her stomach—*petot xadhu thoka khuri*'. The granduncle who bought *seetol* fish and invited us for a meal was Long-Boned Fish Koka. Whenever we visited, the Koka who enquired whether we had set up thorny fencing around the pond, the Pukhuri behind our house was Pukhuri Koka. Ukeel Koka, or Lawyer Grandfather, Daktor Bordeuta or Doctor Uncle, Judge Uncle, Mouzadar Khura . . . I named these sober and serious men according to their professions and the posts they occupied.

Whenever I close my eyes, I see these people. Memories and stories run through my mind as if they are playing on a movie screen. They bring a multitude of emotions to my mind.

My father's mother's eldest brother was our Judge Koka. Yes, he was a judge. Once, when I was still a little girl, he had taken me to see the High Court. He pointed out the throne-like chair on which the judge sat and presided over the court. I had sat on it for a bit. In a serious voice, Koka had told me that one should not sit on that chair in that manner. I had bowed then, in the same way I did in front of the altar in the Naamghar, the prayer hall. Koka had said, 'You are already serious about your studies. One day, you shall come here as a judge and sit on this chair.' I had gazed at the chair for a long time.

One day, I had gone out with Daktor Khura. After some time, we reached the path that went up to the graveyard that dated back to the British era. Daktor Khura alighted from his ricksha, and I too did the same. Khura went to the back of the ricksha and pushed it up the hill road. Seeing him, I too did the same. Daktor Khura told me that the ricksha-pullers got heart disease if they had to keep pulling their load of passengers on steep roads like this. Whenever they reached this kind of road where the ricksha had to be pulled up, it had become his habit to jump down and help by pushing it.

Yes indeed, so many stories, so many memories of those people whom I had called by special names. Wrapped up in each name was a particular time, particular period and memories entangled in these nicknames. Each one was flesh and blood, a real person. But now when I look back, I can't touch or hold them. They look like shadows on a screen. But when the shadows on the screen receive a bit of warmth from the heart, the people thaw out. They come to me. I can place my hands on that warmth, I can move around very easily with them. I can speak with them, and I can tell them about my thoughts and feelings, and they can do the same.

A peal of laughter and a question. 'A doggie prince?' A request that came through suppressed laughter, 'Teach me how to make a double-fry egg.'

Long hair and a fairy tale.

A plump woman with a potbelly and lots of stories.

An unconscious smile on a sober face . . . 'You already study hard . . .'

A compassionate healer who pushed a ricksha on a steep, uphill path,

How can I forget any of them?

And how can I forget Ghori-Koka Aita? The Koka and Aita of the Clock? Ghori-Koka was the kind of person one can never forget. The picture of that enormous clock is still stuck in my mind—it is impossible to erase. Along with it, the resonant chimes of that clock. It is not easy to forget these things.

The person whom I had named Ghori-Koka was my father's sister's husband. His Peha. This particular aunt, his Pehi, had practically raised my father. We had noticed that there had been a special bond between our father and this pehi right to the end of their days. Most of our visits were to their home.

My father's Peha, my Ghori-Koka was my Grandfather of the Clock. He was also a well-known criminal lawyer who went by the name of Shri Kailashnandan Barboruah. His father, the Late Durganandan Barboruah was a powerful Mouzadar in charge of a fiscal division called a Mouza. Ghori-Koka was born with the proverbial silver spoon in his mouth. He completed his BL from Calcutta University successfully and came into his own as the heir to considerable wealth and property.

He started his practice from his father's main house and despite his inheritance, made his own money. People said that if a case was taken up by the lawyer Kailashnandan, victory was guaranteed. This was not untrue. Until today, lawyer Kailashnandan had never come face to face with the word 'defeat'. He doubled, even tripled his father's wealth as his fame spread far and wide. At a young age, Kailashnandan acquired mythical proportions. People said that if the lawyer Kailashnandan just stuck a twig on the ground, it would sprout, become a tree and begin to bear fruit before the very eyes of onlookers.

He established the first printing press in town, the Durganandan Printing Press. He also established the town's first flour and rice mill, Nandan Rice Mill. And there were several other such ventures that were so successful that they were bent over like fruit-laden trees. He renovated the house that his father had built and turned it into an eye-catching mansion. Many stories were told about him. His punctuality was legendary. He was never late or early, even by a minute. The clock could show the wrong time, but lawyer Kailashnandan Ukeel was never unpunctual.

People often talked of his fitness routine. It was said that along with his legal books, he also read books on Ayurveda. He grew many kinds of plants used to make herbal medicines. He himself would consume various herbs and the juices of different roots and plants. Even though he was of medium height, Kailashnandan was a vigorous man with a powerful physique. He hardly ever spoke, only opening his mouth when it was imperative. And these words were almost always orders and commands. Several people were ready to carry out these commands in the court, printing press, rice mill and at home. And in the centre of all this was Kailashnandan Ukeel, a sober, serious man who did not recognize, or did not wish to recognize, defeat as he moved around like an emperor.

Once, while still a student in Calcutta, he had gone to an auction house. When British officers left the country, they often auctioned off their furniture and other goods. Along with other items, a clock was being auctioned. This Swiss clock was as large as the mat on which devotees back home sat in the Naamghar to chant their hymns. The pendulum shone like gold. Even as he gazed at it, the clock struck ten. The sonorous tones of the clock striking the time drowned out all other sounds for a while. He bought the clock.

From that day onwards, the clock became his companion. At first, the lawyer kept the clock in his own office chamber. Later, he kept it near the dining table. It was a spacious table, around which ten people could easily sit, leaving ample room for movement. The lawyer had supervised the décor of the room himself. Besides the dining table, there was a fridge, and an eye-catching sideboard to keep crockery. He kept the clock just beside the dining table, and its face was well above it.

There was a reason for keeping the clock here. At that point, Kailashnandan Ukeel's mother's health was deteriorating quickly. The lady suffered from dizziness too. She would often apply triphola herbal medicines on her head and lie in bed. Truth be told, she was tired. Her entire life, she had rushed around that enormous mansion, and now she was weary. Sometimes, even if she did not feel dizzy, she would apply aloe vera and just lie in bed. Leave alone her son, she would be disinclined to leave her bed even if a God descended from the heavens. There were many domestic helpers to look after the other chores in the house. But who would do the personal chores for her son?

For a while now, her son was not getting anything on time. Kailashnandan Ukeel woke up at four in the morning and drank a glass of lukewarm lemon water with honey. After his yoga practice, he would have a cup of black tea with lemon, along with two biscuits. At six-thirty he would have a spoonful of brahmi leaf juice. At eight-thirty, he would eat two dry rutis along with a cup of milk tea. Before leaving for the courthouse, he would have his meal of rice at ten. But of course, it was not just any kind of meal. He would only have foods recommended by Ayurveda. He had read books on this practice and followed the recommendations rigorously. Even the cooking of these meals had to follow a special method. Certainly, there were many domestic helpers in the house. But the helpers could not really understand these rules. His mother had been punctual and meticulous. But after the passing of her husband, who knows what happened—the lady just could not put her mind to any job. The time she spent on her bed grew longer. She recognized that there was need for another woman in the house and constantly nagged her son about getting married. Someone had to supervise the home. As soon as the daughter-in-law arrived, she would hand over all the responsibilities and would herself travel a bit. Till that day, she had not set foot in the homes of her brothers and sisters. She complained that she was quite fed up.

She tried everything to induce her son towards marriage. She would lie in bed, keenly aware that the household was in a mess. 'I am not feeling too well,' she would say and

take to her bed at odd hours of the day. Her son's hour for
breakfast would arrive but the food would not be ready,
and he would lose his temper. And someone in the house
would say 'Ai is dizzy. Not well at all.'

It was during this time that one day Kailashnandan
met Xonpahi, the youngest daughter of Head Clerk
Jadunath Saikia of the Kopahtoli Tea Estate. Xonpahi was
my father's Pehi, his father's younger sister.

Kailashnandan was going to the courthouse. He had
bought a new Landmaster and had hired Anil as the driver.
He drove very calmly and steadily. It was just past ten in
the morning. Anil had left the driveway of the Barboruah
mansion and steered the car on to the main road. Abruptly,
Anil took the vehicle to the side of the road and stopped.
Over the last few days, the Amar Circus had created great
excitement in the town. Today, the show was leaving
for another town . . . This was no small event. A huge
procession was on the road. Camels, horses, elephants,
cages with lions and tigers, a bunch of small dogs with white
fur, a large number of monkeys, a couple of chimpanzees,
all kinds of packs and bundles were on the road, moving
onwards. People as well as vehicles had parked on the side
of the road.

Kailashnandan was sitting in his vehicle, watching
the procession. He noticed that in the gap between the
camels and the elephants was a girl. She could neither go
ahead nor could she move back. She had been walking
towards her college, when she was encircled by the circus
as it moved ahead. With her reddened face and round

eyes, it seemed as though she would burst into tears at any moment.

Such a foolish girl, this one. Instead of walking ahead, why did she not just step aside like so many others had done? There were elephants in front and camels behind her. And then the horses came up beside the girl and began to march in step with her. The foolish girl kept walking. One of the horses would surely kick her. Did she even know what a blow from the hind legs of a horse could do?

Kailashnandan could wait no longer. He alighted from his car and went to the girl. Holding her by the hand, he dragged her out from the procession.

The girl was trembling. She looked frightened and cowered inside the car, unable to speak. She took sips of water that the lawyer offered her, gradually finishing off the entire bottle. He gazed at the frightened girl with a mixture of amusement and curiosity. Perhaps he felt a tinge of affection that he had never felt for anybody else in his life. She was frightened and all huddled up like a pigeon chased to a corner by a cat.

Kailashnandan scolded the trembling girl, 'If I hadn't been here now, you would have been trampled by the elephants, camels and horses.'

She cowered once more, when he dropped her off at a local Girls' College. She couldn't even raise her head. After her fear had abated, she was now filled with embarrassment. She looked like a leaf of the touch-me-not plant that had been stroked, Kailashnandan laughed. 'Don't fall between horses and elephants anymore.'

In her state of fearfulness and embarrassment, she really did look like a touch-me-not leaf, a lajukilota, that had been touched by a human hand now.

This lajukilota was my Ghori-Koka Aita. She was Xonpahi, my great-grandfather's youngest daughter, my father's Pehi. Pehi's husband, my father's Peha, was the head clerk at Xontoli Tea Estate. After she completed her matriculation, she came to the newly established college and was pursuing her undergraduate studies. Hardly anyone remembered her by the name Xonpahi for she had many pet names and terms of endearment. Her pet names matched her nature perfectly. There were two names in particular that people liked to address her by, Peneri and Peneki, one who sheds tears at the slightest excuse. And a dawdler, somebody who is very slow to complete a chore. They suited her very well. She would take up a chore and continue in a finicky way for hours. After waking up, it took her an hour to wash up and another hour to get dressed. And if somebody said something about it, she would start sniffing and snivelling. She was a crybaby, a Peneri, what else could she be called? As the youngest daughter of the house, there was no great inconvenience with Xonpahi's eccentric habits. Her father would tell her to pour him a cup of tea and go in to have his bath. Her mother would tell her to get ready to go to a wedding, and would, meanwhile, cook the rutis and vegetables. It was all going quite okay. Peneki, or Peneri, would finish her chores while humming to herself. She would do some work around the house, too.

And she would also do what she liked best—reading books. She had, at all times, a book in her hands, which robbed her of her concentration on other chores. She would do the required chores in between reading the book. Her father would tell her to pour him a cup of tea. She would tell herself that she would quickly finish reading a page of the book but would end up reading three. When her mother would tell her to get ready for a wedding, she would read a few pages in between taking out a pair of *paat* silk clothes and wearing them. Obviously, she would be nicknamed Peneki, laggard, dawdler, what else? Even though she was given this name, she continued to read, without any obstruction or hindrance from others.

Kailashnandan Ukeel brought home this girl, Peneri, or Peneki or Xonpahi as a bride. When people got to know about Kailashnandan's choice of a bride, they unanimously commented on her good fortune, 'How many girls are there with the kind of good fortune that this head clerk's daughter has? She's got the moon in the sky, the pearl in the heavens in her hands now.'

Some were envious and gossiped. The head clerk was getting too greedy. Was he so dazzled by the man's wealth that he had to give his daughter in marriage to a man who was ten years older than her? She was quite good in her studies, couldn't he let her enroll for higher studies? He only cared about money.

And what about Xonpahi herself? It came as a shock to her; she had never expected this. While she was still hesitating, she found her life controlled by a large clock that sounded out the hours with a loud, resonant reverberation. It seemed as though the entire household had combined forces in tying her up to the clock.

On the very first day, her mother-in-law explained her son's habits to her: at what time he had which meal, what food, the lukewarm lemon and honey water he had on getting up at four a.m. After that, at six a.m. a cup of black tea and also, vegetable juice an hour before dinner, sometimes, depending on the vegetable, with grated ginger, lemon juice or ground pepper. Dinner had to consist of two rutis along with a bit of boiled rice. The rutis had to be soft, but no oil was to be added. Just before going to bed, at ten p.m. sharp, a glass of hot milk, with less than half a teaspoonful of sugar. There were numerous domestic helpers in the mansion, she herself would not actually have to do any of the cooking, she just had to supervise everything. The elder woman had stroked her face and arms and said affectionately, 'You don't have to bother about me, Ai, just look after your man.'

Xonpahi did try to look after this quiet, affectionate lady. She tried to give her a cup of tea herself when she came out of the prayer room in the morning. The lady was even tempered, and not at all demanding. As long as the other people in the house were happy, she was fine. Actually, as long as her son was satisfied, so was she. What would be required to keep this lady happy? She would be filled with gratitude if a cup of tea was placed in her hands.

And the man himself? The person who had covered her body from head to toe with gold, buried her in expensive clothes, became a clock for her. The timepiece would march on, swiftly, relentlessly, without a pause. She would try to keep up and run in unison.

In the beginning, the man would sit at the table at the set times and call her by her name for his requirements. Later, there was no sound, no request for anything at all, just the presence of a sober and serious person. One glass of lukewarm lemon juice with honey . . . two spoonsful of the juice of the pennywort greens. Two rutis . . . a bowl of vegetable juice . . . a glass of milk with only a bit of sugar . . . a bowl of crushed pomegranate seeds . . . a plateful of sprouted mung beans . . . a large clock, a golden pendulum that swayed from side to side, its sober, resonant chimes, and a man who would come and sit at the table absolutely on the dot. Leave aside berating or scolding anybody around, if possible, he would not even speak to anyone.

Yet he saw everything. He had no physical disfigurement, nothing that could intimidate others. But everybody around was afraid of him. When Xonpahi Aideu got her period, she was barred, by tradition from doing any chores in the household, or even moving out of her room. The horde of helpers would count the number of days for her to resume her duties. Even as she ran around according to the demands of the clock, Xonpahi became, almost without her knowing it, the mother of three children and the 'Aideu', the respected lady head of a large establishment.

The books she had always carried with her slipped from her hands. She clearly remembered the day she had quit reading books. It was just after her wedding. The perfume of the ritualistic turmeric and lentil paste that had been rubbed on her before her pre-nuptial bath still lingered on her body. On the eighth day after her wedding, on the *aath mongola* when she came to her parents' house for the first time after her marriage, they had filled the car with her beloved treasures—the ones she had received as wedding gifts. Ratna Mashima and Sreedhar Mesho from the tea estate her father worked in, had given her a thick volume of *Sahib, Bibi, Ghulam*.

She had sat by the trunkful of books and opened it as soon as she returned to the mansion, her new home. She had taken up that fat volume first. It was eight in the evening. It was time for the lawyer to have his vegetable juice. Rambha bai, the help, had squeezed out the juice of boiled spinach leaves and strained it. But she was unsure about what should be added to the juice of the boiled vegetable. Grated ginger, or ground black pepper or perhaps cilantro? The lawyer's mother had gone to her brother's house, there was a big assembly at the Naamghar. She was not well either. Nou Aideu, the New Bride, was in her bedroom.

The lawyer barely had a sip of the soup and left the table. In the kitchen, there was consternation. And there she was, immersed in her book. When she got up the next morning, once again she took the book in her hands. The lemon juice that Rambha bai served was otherwise all right. The only thing was that it was a little too warm. Peneki was used to running late. She left her book with a practiced gesture and came running to the kitchen. It was late. Late by fifteen minutes! Ukeel Deuta, as he was respectfully addressed by the staff, had left the table without having his black tea. Rambha bai and the others had been waiting in the kitchen for Aideu to come and serve the tea. The usual routine was that they would make the tea in the kitchen, and somebody would come and take it from them and serve it at the table.

After the lawyer left, she went back to the bedroom. But she could not find that book again. She had left it on the bed, marking the page till the point she had read. She understood the hint. Even so, she would sometimes open the trunkful of books, take one out and stroke it lovingly. The intervals between her opening the trunk gradually grew longer. After some time, the lock caught rust. The trunk had been pushed under the bed, into a not-so-easy-to-access place. And after the birth of her first child, it became very difficult to drag out the heavy trunk from below the bed.

Between raising their three children and the numerous responsibilities of the household, she barely kept track of anything else around her. How could she even take the hooked iron rod and pull out the trunk? But every night, as she prepared to sleep, she remembered the trunk. She would think of taking out the books and airing them. But she would forget about it in the morning. The trunk remained where it was. She had learnt to beat the clock, even with a baby on one arm and kitchen utensils in the other hand. The lawyer found everything ready when he came to sit down at the table. She never gave him any cause for complaint. She had easily defeated the clock.

It was at that time that Xonpahi, Peneki or Peneri became my true Ghori-Koka Aita. Often, my father's Pehi would send a written invitation to my father to come and spend a few days of the summer holidays with her. Visiting Ghori-Koka Aita meant lavish meals and gifts of new clothes. I remember that Ghori-Koka bought the clothes for us himself. He had a specific store that he frequented, where he was well known. He just had to say whether the clothes were for a boy or a girl and the child's age, and the items would be put into the car. Everybody praised the clothes that Koka bought for us. But I did not care at all for the dresses he bought. They would be the same colour every time, a shade of grey. I preferred floral prints on colourful dresses. I would get quite irritated, though I never showed it. Why did he have to buy the clothes himself? When we went clothes shopping with our mothers, it felt like a small festival. The salesman of the shop would spread out the clothes. We would feel one with our fingers and examine another before choosing for ourselves. Why would Ghori-Koka not allow us to accompany him to the shop? Ghori-Koka Aita, our grandaunt, always wore those gloomy shades of grey. In their home, too and everywhere else, this colour persisted. Curtains, bedcovers and bedsheets, cushion covers, everything was of that dull grey colour. All right, let Koka wear this colour if he wanted to, but why did he have to make others wear the same hue?

Of course, I never spoke about it to others. One day, I asked Aita, 'Why don't you go yourself to buy your own clothes? Ma goes in a group with Ranu's mother, Punyo Mahi and others. I go with them. It's wonderful!'

Aita smiled slightly and said, 'I don't even know how to choose clothes. If I bring back something that I like in the shops and when I look at it at home, I don't like it at all.'

'Don't you want to go to the shops?'

'No, Majoni,' she said with affection, 'I don't even feel like going. I don't like the crowds, the noise, the jostling at all.'

'You get a headache if you go out in the sun, don't you?'

'Majoni, I've hardly stepped out of the house all this time. I find it difficult to move outside now. My eyes hurt and everything becomes dark. After I return, I feel quite unwell.'

'Are you scared?'

'Yes, I'm scared. Very scared. I feel as though those cars and other vehicles will knock me down and push me into a drain. I'm terrified of even crossing the road.'

'But you used to walk everywhere before. Deuta talks about it. If you heard that your friend had a book for you to read, you would go in the noon heat of summer.'

'I was a young girl at that time, wasn't I?'

'I heard you used to read a lot. Deuta always talks about how much you loved reading.'

Actually, I had brought a couple of my books of fiction for this Aita. I had tried to broach the subject. But at that point, the clock struck six resonantly. Aita jumped up, Ghori-Koka would be here to have his ruti and stir-fried vegetables. Koka used to return home at four, earlier. But now he had established a tea estate. There was a small cottage there, as well. He would often go from the court itself to supervise the work in the garden. He would rest a bit there, oversee whatever work needed to be done, and return around seven in the evening.

At that time, Aita's sons were away from home, studying. Her knee joints and elbow developed chronic pains. She seemed to have shrunk. There were many consultations with doctors and ayurvedic practitioners; all kinds of allopathic medicines and nutritious foods were prescribed. However, she seemed to be neglecting her own health. She was indifferent not just to her own health issues, but also seemed to be indifferent to everything around her. Looking at this woman, who walked with a bad limp now, who could say that she was ten years younger than Ghori-Koka? My Koka, though, was still quite vigorous. He was still forging ahead; he still did not know the meaning of defeat. And keeping pace was the clock and its resonant chimes. It had been taken for cleaning and servicing just once, but it was still going on as before. And limping with clockwork precision, in synchrony with the chimes, without caring for her own health at all, was a lame woman who could not even bend her knees.

Ghori-Koka Aita would get a bit of rest at night at that time. Rambha Bai would massage her knees with a liniment that smelled of fish oil. Aita would doze off. For a while then, she had been able to fall asleep only towards dawn. To get up at four in the morning, especially during the cold, damp winter months, was very difficult for her. But still she arose.

For some time now, she had begun to feel a sense of gratitude towards the man. He had stopped bothering her at night. In the beginning, she had felt a little guilty. Later, she convinced herself that this was quite normal. After all, he too was ageing. He was ten years older than her! She felt a new respect for the serious and sober person. What did she have to do, after all? She just had to arrange a few things for him on time. He had seen to it that she had no worries. He had taken on the responsibility for all domestic requirements. He advised his sons about their studies and career paths. He took care of their admissions to suitable colleges. When she looked around, everybody seemed to be beset with so many worries, they had so many problems, so many troubles and sorrows. They must all be saying, how many are there who have the same good fortune as Xonpahi? She would try to convince herself, after all why should they lie? They were telling the truth.

Meanwhile, Kailashnandan's material worth and his properties were growing rapidly. The tea estate had started yielding profits as well. He had worked really hard to establish it. Sometimes, he would go there straight from the court and even spend the night there. Once, when the boys had come home for the holidays, he had taken all of them to see the estate. She had been astonished to see the verdant Xonpahi Tea Estate. How could this man work so hard? Yes, of course he could. Who else could work like this man, who did not waste a single moment of the day?

The effort she put into beating the clock grew even greater.

Before he died, Kailashnandan Ukeel had set his affairs in order. While alive, he had passed on the responsibilities to his sons and settled everything. He had arranged for Xonpahi to receive money every month. Just before he died, he bought the land in front of his house and built a row of cottages to rent out. A small family would be able to live comfortably in each one. There were arrangements for water and all other necessities. The row of cottages filled up quite fast with small families. They were all young couples from around the country, some with a son, some with perhaps a couple of daughters and some couples with a pregnant wife. They all had a limited income. Some were holding down minor jobs while others had some small businesses. Their furnishings were sparse, too. It had become a habit with Aita to sit on her verandah till Ghori-Koka's return and watch these small families. Unknown to the lawyer, she had developed a kind of relationship with them. The vegetable garden behind the mansion yielded a large amount of produce. She felt a great deal of happiness when she distributed these vegetables, greens and fruits to the tenants. Her three sons were now flying the flag of the Barboruah family high in other cities across the country. She did not see them even once a year. They too, had wives and children, and were happy in their domestic lives. She was satisfied with this.

Kailashnandan passed away in due course. At the time of his death, he was in his house in the tea garden. Along with other relatives, Aita too went there to bring back his mortal remains. Somebody had taken along the lady, stunned as she was, in the vehicle to the estate.

She saw that the house was full of people but did not recognize a single person. They moved aside and cleared the path for her. They wept when the body was taken to the funerary vehicle. In the corner of the room in which the body had lain on a wooden bed was a woman. She was weeping. She was a full-figured young woman. She was taller than the average Adivasi women who lived on the estate. She was fair. On her wrists were two thick gold *balas*, a heavy gold multilayered *chandrahar* with floral designs that reached down from her neck to below her chest, and in her earlobes were weighty traditional gold earrings, *kerus*. Both her sari and the warm wrap she was wearing were grey in colour. The wrap had floral embroidery over it, in a different shade of grey.

The obsequies, the shradha ceremonies were held with great attention to rituals and also grandeur. Many people visited to condole. They thronged the house. They brought with them the ritual bereavement food, fruits, vegetables and other items that were permissible in a house of mourning. These were of such large quantity that even when they were distributed to other people, there was still a lot left. The lame lady was given a pair of white mekhela sador to wear. A simple bed was made for her on the floor, for as a new widow she had to sleep on the ground. She was given an evening meal of ritually permitted foods.

I was studying at the university at the time. I still used to call my Aita, Ghori-Koka Aita. Who knows what happened to Aita, but she would not let me budge from her side. She would often hold on to my hand. Many people came to express their condolences to her. She would only speak in monosyllables. My parents left for home, promising to return for the final shraddha ceremonies. Aita refused to let me go. I had wished to return as well. I had never felt too comfortable with my Koka's relatives. I felt ill at ease with Aita's three daughters-in-law. Unable to see a way out, I remained behind. Through all the many ceremonies leading up to the shraddha, I stayed close to Aita. Often, her hands would sweat, it seemed as though something within her was shaking up her entire being. Sometimes, I felt the shudders that engulfed her. I got the feeling that she would be unable to stand and would soon fall to the ground. I would try to make her drink a glass of water, eat a piece of apple that I had cut and placed before her.

The ceremonies of death, the shraddha and the subsequent blessings given to all were over. The guests, the visitors were preparing to return home. The discussions around Ghori-Koka's will started. It was only then, it seemed, as though people discovered a woman clothed in white, walking around with a limp, putting the house to order, keeping the things that were scattered around in their proper places. She kept me very close to herself. Apparently, this Ghori-Koka Aita was afraid to stay alone.

The clock itself kept up its resonant chiming. Sometimes, Aita would be startled by the sound of the clock. She would get up from her sleep, she would get up even while she was sitting, with a start.

The noted lawyer Kailashnandan Barboruah's will was a watertight one and so nobody could dispute it. Once more, the people began to whisper among themselves. Look at this woman's good fortune! He had made all the arrangements for her to live a life of great comfort. In fact, he had made monetary arrangements for her to go on pilgrimages, too, if she wished. Even the obsequies after her death, the expenses of her shraddha ceremonies were taken into account under separate heads. The sons were satisfied as well.

He had also arranged for an Adivasi woman from his tea estate to have a regular income from the estate itself. He had willed her the house there as well. People talked about his generosity. She would make a cup of tea or cook him a meal when he went to the estate. He had not forgotten even that woman who worked for him. In his will, he had also kept aside some money that could be taken out and utilized for my wedding. Indeed, he had not forgotten anybody.

As Aita got ready to sign the legal documents, she expressed a wish that all the property and money that had been kept in her name should be transferred to her three sons. She was holding my hand at the time, again. At times, when she clutched me hard with her sweaty, trembling hands, I found it difficult to bear. Ghori-Koka Aita had never said anything about herself, or her wants and desires. Now, for the first time, in a firm voice, she was asking for something for herself.

Everybody listened to her in silence. She gave away the huge mansion that was now in her name to her sons, as well as all the other property. All she asked for was the row of houses. She planned to live in one of those herself.

All the assembled people expressed their shock. This lady would be making her home in proximity to those people who lived there. But Aita did not listen to anybody. She had asked the tenants of one of the cottages to vacate the place. She now chose a few select items from the mansion and went to live there. Her sons decided to rent out the mansion to a large private company for their Guest House. They were planning to remodel the house in order to make it more suitable for a Guest House.

One day, Aita got two men to drag out that trunk from under the bed. It was very rusty. The trunk was taken to Ghori-Koka Aita's new home. Everybody was curious about its contents. They all assumed that the greater portion of Kailashnandan's undisclosed wealth was in this trunk itself.

My Ghori-Koka Aita took me with her to settle the new house. Perhaps Aita herself did not realize it, but after she moved into this house, the affection that her daughters-in-law felt for her seemed to overflow. All their talk, their discussions would ultimately come to a rest on the topic of the trunk.

'Why do you need to keep this old, rusty trunk?'

'I'll buy a new one for you.'

'Give this one to Rambha bai.'

'This lock is probably jammed.'

'The planks on which it had been placed under the bed have rotted away.'

'The whole floor will be spoilt.'

'She's a woman living alone, why does she need to keep the trunk with her?'

'People will suspect that it's stuffed with valuables.'

Ghori-Koka Aita called Jeebon from next door. He had a fruit stall at the nearby crossroads. She asked Jeebon to push the trunk under the bed. He couldn't even budge the trunk. He called two more men and pushed the trunk under the bed. Aita sat on the floor, and tried to see if she could reach the trunk. She directed the men to pull it out a little.

Ghori-Koka Aita's new home was now more or less settled. The sons and daughters-in-law were clearing up Ghori-Koka's bedroom. They were bundling up some items. I was sitting in the next room, stitching the ends of two of Aita's plain sadors, without *paris*, woven borders. Suddenly, I heard my own name, Jupitora, being mentioned in the conversation that was taking place in the other room. The words came to me even through the sounds of the room being cleaned up.

'The old woman is hanging on to that trunk as though it has all the treasures collected by the God of Death himself.'

'I wonder what's in it?'

'Her grandniece must know.'

'She's put on this show of not wearing any jewellery, but what's the use?'

'Tell me, which woman doesn't desire gold and jewels?'

'I love old Assamese jewellery.'

'I've heard that Deuta gave the old woman a huge amount of gold. The heavy gold jewellery covered her from head to toes.'

'How much antique jewellery did we get at our wedding?'

'It's all stuffed there.'

'Wait and see, we'll be leaving, and then Jupitora will make off with all of it.'

'She's a sharp one. Good at her studies and intelligent too.'

There was a huge thud from the next room, the sound of something falling. From Ghori-Koka's room came the deep, booming sound of the clock striking three. I quickly packed my things and went to Ghori-Koka Aita. Trying to sound as normal as possible, I said, 'Deuta has sent for me. There's some job interview tomorrow.'

Ghori-Koka Aita was silent for a while. I felt the touch of a weak palm on my cheek.

'Go, then. Come again during your holidays,' Aita's lips quivered.

Some people entered the room. They were carrying that huge clock and also a bundle. Aita told them to take back the clock. 'Tell Borbopa to keep this,' she said, referring to her eldest son. 'He's got the habit of punctuality from his father.'

Aita opened the bundle. Inside a polythene packet were some books. I recognized a few of them. I myself had brought these story books from my own store for Aita to read. *Stories from Russia, Stories from Greece, Stories of the Blue Sea.*

There was also another book, a fat volume. Ghori-Koka Aita picked it up. *Saheb, Bibi, Ghulam.*

Aita opened the book. Bookmarked on the thirtieth page was a lace-edged silk handkerchief, with an embroidered butterfly in one corner. The handkerchief was stained in some spots and was stuck on the page. Very delicately, Aita prised the handkerchief free. The material came apart into four pieces along the creases. Aita took the edge of her white sador and wiped the book. As she did so, Aita looked at me and laughed.

I gazed at Aita's radiant face creased in laughter. After which I hurried out to catch the four o' clock bus.

THE YELLOW FLIPFLOPS

(Originally published as 'Halodhiya Hawai Sandal')

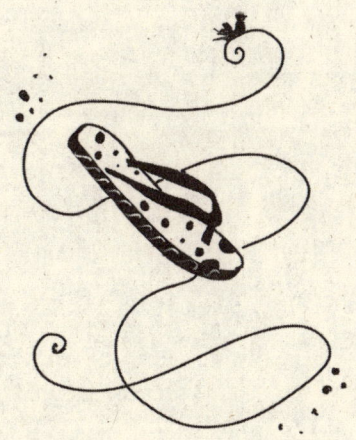

The bride let go of her father and went and hugged her mother. 'Ma! Where are you sending me!' she sobbed, as she slumped on her mother. The gold-worked sador she wore fell off her shoulder. The vermilion phot of xendur on her forehead and the line drawn with sandalwood merged. The bride's mother, too, was quite distraught. The people who had come to see off the bride wept piteously.

Suddenly, over the sobs and the wails came a shout, 'Hold on to the mirror carefully! It was about to fall just now!'

The people surrounding the bride looked to see where it came from. The bride's elder brother was Bhargob Choudhury, an important official posted in the oil town of Duliajan. He was supervising the loading on to the truck of the furniture that would accompany the bride to her new home. The bride's Bordeuta, her father's elder brother, Headmaster Rammohan Choudhury was giving directions to her second eldest brother, Dr Ranjan Choudhury in a soft voice. The bride's elder Khura, Murulimohan Choudhury, her father's younger brother, who was an officer in the Agriculture Department, was, with her younger Khura, Krishnamohan Choudhury, the land revenue officer, organizing the vehicles in which the people who would accompany the bride to her in-laws' home would travel. The bride's elder brother Bhargob would have to return to Duliajan this very day. There was no question of them travelling in his Maruti. Ranjan had not yet bought a car. He travelled everywhere on his motorbike. The headmaster's car was a second-hand Ambassador, how could they send that? There was a dent in the place where a cow had bumped into it last year. Besides, there was a danger of it stalling and coming to a halt on the road. The land revenue officer and the agriculture officer had brought their jeeps. Naturally, it was a matter of prestige, and they could not possibly use the vehicles brought by the groom's family to send the bride away.

So, who could they ask to send a vehicle to take the bridal party to the bridegroom's home? No doubt there were three cars at the wedding venue. But how could they ask some distant relatives for the loan of their cars for two days?

'Dada, the person who had supplied the firewood is asking for payment.' A thin man wearing filthy clothes, covered with a variety of stains was cringing before the land revenue officer and agriculture officer.

'Didn't we give you three hundred rupees yesterday? Why don't you give him from that amount?' The land revenue officer's forehead wrinkled in irritation.

'The fees for the handcart, the electric wires from that amount . . .'

'Okay, okay, there's no need to give a list, here, take the money.' The agricultural officer threw a hundred rupee note in the direction of the thin, withered man.

'Really, this man is becoming impossible . . .' The agricultural officer's face, too, showed a great deal of annoyance.

Indeed, the presence of this man who did not know how to speak with respect or do any kind of work properly was annoying almost everybody at that wedding.

'He was going towards the bridegroom's people, saying he was the bride's youngest Khura, her father's youngest brother. He had a *gamosa* around his neck, and he was approaching them with folded hands. It was I who somehow managed to send him off to the back . . .'

'The bridegroom's maternal uncle, the Forest Ranger Bora in fact asked me how that person was related to the bride. Somehow, I managed to change the subject. What was the need for him to go around with the *bota* of *tamol* paan in his hands, offering them to the bridegroom's party and introducing himself as the bride's youngest Khura?'

'He's inherited all of our Deuta's property, can't he stay in a decent way? And the woman he married! They have a large brood of children.'

'Stupid!' The land revenue officer crushed his lit cigarette with his shoes on the ground.

The bride had, in the meantime, reached the gates. She was throwing fistfuls of rice behind her without turning. This was essential or the Goddess of Wealth, the Lokhimi who resided in her father's home would leave. Her Borma, the wife of her father's elder brother, held her hand firmly and directed her while she flung the rice back with trembling hands. She wept so hard that her whole body shook. A woman around the bride scolded her, as she seemed reluctant to go to the bridegroom's house, 'Don't take the Lokhimi from your mother's house, pay attention now and scatter the rice behind you.'

Another woman added, 'Your aunt is right. Now you can't see the path ahead because of your tears, but once you are in your husband's house, you'll forget everything.'

The people who were to accompany the bride approached the land revenue officer to find out about which car they would be going in.

The land revenue officer looked around and called out to his younger brother who was sitting in a corner of the decorative canopy and smoking a bidi. Throwing his bidi away with alacrity, Horimohon came running up.

'Go quickly, get Nimai driver's car. I've already spoken to him.'

'Going, Maju Dada,' said Hori to his middle brother, and looked around helplessly.

'What's the matter? Why are you shilly-shallying?'

'I mean . . . a bicycle . . . and I wonder where Nimai lives . . .'

'Take a ricksha. Ask around for directions to Nimai's home.'

Hori scrounged around in the pockets of his lopsided kurta.

'You don't even have the fare for the ricksha, didn't Dada just give you a hundred rupees?' On hearing the officer's rough voice, Hori hung his head. 'Well, the supplier of firewood came and asked for some more money . . .'

'Okay okay . . . here take this . . . twenty rupees.'

'Stupid.' This time round, the agricultural officer pronounced the word.

The bride was escorted to the car by her brother-in-law. Once more, there was a fresh round of weeping and auspicious ululation as she departed from her paternal home. A few people climbed into Nimai driver's vehicle to accompany the bride to her marital home. The truck loaded with the household objects that the bride was taking with her also started. The gate to the compound which till just recently had been thronging with people emptied. It was still adorned with auspicious strings of mango leaves, plantain saplings and brass *xorais* but now, it was as though a weariness had descended on all.

Near the hearth where the hired cook had worked sat Reboti. She had put a saucepan with water on for tea. The lack of sleep and hard work of the last three days had brought on drowsiness. Yawning repeatedly, she put tea leaves into the boiling water. Her arms ached while straining the tea into the cups that were arranged on a tray. Her joints hurt; her feet were tingling. She stretched her legs forward on the ground to sit. The woman who had come in to take the tea tray out scolded her. 'Your legs are too close to the teacups, remove them.' She quickly folded her legs. Yes, certainly it was disgusting, her feet looked as though they had been buried in soil. After the half-day bus journey, she had taken off her sandals and put them under the *alna* in the bedroom. She had come here because it was her elder brother-in-law's daughter's wedding. Since then, she had practically no rest for three days. It seemed as though all the utensils, the large and heavy *kerahis* had been heaped up just for her to wash. The whole house and courtyard were piled up knee-high with rubbish. People were waiting with thirsty throats just for her to make tea for them. She had gone back and forth from the pond so many times that her feet were caked with mud. They were tired out. Leave alone her feet, she did not have time to wash her hands either, properly.

But she needed to wash them. The mud was clinging to the gaps between her toes. She was about to leave for the *pukhuri*, the pond, again, when a deep male voice made her pause. She pulled up the edge of her sador, the *oroni*, over her head. It was her eldest brother-in-law's voice. 'Twenty cups of tea, needed outside.' She had got up to wash her feet, but now she put the used cups into a bucket instead. She did not wish to walk down the muddy path this early in the morning. There were two full green water tanks outside. Water flowed out smoothly at the turn of the tap. On the first day, Reboti had washed up the utensils there. While she was washing the kerahi in which mutton had been cooked, somebody had growled at her, 'Why are you wasting this pure water? Go and wash these utensils in the pukhuri. Where will we get water for the people, who have come from the bridegroom's house for the *joron* ceremony, to wash their hands?'

On the day of the wedding, Reboti, tired out and thirsty, had started to go to the tankers for a drink of water, but had stopped. The sound of that harsh voice echoed in her ear. She drank the muddy water of the pukhuri instead. Rubbing her eyes, she set foot on the slushy, muddy shore of the pukhuri. Sitting on the bridge, she washed the cups as well as her feet. After sprinkling water on her face and eyes, she felt a little less tired and refreshed. She had scrubbed her feet clean, and now she paused as she looked at the muddy path before her. Should she go to the other bank? She could cover herself up and walk under the jackfruit tree to reach the covered area inside.

'Reboti! Oi Reboti! We need some cups of tea!' She recognized her sister-in-law's voice, her husband's elder brother's wife.

'Coming, Baideo!' she said, and walked down the path, placing her feet on the depressions created by her own footprints on the mud. She reached the temporary shed that had been put up for cooking.

The agricultural officer's wife was waiting with an irritated frown on her face. 'Your elder brother-in-law had asked for some tea . . .'

'It's almost done, Baideo.'

Reboti hurriedly prodded the dying embers of the fire. The prime firewood had been used up by the hired cook, only the small bits were left. But she was used to cooking on the fire made by the husks of betel nuts. The fire came to life again. The tea was soon made, and her sister-in-law went away with the filled cups.

Reboti went and sat on the pile of firewood behind the shed, with a cup of tea in her hand. The temporary roof over the areas meant for bathing, cooking and the canopy created a kind of private corner here. Like a kitten that was hiding from the dogs chasing her, she sat sipping her tea. People were searching for her, 'Tea, we need some tea, where has that woman gone?'; 'Reboti! The rooms need to be swept.'; 'Reboti! You've scrubbed these clothes with soap, now go and rinse them in the pukhuri!'; 'Reboti! Fetch a couple of pails of water, will you?'; 'Reboti! Reboti! Reboti!'

She remained sitting quietly. She was crushed by the lack of sleep over three days, and hunger and tiredness. She dozed off even as she sat there. She was awakened from her slumber quite suddenly by the dogs barking and fighting over scraps of food. A familiar voice seemed to be saying something to her. 'Where are you, do you hear me? It's time to leave, get ready.' Her husband's voice now came clearly to her. 'Here, do you hear me? It's time to leave, get ready.'

On hearing her husband's voice, Reboti came out from the corner.

'What's the matter?'

She looked sideways at her husband's clothes. They were his best clothes but were now completely soiled and covered with stains from the banana stems, mud and grease from the car.

'Come on, let's go. We'll be able to reach by daylight only if we catch the bus now.'

Suddenly, a voice called out. He ran back the way he had come.

Yes, she would have to go. While trying to rearrange her clothes and attempting to rub out the dirt from her clothes and body, her thoughts went back to her home and the family she had left behind. She had left her two sisters there. Who knew what they were doing? Were they able to manage the mischievous boys? The cow would soon calve, the paddy too needed to be put out in the sunlight. If it clumped up in the grain basket, the *duli* itself, it would be a huge crisis. Some pumpkin plants were growing vigorously near the marshy area where the leftovers were thrown. Some bamboo supports needed to be put up there. When the gourds ripened, they would cover the cost of salt and oil that they had to buy. She visualized the small details of her home. The bustle of coming to her elder brother-in-law's daughter's wedding, and then the many chores that had fallen on her had given her no time to think about her own home. She suddenly grew agitated. Her children, the ducks, the cow, the paddy, the gourd plants . . .

She got ready to leave quickly. She had not brought any box or case with her. She could carry the pair of mekhela sador she wore while bathing in her bag. These last three days she had been wearing her only good pair of clothes. While setting foot on the verandah, her eyes fell on her feet. The gaps between her toes had become pale and wrinkled by constantly being in the water. It would be painful to place her feet on the stony path.

But of course, she had quite forgotten that she need not painfully walk bare feet on the pebble-strewn path. She did have a pair of sandals, a pair of soft, yellow Hawai flip-flops with red polka dots on the upper soles. When she had arrived, she had been quite distraught at the thought of being separated from her suckling infant for a considerably long time. She had kept her sandals on the lowest rack of the wooden alna. She went to that alna. As soon as she set her eyes on it, her heart missed a beat. No, her sandals were not where she had kept them. She had kept the sandals just there, in that very corner, when she had come here. She had then gone to the pukhuri to wash her hands and face. She had not come this way for the last three days. What could have happened to the sandals? Her heart began to beat rapidly. The yellow Hawai flip-flops with the red polka dots; what could have happened to the pair? Could somebody have taken them? Her throat went dry.

The land revenue officer, the Hakim's family would be leaving this evening. His two daughters were packing their clothes up. Reboti came and stood near them. The elder one abruptly shut the case. The half-folded *muga* clothes were caught at the side of the box, and there remained a gap between the lid and body of the case. The young girl covered that gap with her hand and asked Reboti, 'What do you want?'

'I had kept my Hawai sandals under that alna, did you see it, Majoni?' asked Reboti, using an affectionate appellation for the girl.

The Hakim's wife had now entered the room. Reboti went up to her. She barely reached up above the waist of the tall, well-built Hakim's wife. A strong odour came from Reboti's body, an odour that was a mix of sweat, ashes, mud, soap, turmeric, oil and much else. The Hakim's wife automatically stepped back. Rebati asked, hesitatingly, 'Baideo! I had kept my sandals just there . . .'

'What sandals, how will I know where they are?' At these harsh words, Reboti went once more to look below the alna. She went down on her knees and dragged herself around to look in the corners behind the almirah and under the bed. The Hakim's wife was about to take off the new set of gold jewellery that she had worn during the wedding. She had bought it for this occasion. But now she paused. How could she take off her precious jewellery in front of this woman? Who knew with what motive she had entered this room? The Hakim's wife said impatiently, 'Listen, there's no sandal or any such thing here, do you understand? We were right here at night, there's nothing here. Go and look on that side, somebody may have worn it and gone off.'

Reboti left. The Hakim's wife looked at the dirt-encrusted woman as she went out, and in a low voice scolded her daughters, 'Shut the suitcase quickly, can't you see there are so many people just walking about here?'

Reboti went to the other room. Several people were sitting on the carpet and sorting through the gifts that had been given at the wedding. Placing the wraps in a heap to one side, they put the gifts inside a steel almirah. Reboti went and stood right there. Her husband would arrive any moment. The bus left at ten, it seemed, and here it was almost nine o' clock. Reboti's throat was dry as wood. Would she ever be able to find the sandals?

The women who were sorting out the gifts gave a sidelong glance at Reboti.

'This is Horimohon's wife . . .'

'Is that so?'

'Issss Ram!' one exclaimed. 'If I had known she was the daughter-in-law of this house I would never have made her wash my clothes.'

'It's not your fault. Just see what she looks like.'

Reboti paid no heed to what the women were saying. What had happened to the sandals? She had only that one thought in her head.

All these days, the other women had not heard a single word from Reboti as she had silently shouldered the burden of work. Now, they heard her voice. 'Did you see a pair of sandals? Hawai sandals, with red polka dots.'

'Look around, maybe they are under some furniture somewhere.'

Reboti began to search under the bed, under the boxes stacked together and in the corners between the walls and the steel almirahs. No, they were nowhere to be seen. Reboti was almost in tears. What could have happened to her sandals? She began to poke agitatedly at the heap of gift wraps of many colours that had been piled to one side. Maybe the sandals were under the wrapping paper. Dragging herself, she sifted through the papers and neared the carpet where the gifts had been spread out.

One of the women whispered to the bride's Mami, her mother's brother's wife, who was opening the gifts, 'Give this woman something, just look where she's looking for her sandals. She seems to have come here hoping for something.'

'Yes, give her this flower vase,' said another woman sitting nearby.

Reboti's eyes were filled with tears. She did not see the vase that the woman proffered. In her distraught condition, she did not even hear properly what the woman was saying.

Maybe somebody was wearing her sandals. Reboti leaned against a pillar and started to look at the feet of the people who were coming and going. Suddenly, she felt dizzy. She had worked unbelievably hard for three days and nights, barely eating a thing. She sat with her back to the pillar. Could somebody have worn those sandals? Suddenly, she visualized a smooth, fair, plump and unblemished pair of feet, with pink, gleaming nails. On the feet were a pair of Hawai flip-flops. When she had gone to give the pails of water in the bathroom, that pair of fair feet had emerged from the toilet. On the feet were yellow sandals. Who was that? A pair of fair, smooth legs with pink, gleaming toenails passed by before Reboti as she sat there. Reboti lifted her head and saw that it was the wife of her husband's nephew. She looked quite like a foreigner, a white woman.

Reboti approached her. 'Bowari!' she said, referring to her endearingly as a daughter-in-law, 'Did you happen to see my sandals? A pair of yellow Hawai sandals, with red polka dots . . .?'

'Hawai sandals? No, I haven't seen them.' Saying this, Bhargob's wife tried to move away. But Reboti stopped her. Her mind was not working. 'How can you say you haven't seen them? Hadn't you worn them to go to the toilet?' Her voice had a fierceness, a burning urgency like that of the earth heated by the hot sun.

Bhargob's wife flushed. Angry and affronted, she came and stood with head downcast in front of the filthy woman, her aunt-in-law.

'What's the matter, Reboti?' asked the bride's mother, who had wept so hard that she had almost fainted. She had now recovered. She paused when she saw her daughter-in-law standing in front of Reboti with bowed head. This girl's husband, her son Bhargob, had borne almost all the expenses for this wedding.

'She wore my sandals and . . .' Hearing Reboti's words, the bride's mother voice grew shrill. 'Why would my daughter-in-law wear your sandals? For what reason?'

Reboti quickly left. Had the sandals really vanished? She felt a buzzing in her ears and went now to the marquee outside, it could be that somebody had worn the pair and kept the sandals outside.

As soon as she went outside, she came face to face with her brother-in-law's son, Dr Ranjan. 'Bopai,' she said, addressing him affectionately, 'Have you seen my sandals? Yellow, with red polka dots . . .'

Astonished, the doctor looked at the dark face before him. What was this idiot blabbering on about? He was in the middle of a thousand chores, with a thousand worries, and here she was, asking about sandals?

Reboti lost all sense of time and place and hunted for her sandals. Her face was flushed, her eyes were full of tears. The oroni, the end of her sador that covered her head as a mark of respect for her seniors, was falling off. Her sador itself was undone and was dragging on the ground. Agitatedly, she asked everyone she happened to meet, 'My Hawai sandals. Yellow, with red polka dots . . .'

In the house, the people wished to rest a bit after the wedding that had just taken place. They wanted to discuss all that had happened, there were some chores left that needed to be completed, and here was that irritating Reboti, rushing around asking about the whereabouts of her sandals. By now, they all knew that the woman had lost a 'pair of yellow Hawai sandals with red polka dots'.

Reboti's husband was to arrive at any moment. She grew more frantic by the minute. Getting rebuked by one, scolded by another, she rushed around asking, 'My sandals . . . yellow, with red polka dots . . .'

The marquee outside was being dismantled. Under the bit that was still standing, several people were sitting and talking. The hakim, the agricultural officer and the bride's father too were there.

Reboti went to where the materials were piled up after the marquee was dismantled. There were heaps of carpets, tarpaulins, chairs, glasses, lights and many such items. Reboti began to search for her sandals in that pile, sometimes dragging herself, sometimes bending over, sometimes kneeling. In a beseeching tone she asked the boy who was dismantling the temporary lights, 'Bopai! Did you see a pair of sandals while you were getting these lights down? Yellow . . . with red . . .'

'I don't know,' said the boy in Hindi. He sneered and went back to work.

The headmaster caught sight of Reboti, and called out, 'Xoru bowari!' referring to her as the youngest daughter-in-law. 'What are you doing there? Isn't it time for you to leave, I gave Hori the fare for your return quite some time ago.' He said the last few words louder than was necessary.

Drinking their tea, along with sweetmeats, the people sitting around idly were discussing the wedding that had just taken place.

'The wedding went very well.'

'She's the only daughter, it has to be done well, hasn't it?'

'The father is fortunate; the bridegroom is well suited.'

'The bridegroom's family is very good.'

'The fish that the Hakim provided for the feast will not be forgotten for a long time.'

'You haven't mentioned the cream . . . the bridegroom's people praised it greatly.'

'Our eldest boy has captured the whole wedding through a camera it seems.'

'Indeed, yes! You'll be able to see it this very evening.'

A gale of laughter revived the surroundings that were drooping with tiredness.

A ricksha came and stood near the gate. Horimohon alighted from it and immediately went inside.

Reboti began to tremble when she saw her husband getting down from the ricksha. This meant that they would have to leave immediately, otherwise he would not spend money on a ricksha. Her husband would come looking for her here and rush her into leaving. But the sandals! What would happen to her sandals!

She walked with the unsteady gait of an intoxicated person towards the people who were sitting and relaxing over cups of tea and sweetmeats. She had lost all sense of what was appropriate, what was not. All around her whirled the colour yellow and red polka dots. She suddenly asked the assembled people, 'Did you see my sandals? Yellow, with . . .'

It was as though Reboti had placed her hand inside a wasps' nest. The people all said angrily, 'What is this woman talking about? Going on about sandals . . .'

'It seemed she accused Bhargob's wife of stealing.'

'She questioned the bride's mother as well about her sandals even though the poor woman had fainted with so much weeping.'

In a soft voice, the bride's father said to Reboti, 'Xoru bowari! What are you doing? In order to take one's place in society . . .' He seemed as if he was about to give some advice to Reboti. To the astonishment of all present, she sat on the ground, took the oroni on her head and began to sob. She was enveloped by the stained, soiled clothes, which began to shake to the rhythm of her sobs.

In a broken voice, she said, 'That's not my pair of sandals. Your brother does not have the means to buy sandals for me to wear. I've borrowed these from Bhadoi's mother for the wedding. And she herself bought this pair with the money she put together by selling her pigeons.'

Reboti broke down completely. 'What shall I tell Bhadoi's mother when I return?'

TANGLE

(Originally published as 'Jot')

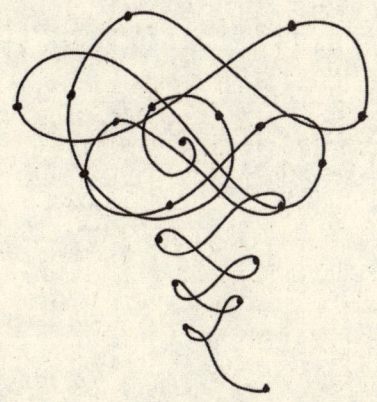

Old Bogi was on her deathbed. People kept vigil around her in turns. She would be leaving this world anytime now. The people around her saw the signs of impending death. One said that her earlobe had drooped, another commented that her lips were turning black and that there was phlegm in her throat. And yet the real hour of death didn't seem to be actually near. But she was completely bedridden. All her bodily functions were carried out on the bed itself.

It was a busy time for those who worked in the fields. Everybody would eat a frugal meal of rice very early in the morning and rush off. The ones who remained at home also had chores to complete. Nobody had any free time. In this situation, there was a bit of a problem with regard to Bogi Buri, Old Woman Bogi. Even so, they kept vigil by turns, as much as was possible.

Bogi Burhi's name said it all. At one time, her skin was as smooth as the petals of a gardenia bloom. She had been a fair girl, youthful and attractive, and it was said that nobody could gather up this girl's hip-length hair into a bun on her wedding day, so heavy and thick was it. The bride had to tie up her hair on her own. Coming from a very poor family, she had been sent off to her husband's home wearing a pair of very ordinary clothes without a single gold ornament adorning her body. The bridegroom, too, came from the same economic background. Even so, they had a house of their own and enough cropland to give them their simple meals.

Bogi had grown up listening to the same kind of remarks: 'This one is a lotus from the mud of a pond', 'this one should go to a royal house', 'only a pucca house of cement in the city will suit her', 'it would have matched her appearance if she had been moving around in motor cars', and 'just watch, this one will live like a queen one day'. And she too had secretly begun to believe that one day, a prince would surely come and take her away. She would be buried in gold ornaments and rich clothes, fit for a queen. But she had nothing now. Not a pair of good clothes, no ornaments for her ears, no bangles for her wrists. Indeed, the prized golden-hued stone necklace that had been seen at the bazaar during the festival of Holi was also out of her reach. Despite all the money she saved from rearing poultry, her household was always in want of something. One of her siblings would fall ill, or something would happen to her mother. Her father's shop would teeter on the edge of closure because of his inability to replenish his dwindling stocks. What could she do? The Holi bazaar would come and go, but all she could buy were a few glass bangles . . .

The dark house dated back to her grandfather's time. In the evenings, a small lantern hung from the little shop that her father had set up in front of their house. The field ahead yielded enough food for only three months. Her invalid mother kept falling sick, and the father would thunder at the children for no rhyme or reason. All of this put tremendous pressure on Bogi. She would fill a small earthen saki with a bit of mustard oil, smear a light film of mustard oil on a plantain leaf and make some black kajol. She would shape a small round phot between her eyebrows with this collyrium. Her mother disliked this. She, too, knew that this bit of mustard oil could very well be used to flavour the mashed potatoes. Bogi would wipe away her occasional tears and wait patiently for her prince.

There were no books. Even buying school uniforms was difficult. And yet, amid all this, Bogi passed her matriculation examinations in the second division. In Bogi's village, girls did not usually go to college. The college in the nearest town was thirty kilometres away. In between were seven rickety bamboo bridges and huge potholes on the road. A bus used to ply between her village and the town, but it had overturned on the side of the road. Those for whom it was necessary, would commute on bicycles. Hardly anyone from outside came to the village, nor did the current residents go out. Because of the lack of interaction with the world outside, Bogi's village had many unmarried girls. Nobody came from outside to marry girls from this village. And nobody who came here for some reason, ever wanted to return.

Finally, Bogi got married to Dimbeswar, the son of Monuram Bayon, resident of her own village. There were minimal ceremonies. The bridegroom's family came one day and applied oil and xendur on her head and took her away. For a long time, Bogi's mother took pride in the barn, the pond and thickets of bamboo in the Bayon house. It was a proper house with a roof of corrugated iron sheets which sloped down from a central wooden frame—a batten. In a village where almost all other houses had roofs of straw and sometimes leaves, this was indeed something to be proud of.

Bogi was deeply disappointed by the clothes which Bayon's wife ritually gifted her while accepting her as a daughter-in-law. The older woman put a ring on Bogi's finger, and this too disenchanted her. The clothes were of a dull colour with small woven flowers spaced far apart. The thin ring with its small stone made her heart heavy. She had always wished for a red pair of mekhela sador with intricate woven work right up to the waist. She had assumed that she would be getting this at her wedding. The bridegroom's Khuri, his father's brother's wife, put some cheap readymade gilded jewellery on her ears, neck and wrists. They would lose their sheen and turn dark in just a few days. Bogi had never lifted her head once during this Juroon ceremony in which the bridegroom's mother applied xendur on her head. The newly applied vermillion powder brought such a glow to her face that everything else around her seemed to be dull in comparison.

Just like the jewellery which lost its sheen and grew dark, Bogi's heart and mind, too, gradually turned dark. The coils of disillusionment wrapped themselves around her. Her new household had three sisters-in-law, two brothers older than her husband and two younger. The two daughters of the house had been married off and were now in their marital homes. Along with her father- and mother-in-law, there were hordes of ploughmen and labourers. Among this crowd of people, she drooped and wilted. She was in any case not in the habit of speaking loudly. When her mother would berate her soundly for using the mustard oil to make kajol, she would, at the most, groan once. Now even her mother was not around to listen to her groaning.

She did not like anything around her, nor was she ever in a good frame of mind. She disliked her handwoven clothes, which had turned a dirty brown after being washed in the water from the handpump which contained a lot of iron. A silver chain had been bought for her because the jewellery given to her earlier was tarnished. She disliked the smell of the coconut oil which was bought in bulk for everybody. She hated the smell of soda that came from the soap that was bought from the grocer and cut into pieces for all. She even disliked the rice in this house. The barn was filled with paddy, enough to last this large family through the year. There was no shortage of rice. Thrice a day, her mother-in-law would cook rice in an enormous *degchi*, and with every meal, there were leftovers for at least two people. She would cook a curry in a huge round-bottomed iron kerahi. From the moment she had set foot in this house, she had observed that there were no fries served at meals. Usually there would be just one curry. In the summer, a curry would be made of the small *botiya* fish, the loach that had been strained from the water in the fields, along with stalks of colocasia. She could barely swallow this curry. In winter, the curry of mustard greens, which were cooked without any oil, hurt her mouth with its abrasiveness. The presence of her husband when he returned from the card sessions before the neighbourhood Konti's shop, smelling of bidi and cigarettes was as revolting to her as was the summer fish curry.

But what could she do? As soon as she placed the food in her mouth, it slid down to her stomach. When her husband returned, she would lie on the bed and crawl on the dusty roads that had taken root within her. Her tears dampened the lanes and roads around. She would crawl through the dampened lanes. Nobody had any inkling about it. She would enter some small lane and straighten her back. She had always thought her father's house to be a jail, the root of all disappointments. But her soul had not been so dusty, so filled with sand when she had been there. Her mother, in spite of scolding her about the kajol, would not sell the eggs from the ducks and chickens they reared, and save them for the children to eat instead. Once in a while, she would cook pigeon meat with potatoes. During long holidays, there would be a shortage of rice in the house. But in the winter, her father would sell vegetables in front of his shop, on a platform made of split bamboo. If the profits were good, he would bring back sweetmeats such as jilepi and goja for them. After coming to this house, she had never been able to mash up a boiled egg with salt and oil and have it with her rice. She had never had a full bowl of meat curry here, even if only once a month. The curry that was made from the tiny amount of meat that came to this house when a goat was slaughtered at the meat shop near the crossroads, had more pieces of raw papaya in it. She had never, in this house, had a ruti, a wheat flatbread, with her morning tea. She knew that in this house, amid this crowd of people, she would never get a ruti with her morning cup of tea, nor a boiled egg at the side of her bell metal *kanhi* of rice, a curry with several pieces of meat, a piece of fragrant soap or a pair of clothes made of soft fabric. These things became like stars in the firmament, clouds in a blue sky or a flock of birds flying off into the horizon. She would never be able to experience these things again. There was only a memory of them and regret. Even as her disappointments and sense of hopelessness grew, her silence, too, became more pronounced. The dry sand within her sucked up her voice, her talk, her laughter. In the meantime, she became the mother of two children.

That same Bogi is now lying on her deathbed as Old Woman Bogi. Bogi Burhi. Her parents-in-law had died a long time ago. Her husband, too, suffered a respiratory problem, and passed away in middle age. Her daughter was married, and her son had joined the army and gone to his posting. Both her children had come here with their families when they learnt of their mother's condition. The old woman was breathing laboriously. The season for working in the fields was over. It was almost time for Durga Puja. The autumnal *xewali* flowers were budding. The old woman remained bedridden. She was beginning to get bedsores on her back. The family visited often but was worried and strained over the task of taking care of her and nursing her. Her son had already come to visit his mother on her deathbed thrice. The daughter lived nearby; she visited frequently.

The old woman's voice, too, gave way. Only the gaze that clung to her eyes remained. She would stare with eyes wide open at all that was going on around her. It looked as though she was about to say something. What could she have to say, this voiceless woman? What was she thinking? Did she think at all? Did she remember what was said to that girl who used to take that black phot with freshly made kajol? Nomal's mother would tell her daughter if she left her hair open, 'who knows which palace this girl will adorn?' Her youngest uncle, Konpeha would say, 'If a person of means takes home this girl, she will be a Queen, no less.' This Bogi, this fair girl whom everybody agreed would be a queen one day, was now this Bogi Buri, just a bag of bones, lying in an unbearable state on her deathbed.

Perhaps the old woman would not have come to this state if the government had not repaired the bridges that were balanced precariously like an old person's teeth. One couldn't really say. Even so, would a city girl like Nomita Chaliha have come to this godforsaken village to teach in the newly established higher secondary school here? It was only after the bridges were built that public transport such as buses, trekkers and cars began to ply on the roads. And would Amol Barua, who came from a wealthy family in the city, have come here as a teacher in that case? Despite acute unemployment, one doubts whether this primitive village would attract their likes. A place still stuck in the stone age.

But they did. The city-bred boy and girl, each with a university degree, joined work. They got to know each other and developed a relationship, and one day, got married. Just after their wedding, they bought a bigha of land from the Bayon family and set up a home next to Bogi Burhi's house. A lot of modern stuff came to their home, over the newly repaired roads and bridges. In no time at all, the shiny new house was filled up with shiny new things.

In the meantime, the village too saw many changes. Every day, new shopping outlets came up and new institutions were established. It was as though everybody had been waiting for the bridges to be repaired. As soon as this was done, everybody came rushing in. But this new wave could not touch all of them; for some, these waters simply moved around and away, leaving them unaffected by change.

The home of the Bayons was one of those untouched by the wave of change. The previous generation was now elderly. The next generation now consisted of young people. Some bits of land were sold off in the same way as had been done in the case of Amol and Nomita. But all else remained the same.

Everything happened quickly. Bogi Burhi had been quite young when Nomita and Amol had set up their home. She herself had been married off at seventeen. After a year, she became a mother of a girl and then a boy. When Nomita and Amol had built their house next to their backyard, her daughter was in high school. She hadn't yet reached the stage in school when the school uniform would change from her skirt and shirt to mekhela sador. Her younger brother was still in the lower primary school.

It was at that time that Bogi became close to Nomita. One night, the girl who worked as a domestic help in Nomita's home came rushing into the Bayon home. Amol had been away from home that day; he had gone to the city for some work. Nomita had vomited repeatedly throughout the night and had become very weak. She had fallen with her head to one side. The girl who worked there had come running fearfully to the Bayon house . . . It would be quite some time before Bogi's husband would return from his *bhang* and card gatherings. Bogi went to Nomita and did everything necessary to help her.

It was from that day that Bogi's relationship with Nomita's household began. It was almost as if visiting Nomita's home had become an addiction for her. She would keep her ears cocked for the sound of a motorbike in the afternoons. As soon as Nomita and Amol returned home, she would go through her backyard and into their home. With her weak physique, Nomita found it difficult to carry out all the household chores. But Bogi tackled these effortlessly. She would swab the smooth, colourful floor, wash the crockery with their floral designs, fry up brinjals in the oil from the large containers, make soft rutis, pour out cups of sweet, milky tea that looked like molten gold. Even though Amol and Nomita kept saying, 'Baideo, you don't have to do all this,' referring to her as elder sister, they loved it secretly. If for some reason Bogi did not come someday, they called her over.

When Nomita was pregnant, Bogi became indispensable for them. Bogi began to cook the evening meal as well for them. There was no need to set up any rules; Bogi simply began to cook their meals, and would come and go as required. They began to consider her as part of their family. Bogi was tied to Amol and Nomita's world. They, too, truly thought of Bogi as their own. They treated her with respect. At first, they had planned to pay her but had felt very uncomfortable at the thought of it. Still, they held out the money and told her it was to buy some clothes for her children, since Durga Puja was approaching. They were relieved when she took it without protest.

The rigidity of the Bayon household that had existed during her father-in-law's time had relaxed and nobody commented on the fact that a daughter-in-law of the house was visiting a neighbour every single day. Her husband, who was getting more useless by the day, was relieved to see that his wife did not bother him so much now that she had begun to spend so much time at the neighbours' place. He did not have to worry about providing his children with books, or his wife with a blouse, anymore.

And Bogi? The silent, morose woman who had entered the Bayon household and who took care of the household chores? Nobody guessed that those rough, sandy roads and lanes were not within her anymore. In their place was a fire that blazed and flattened everything in its path. Within her, the flames stretched in all directions, joined the hot desert that originated from her sighs.

Durga Puja was over. There was a slight chill in the air. The old woman Bogi was still stuck to her bed. Gradually, bits of her reddened skin had begun to peel off. Sores were beginning to form on the spots that constantly rubbed against her clothes. At least, there was some relief. It was a joint family with many members. All of them took care of the old woman the best they could. Somebody came and quickly changed her clothes in between their other chores, somebody else sprinkled some talcum powder on the parts where bed sores were developing, somebody else soaked a bit of cotton in the liquid medicine and wiped her down. The old lady's son stocked her medicines every time he visited, her daughter too brought a bottle of Horlicks or a few packets of biscuits every time she came. The people in the household could not neglect this woman who instead of complaining had worked hard throughout for them.

The old woman certainly got the care she was entitled to. But the more she lost weight and became thinner, her eyes seemed to become larger and their gaze sharper. They appeared to pop out of her face. Nobody could meet her gaze. Looking at her made them uncomfortable. At times, her son, daughter or other members of the family asked her, 'Do you wish to say something?' But the only reply was the same unblinking stare. Unable to bear it, somebody would say, 'Shut your eyes, what are you staring at?' The pupils of her eyes would stir a bit, but again, they returned to that same gaze.

Within this discomfiting stare was trapped a simple, straightforward woman—that woman was Nomita. Nomita, during her pregnancy many years ago, had become very dependent on Bogi. The latter, too, had grown close to Nomita. But even as, outwardly, she seemed to grow closer to Nomita, the fire within Bogi blazed even more fiercely.

Bogi saw in Nomita that woman she had dreamed of becoming years ago. All that the people had said about her, Bogi, when she was young, was now evident in Nomita. What they had said she would get, Nomita had. She lived almost like royalty. Her home, her clothes, her jewellery together combined to create a regal aura. Everybody around pampered Nomita no end. Her parents and parents-in-law, her aunts and uncles, everybody cosseted her. Bogi looked on with astonishment. How could a single person receive so much love? And Nomita's husband, Amol? Bogi's eyes would begin to close when she looked at him. Where was this light coming from? This man, what does he not do for Nomita? Unless she had seen it with her own eyes, she would not have ever believed that a man could love his wife, could adore a woman so much. While completing her chores, Bogi would glance at Nomita every now and then. What did this woman have in such abundance?

Here she was, without even a fraction of what Nomita possessed. And there was Nomita. What did she not have? Nomita would wear soft, beautiful clothes and go to work sitting behind Amol's bike. After her return, she would wear a loose-fitting blue kaftan and sit, watching TV with her feet up on a cane stool. She would eat whatever she wanted to on those white platters. She could buy whatever she desired. And that man, whose presence one could not look away from? He would constantly be hovering around Nomita. Bogi noticed that Amol sometimes stroked Nomita's hair. He would gently massage her back. Whenever he went out, he always brought back something or the other for Nomita. Bogi often heard the two of them talking about their coming child. This man would really love and care for his children.

Whenever she looked at Nomita, the arid streets within her would blaze up anew.

The eldest son of the Bayon household shifted out along with his family. The middle son and Bogi's husband were left at the place. The youngest son lived close to his workplace, which was away from the household. After the eldest son, a schoolteacher, left, there was a great deal of financial hardship in the family. He had been taking care of the expenses, from the larger ones down to even the small items such as salt, sugar, cooking oil and tea. Because the middle son looked after the fields, there was no shortage of rice. Bogi's husband had more or less turned his back on domestic responsibilities and spent most of his time with Shibnath's group of bhang addicts. Her younger brother-in-law and the middle one's wife hurled barbed words at Bogi. The more the people around her complained about her husband, the more Bogi put all her energies into the domestic chores. After her mother-in-law passed away, Bogi took her place at the kitchen fire. Like a cat that lay comfortably in the warm ashes near the kitchen fire, Bogi, too, seemed to permanently stay there. She always cooked the alkaline *khar* without oil of mustard greens, a curry of botiya fish and loach with arum stems. The only difference was that there would be no leftover rice. Quite often, there was a little bit less, in fact.

Bogi's children found it difficult to study. There were no books, no clothes, no pens, no paper.

It was at this time that Bogi began to regularly visit Nomita and Amol's home. The children now at least got their books and paper. And every day, the fire within her burnt even more fiercely. Without anybody knowing it, she was getting scorched. Like a drowning person clutching at straws, she tried to escape this scorching by working herself to the bone in her own home, and in Nomita and Amol's.

Nomita was now in the fifth month of her pregnancy. She became even more sickly. She would often feel a pain in her stomach. Relatives from both hers and Amol's sides came and conducted the Ponchamrit rituals that are done in the fifth month of pregnancy with quite a bit of fanfare. It was Bogi who took care of all the details of the ceremony.

A woman was preparing to give birth to a new life. What was so great about that? When Bogi looked at Nomita sitting with her new clothes, new jewellery and being fed all kinds of delicacies, she was again charred by that fire inside her. After wrapping up all the chores in Nomita and Amol's home, Bogi went back to her own house and began to cook. She cleaned the house till late at night. Her younger sister-in-law, upon seeing Bogi swabbing the kitchen floor in the middle of the night, was unable to sleep as well. She kept saying, 'What's the point of working like this till you drop? Baideo, go and sleep.'

In response, Bogi would look at her sister-in-law. When she had come as a bride, she had resembled a pitcher that was filled to the brim. Now she looked like a dry bundle of straw. But who in this house noticed this?

And she, Bogi herself? After she came into the Bayon household, her skin, which was smooth and fair as a gardenia, took on an ashy hue. Her hair, which had reached to her hips, what had happened to that? Had anybody been bothered to notice these changes? She remembered Nomita. If she uttered even a tiny sound of distress, her man would come running to her side. The people from both her own side, and her husband's, were always eager to make her comfortable. Bogi's sister-in-law had grown alarmed after seeing her mopping the floors in the middle of the night as if she was possessed. To her sleepy sister-in-law, Bogi had said, 'Go and sleep. I'll also have a quick bath and go to bed. I don't get much time during the day.' Revealing her blackened gums, she tried to smile.

Nomita was now almost bedridden. There was some problem, the foetus, too, was not growing as it should. Twice, Nomita was taken by car to the doctor in town and often, he was brought home to examine her. Bogi started to go to Nomita twice a day. She was now Bogi Baideo, the Elder Sister to the household, which was completely dependent on her. Amol too looked to her to get his morning tea, his afternoon meal, his clothes, even his shopping bag. Bogi would serve him his meal with four or five different curries and side dishes with a great deal of satisfaction. She would wash Amol's clothes till

they were as white as a heron's wing, and carefully fold
them away. After his return home in the afternoon, Amol
would get a bell metal kanhi full of puffy fried lusis with
a curry. A pail of hot water would be waiting for him
in the bathroom, along with a fresh gamosa to wipe his
body. Bogi was no longer the same woman, the daughter-
in-law of the Bayon household, with badly receding hair
which revealed her forehead and temples, a mouthful of
blackened teeth that revealed her gums while she was
pampering Amol. At that time, unknown to the world,
Bogi would become that girl with hair falling to her hips,
who would put a phot of black, freshly made kajol on a
plantain leaf and transform into the lotus blooming in the
mud. The daughter-in-law of the Bayon household would
melt away at these times.

Sometimes, while Bogi was serving Amol his tea, or his
meals, Nomita, too, would come and sit with them. With
a great deal of affection, she would ask Bogi, 'Baideo, have
you eaten something yourself?' Bogi would silently place a
cup of hot milk before Nomita.

'Bogi Baideo must have been my own elder sister in
some previous birth. Without Baideo, I can't imagine what
would have happened.' In Nomita's presence, the wife of
Dimbeswar Bhonguwa of the Bayon household, the bhang
addict Dimbeswar, came to life again. She would yank out
Bogi's tresses which had reached her hips, and resembled
the glossy wings of a crow, smear her gardenia-like skin
with ashes, make her slim fingers knotty and coarse, wipe
away the phot of kajol from her forehead, and crush and

pull apart the petals of this lotus that had bloomed in the mud.

As the days passed, Bogi found it more and more difficult to tolerate Nomita. When she was in that beautiful house filled with pretty things, near that man whose appearance made it impossible to turn her eyes away, Bogi came out of the shell that she wore in the Bayon household. She transformed into that young, restless girl with the black phot of kajol on her forehead. One day she would be Queen, she thought. Her whole life lay ahead of her. But Nomita's presence hindered those dreams, pushed her back inside her shell, in which fire burned within her, waiting for death. As her envy and bitterness against Nomita grew, her attention to Amol's needs increased. She noted with great satisfaction Nomita's declining health.

An enormous, tangled knot grew inside Bogi.

Everybody noticed it when the cattle used for ploughing the fields went off their feed. When the pregnant goat was a little late returning home in the evening, everybody went out to search for her. When the hen sat brooding, there was a commotion as everybody tried to find out why this was happening. In fact, even when the tender, immature coconuts fell from the trees, there would be accusations about over-trimming the leaves of the tree, and cutting them off causing the unripe coconuts to fall before time. But no one cared when a living, breathing woman went around carrying an enormous tangle within her, a knot that could not be unravelled. Who could make others understand this? Dimbeswar, the bhang addict? Her young children? Her sister-in-law, who had dried up like a bundle of straw? Her husband's brother or sister? Why would anyone waste time on this woman who, with head bent, was constantly at some chore?

That young woman, Bogi, was not the one lying in bed. This one was Old Woman Bogi. Bogi Burhi. But in her eyes was reflected that knot that remained tangled. Her mind, full of those worms, and blocked by a damp, putrid darkness, had now come to rest in her eyes. The people around her clearly understood that the unbearable gaze of this woman on her deathbed was not normal.

One day, her daughter came and started washing her. She turned over her mother, and was about to powder her back, when she screamed out loud. Maggots were wriggling around in one of the bedsores. The daughter powdered her mother's back and changed her clothes. It was maybe Romola Baideo who advised them to lay Bogi Burhi on a bed of freshly cut plantain leaves. The bedsores would not rub against her clothes anymore and would not worsen. Romola Baideo's father-in-law had been completely bedridden for almost three years. And in truth, after they began to put plantain leaves on the bed, the family got some relief. Even those who came to enquire about her condition began to bring with them a few freshly cut new leaves of the plantain with them.

The tangle in her mind had not yet reached Bogi's eyes at that time. It was her soul that was in its grip growing larger by the day.

Nomita had been very sick and there were quiet discussions about taking her to the city. Bogi packed her trunk with her necessities, though she wondered why were so many clothes required for just one person? She would need to stay in the hospital, and therefore, Amol had bought a large number of new clothes from the city for her. Bogi had fingered them as she had put away the clothes in the cupboard. While she did so, she felt a deep resentment against this woman lying in bed. She was loved and cared for even though she did not lift a finger. While getting ready to give birth, she had become very sickly. She was constantly unwell, no matter what was done for her. She was overly delicate. She had a thin and emaciated body, and yet she had come to set up a home. She had got stuck to the man like a leech and was sucking out his blood. She should have been married into the Bayon household; her lot should have been with Dimbeswar Bhoguwa. By now, plants and grass would have grown from the remains of her body.

All of Bogi's anger and resentment glued themselves to Nomita. But, at the same time, Nomita and Amol, the people of their families, and the neighbours from the village were amazed at the care that Bogi took of Nomita at this time. Who looked after a person who was unrelated to them in this way? Indeed, people did not even take care of their own people like this. Nomita and Amol were grateful to Bogi.

There were just about four or five days left for Nomita to be taken to the city. Everything was packed and ready.

While Amol and Nomita were away, Bogi, along with her son would come and sleep in their house. All arrangements had been made.

Without warning, the unimaginable happened. Suddenly, Nomita's labour pains started. Their domestic help called Bogi at midnight, a full moon night. There was a huge commotion. Doctor, traditional medicine practitioner, saline, medicines . . . the only doctor from the health centre of this remote rural area, Jayanta Sarma, did not leave Nomita's side. Bogi ran around, making sure that whatever they asked for was given to them. Amol was sitting on a chair outside, his head in his hands. Bogi stood near him. Silently, she handed him a cup of hot tea.

And then Bogi did something that she never had, in her whole life. She seated herself on the chair in which Nomita had always sat and put up her feet on a cane murha in exactly the same way that Nomita did. With her feet up and her head bent, Bogi looked at the world outside. Everything was silvery in the moonlight. She had come out of the carapace of Dimbeswar Bhonguwa's wife. She had lit an earthern lamp filled with mustard oil and collected kajol on a tender banana leaf. With this, she had fashioned a phot on her head. She floated on an unfamiliar happiness.

The doctor came out and told Amol that the mother was all right, but he could not save the baby. Leaving his tea where it was, Amol rushed inside. Even while it was still dark, people from both their families had rushed in, weeping and wailing. The dead baby had been placed on a table. Nomita kept trying to touch the baby girl. The baby had turned blue, her skin was wrinkled. Nomita was howling with grief and despair. She went repeatedly towards the dead girl, her hands spread out. All the people surrounded her with love. They spoke soothing words.

'*Ai*, dear one, you will have a child in your lap again . . .'

'If the tree remains, it will surely fruit again.'

'She had some birth defects, if she had been born alive, she would have been disabled, challenged.'

'Before this year is out, you will conceive again.'

'If you carry on like this, what will happen to the man?'

Amol wept too. Bogi cooked a curry with plain dail, potatoes and some rice. Even though they all said that they would not eat without Nomita and Amol, ultimately all the visitors did have a bit of food. Amol spoon-fed Nomita the freshly squeezed mosambi juice that Bogi brought to him.

The table was empty. Somebody from the village arrived, took away the dead baby, and buried it in the field behind Bogi's house. How long could it take for the earth to embrace this tiny body that had emerged lifelessly from the womb? Nomita had wailed hysterically when the dead body was taken away. Bogi kept glancing at the weeping, broken Nomita as she went about her chores. She was crying and making a huge fuss now, but what else could you expect of a woman who had spent her entire pregnancy lying in bed, without moving a finger to carry out some domestic chores? She was born a woman; she couldn't even give birth to a boy and place him on her husband's lap. All she knew was eating and dressing up in a variety of clothes. What was she so proud about? Her education? After a long time, Bogi remembered that she had cleared her matriculation examinations in the second division. If she had got the opportunity, like Nomita, she too would have passed her BA and MA examinations. These thoughts sputtered in her mind like mustard seeds. They burnt inside her, and she was overwhelmed by the unpleasant smell of burning.

It was almost midnight by the time she returned from Nomita and Amol's house. She had taken upon her shoulders all the work involved in feeding and looking after all the guests. She had spent half the night completing the chores in Nomita and Amol's home. It was not obligatory for her to do this. Bogi would go to Nomita's home at daybreak. The house had become quite chaotic with the presence of so many people. Throughout the day, Bogi would spin like a top, bringing order and completing her chores. Everybody was rushing around, pampering Nomita. Throughout the day, Bogi would give a sidelong glance to Nomita as she rested her body on her husband, and weep with her head on his shoulder; everybody around her pitied Nomita.

That old fire arose within Bogi. Nomita had given birth to a stillborn baby, but the way they were carrying on, it was as though she had brought home the Lord Krishna himself. The crowds of people kept consoling Nomita with the same words. *Before the year is out, your lap will be filled, if the tree is there, how long could it be before it bore fruit again?*

And Amol? He did not leave Nomita's side for even a moment. When Bogi had spoken to him about putting some food into his mouth, Amol had cried out, 'Nomi hasn't eaten anything since yesterday, in this condition . . .' He couldn't finish his sentence. Bogi silently brought milk and a few bananas for Nomita and Amol and left the room.

Nomita, still leaning on Amol, had milk and a banana. This woman drank the milk and ate the bananas, but it was as though the Goddess Lokkhi herself had descended from the sky to partake of the offerings. The man was happy, so very happy. The other people around her were full of joy, too.

Mustard seeds sputtered within Bogi. Nomita's weeping was gradually diminishing. Once, Bogi noticed that the weak Nomita had smiled at something somebody had said.

By the time Bogi finished her chores, it was almost midnight. As always, she stood at the door of their bedroom to tell Nomita and Amol that she was leaving. Placing his hand on his mouth to indicate that she should be quiet, Amol came and stood by her. Nomita was sleeping. Afraid of waking her, Amol had not even worn his sandals. Amol gave Bogi some money. 'You've had to work very hard these days.' Bogi took the money and left.

The path behind Nomita and Amol's house led straight to the Bayon home. That huge field started from just behind the Bayons' home. Bogi looked at the field. It was dark. A large swarm of fireflies was hovering around in the darkness. For a while, she gazed at the dance of the fireflies over that dark field. She had no desire to return to the Bayon home. After all, who was there? Who would be waiting for her to return there? A woman had not returned home this late at night. Was anybody worried about this? Her children must have gone to sleep. They knew that when their mother went to the teacher's home, it meant that a lot of their needs would be met. And that man, Dimbeswar Bhonguwa, the addict, who was the reason she had come to this house? For quite some time now, he had started to lie around in the Shiva temple. He could not be bothered about the whereabouts of a woman from his household, his wife. He too knew that when his wife went to the teachers' home, even the little bit of responsibility that he had towards his family could now be relinquished.

Who knew what happened, but Bogi, instead of going back to the Bayon household, started to walk towards the field. In the darkness, the Bayon house seemed to be a sleeping elephant. Nobody in that dark household had lit an earthen lamp in anticipation of her return. She went forward to the field over which the fireflies were dancing. She felt that in this whole wide world, there was nobody she could call her own. At that time, she forgot the world. She was now immersed in thoughts of that angelic girl with skin as fair as a gardenia, hair as black as a raven's wing. Why had she not been given the chance to live like a queen? Why had she not been able to live in a setting that matched her jewel-like appearance? Everybody had agreed that she would do so. What was her fault?

Bogi saw that otherworldly, angelic girl flitting about in the flock of fireflies. The fireflies decorated her flowing hair with golden flowers. By the pale light of the sinking moon, her milky hued skin glowed in the darkness.

Suddenly, she tripped on a mound of earth that had been freshly heaped there. In a trice, she understood how that mound had come to be there. She had stubbed her toe on it. In that darkness, she could not see if it was bleeding, but she felt a liquid wetting her toe. She seemed to see that otherworldly beauty garlanded with fireflies, moving in the darkness to sit on that verandah. She was wearing a loose blue garment. She had put up her feet on a cane murha. The prince was gazing at her face. Another person came and stood near them. As soon as she approached, the otherworldly beauty's hair fell out and clumped together so that it resembled dried jute fibres. Her gums blackened, her teeth loosened and protruded from her mouth. Her skin turned ashen, the blue garment that she was wearing fell, and in its place, there was a frayed, coarse mekhela sador in a colour that had turned grey. She remained standing there with lowered head. In her hands were two cups of tea. The man had tenderly run his fingers through the woman's hair. And the woman who remained standing with two cups of tea? She quickly went away from there.

This woman, who was always smiling, had wailed and wept on seeing her dead baby laid out on the table. The woman in the faded mekhela sador had looked with astonishment at the contorted face of this woman who always got everything she wanted. In the silent darkness of the field, Bogi seemed to hear those heartrending cries. The wails had become a gust of wind and entered her soul. It had put out the fire that had been burning constantly within her.

Bogi sat near the mound of earth and took long, deep breaths. The man had slowly fed sips of milk to this woman who had almost fainted from weeping. A small ray of a smile had come unconsciously on the woman's face. The smile had remained hanging in the dark surroundings.

The embers of the dying fire within Bogi briefly flared up into a blaze again. Within the tangles of her mind, Bogi seemed to see these pictures dancing up and down. The light of the waning moon seemed to add to the knots within. Forgetting everything about the reality of the world around her, she picked up a split bamboo that somebody had discarded. She began to dig at the soil of the mound. A jackal passed, another creature like a wild cat also passed her, but she did not notice either of them.

It did not take her very long. The girl who had arrived dead into this world emerged from the mound. The soil was falling apart, revealing this buried girl. Her stomach had swollen up like a balloon. A mass of ants swarmed on her wrinkled skin. Her eyeballs had been half-eaten by ants. Bogi did not shiver in the least as she lifted the corpse. At that time, her clammy mind wanted only one thing: the sound of a particular woman's wails. Let her howl. Let her wail, too. Why did so many people have to come over just for the sake of one woman? And why should another woman remain sighing always? Without being aware of it, she rolled about on the field and from her mouth, came the same sounds. She lay on the freshly dug mound and was soon covered in mud. In the light of the waning moon, the night seemed even more haunted. Rolling about, she kept saying, 'Let her cry, let her cry.' Bogi's eyes burned darkly like embers.

She brushed aside the ants and hid the dead girl under her sador. Pushing all the darkness of that haunted field into her mind, she roamed around the ground. There was an odour coming from the dead body. A few jackals were sitting at a little distance. Rending the silence of the night to shreds, they began to howl.

Abruptly, Bogi started to walk towards Nomita's house. She went and stood near the verandah to the south of the house. Nomita and Amol's bedroom was adjacent to this verandah. There were several earthen pots on this verandah, in which different varieties of flowers were in bloom. Nomita cherished these plants. A sweet aroma was coming from the white flowers of a plant that had been newly brought here. Bogi wrapped the dead baby in the end of her sador and stood at the bottom of the verandah. She seemed to see Nomita, hazily, in the dim light of the waning moon. Nomita was sleeping with her head on Amol's shoulders. Amol was stroking her hair. There was nobody around except for the plant with the white blossoms that Nomita had planted. Its fragrance was everywhere. Nomita looked after this plant herself.

Bogi took out the dead baby from under her sador. In the darkness of the waning moon, there was not even a bit of light in her eyes. She placed the corpse exactly in front of the door. She knew that no matter what happened, no matter how ill she was, Nomita always came out to this verandah after waking up. She would look to the eastern sky and give her salutations to the sun. Bogi rubbed the plant full of blossoms. She took the blooms that had fallen off and sprinkled them on the face of the dead baby. After this, she went straight home. Sitting by the side of the well, she poured bucketfuls of water over herself. Bogi fell into a light sleep towards dawn.

By then, Nomita had been covered in a white shroud and placed outside. Bogi listened covertly and came to know how Nomita had got up from bed and placed her foot on the body of the dead baby, how the corpse's stomach had burst open, and after that, how and where she had fallen on the ground. And how that fall had proved fatal. Bogi also heard how Nomita had looked down for a moment at the body with its intestines spilling out and had lost consciousness.

The assembled crowd took the name of the Almighty and wondered how the dead baby had come right into the house. They all shivered in fear. Somebody cut a young leaf of a banana plant, and lit a saki, an earthen oil lamp, on it. They came and looked fearfully from a distance at the spot. Nobody came near it. Not just on that night, the people could not sleep for several nights in a row. Somebody else lit a saki on the path leading into the house also.

There were no ceremonies of death, no obsequies. Just a few elderly villagers came and lit a saki on that southern verandah. They burned some incense and sang hymns of devotion, naams.

For a long time, people did not go that way after dusk. Amol resigned from his job and left the house that looked haunted. After several years, a Marwari businessman bought it and converted it into a warehouse. Many stories about the house floated around. But after a while, even these died down.

And Bogi? The tangles within her rotted till a point in time they died out. There was only nothingness in her mind that had once been filled with damp and rot. The live embers had long turned to ashes. There were no mustard seeds to pop on the embers. Here was no air, no light. Just a terrible, fearsome silent emptiness. That girl who had once put a phot of kajol on her forehead was long dead now. There was nothing left, only an emptiness that could not be touched or held. She had lived with this emptiness all this while, and here she was now, Bogi Burhi, on her deathbed.

In between, a few incidents took place. The addict Dimbeswar Bhonguwa went missing a couple of times but eventually returned. One day, he vomited blood and died at the Shiva shrine itself. His liver was riddled with holes, a result of all the intoxicants he had imbibed. Her son could not continue with his studies and entered the army instead. He arranged for his elder sister's marriage, too. Bogi's parents, mother-in-law, her elder brother-in-law had all passed away. A nephew joined the banned insurgent organization ULFA and died of bullet wounds. Others got married. The village grew till it resembled an urban centre. None of these happenings could touch Bogi in any way. She was oblivious to it all. She became careless about her food, her clothes, her appearance. A terrible apathy, a vast emptiness. A complete stasis. Nobody could come through the windless, lightless emptiness to touch her anymore. She took upon herself all the household chores and survived.

Before she took to her bed, Bogi's work also included cleaning up the earth thrown up by the termites that were now everywhere in this crumbling house. These termites would throw up earth overnight, all over the house. Even before she began to work on other chores, Bogi would take up a trowel and a cracked container and scrape the piles of earth thrown up by the termites. She would then bring mud from the small pond in the corner of the backyard and wipe the floor with it. Sometimes she would even appear at night with the trowel and container. The others who lived there often thought of cementing the floor. But with so many other problems to sort out, this plan was always shelved. And a woman was constantly cleaning up the earth thrown up by the termites. After some time, the odour of the earth thrown up by the termites stuck to the woman's body.

Bogi Burhi's bedsores grew more severe. Her son would parcel cotton wool, powder and ointments for her. If he found someone going to his home, he would send those through them. Nothing seemed to work. These days, the old woman had begun to mutter something unintelligible and shake her hand.

A senior and respected person from the religious centre, the Xattra, said, 'It's not possible to just keep looking on like this. Some formal rituals should be conducted.'

Her son and daughter came home. Bogi's elder brother-in-law, the teacher who had lived in town, had died long ago. His son arrived. People from the village came, too.

Devotional songs were sung and chanted in Bogi Burhi's bedroom. She was wrapped in a new sador and placed in a sitting position near the altar that had been temporarily put up there. Her son had called the compounder, a paramedic and had got the sores washed. She was all skin and bones now. Her skin was now the colour of an old *eri* cloth and resembled a faded, rough wrinkled sador. On this were the bright red sores all over her body, the sores were peppered with white boric powder.

Throughout the duration of the prayers and devotional songs, the old woman remained with her hands clasped together in an attitude of reverence. The Bhokot, who led the prayers, began to chant the final blessings.

'Please forgive all sins, and gather this virtuous soul to yourself. Free her from the anguish of this life, of being born human on this earth, take her to the heavens. *Joi Ram, joi Hori*, chant with me, *joi Ram, joi Hori*.'

All those who had assembled there chanted the name of Hori aloud. The old woman's son and daughter knelt in front of the altar. The old woman remained in that sitting posture with folded hands. Everybody knelt and prayed at the altar, then got up. The Bhokot's blessings, too, ended. It was time to distribute the ritual offerings that had been placed at the altar and were to be dispensed among the gathering. The respected elder from the Xattra had already tied his gamosa on his head as he prepared to leave.

The assembled people observed that tears were falling from the old woman's eyes. It seemed as though she wished to say something. Nobody remembered when she had last spoken. What could Bogi Burhi, who had spent her whole life in silence as the daughter-in-law of the Bayon household, have to say at this point?

Bogi's voice had an unnatural strength. In a clear voice, she said, 'I did not kill the Mastorni.' Which Mastorni? Which lady teacher was she referring to? Immediately, the crowd began to murmur. The younger generation remembered nothing. And even the elder generation could not recollect what Bogi was referring to. It was Bogi's middle sister-in-law who reminded them. She was probably referring to that teacher who had trampled on the dead body of her baby and died. Once more, they lit the lamp that the Xattra senior had extinguished. All of them chanted in praise of the lord: 'Glory be to Ram, to Hori! *Joi Ram, joi Hori!*'

They all reassured the old woman. Whatever it was, she should tell them about it. She had one foot at Death's door, what was she afraid of? Somebody pushed in some new incense sticks into the holder made of a plantain stem.

'I was the one who brought the dead baby that had been buried. This sinner put it in Mastorni's home.'

There was commotion among the people.

'I dug up the dead baby.'

Bogi Burhi started to pant as she said this.

A week after the ritual ceremonies, Bogi Burhi died.

AUSI OR HAUSI

(Originally published as 'Ausi Othoba Hausi')

If the definition of a beautiful woman means that she has fair skin, a tall, lissome body, thick dark eyebrows, doe eyes, delicate hands and feet with long, slim fingers and lustrous hair and skin, then Ausi or Hausi could not be termed beautiful at all. In fact, one could even call her ugly; and, not even a girl, really. More a woman. It was as though the caress of youthfulness had never touched her; it seemed as though she had always been crushed by age. Her skin was rough, coarsened by the harsh sun and rain. She was short, sturdy and dark skinned. Her curly hair had become scanty as it had been washed, since her childhood, with harsh soap meant to clean clothes. Her fingers were knotty, and her feet and hands were chapped, dirt-encrusted and rough. She had never in her life trimmed her fingernails and toenails. They would wear down through constant exposure to soap, ashes and earth.

At first glance, there almost seemed to be something wrong with her—a kind of mental illness. She seemed hard of hearing, and slovenly in speech and cognition. But there was nothing wrong with her, really. She was not underdeveloped. She had perfect limbs and could work harder than anybody else.

How could 'Ausi' be a name at all? In the course of time, the name itself had morphed to Ausi from another, since it was easier to pronounce. Did her parents give her this name after seeing her dark, dull appearance? But no, that was not it. The names of women like her usually have a back story of suffering and neglect. A woman who was born with a bad leg was *lengeri*, lame. If she was left to die, she was referred to, as *felanee*, she who was thrown away. The daughter of a woman who died at childbirth was Mauri, somebody who had killed her mother.

But behind Ausi's name was joy. The joy of becoming or receiving happiness. The name that Ausi's mother had given her was actually Hausi, rejoicing. She had been born to her parents after five boys. Her mother had longed for a daughter and had affectionately named this longed-for little girl Hausi. But people called her Ausi: the night of the dark moon. The name Ausi matched her looks and her life, which appeared sunk in darkness, the sorrows which clumped together into gloom. Hausi died. And in her place was Ausi who stayed alive.

Ausi was ten or eleven years old when her mother died. She had had six children; she had worked extremely hard ever since she could stand on her feet. How much longer could she remain alive? By eleven, Ausi also resembled an old woman as she spent her days looking after her ailing mother, doing all the domestic chores, taking care of the requirements of her father, her elder brothers and her sisters-in-law. All these thousand-and-one responsibilities weighed her down and aged her.

After her mother's death, she lost even a home where she could bow her head and work ceaselessly. What, after all, was this home? A hut had been built on a small plot of land. The owner of that land had permitted Ausi's parents to live there. Ausi and her mother had together turned that into a home. But when the owner of the land started to build a house there, Ausi's home was demolished. Three of her elder brothers had already left. Now the other two left as well. Her father too went with a group of workers to Kerala. Only Ausi remained. She could not go off to Kerala or Delhi like her brothers. Her father had come to know a lady, Nabanita, whom he called Baideo, elder sister, out of respect, when he had worked as a daily wager for her. He left Ausi with her and went to Kerala. Baideo had expressed a wish to have a girl who would help with the household chores. Where would she stay, what would she eat otherwise? There was no way out of the situation. Ausi's father swelled the ranks of those people leaving for work and went to Kerala to find employment.

When Ausi came to the household of Nabanita Barua and Gourob Barua, Nabanita was in the third month of her pregnancy and was frequently unwell. In any case, Nabanita was not a very sturdy lady. The thin, pale woman had become very weak in her third month. A pair of twins had come to her womb. It was at that time that Ausi came to Nabanita Barua. The Barua household was a mess. The young girl lavished the pregnant Nabanita Barua with a mother's care. There was a woman who came to work part time—in the morning and evening. This helper swept and swabbed, washed clothes and utensils. Nabanita cooked the meals. Or tried to. But she would leave everything midway and go to bed. Later, Gourob Barua took care of the kitchen himself. Within a month, the thin, dark-skinned girl brought order to the chaotic household. She told the Baruas that there was no need to keep the lady who swept and swabbed. She could do this much herself. Why spend so much on her for no good reason? On top of that, there was some brother or her father who came regularly to take the woman's pay. His fare, too, had to be paid.

Listening to the girl, Nabanita had only smiled. She felt a deep affection for this homeless, motherless girl who was able to love and care for a stranger's home. At that time, Nabanita had taken leave from her job and stayed home. Pregnant with twins, she was always completely exhausted. The skin of her stomach had thinned. Towards the end of her pregnancy, this thinned skin would itch unbearably. Her stomach would constantly prickle. After finishing the household chores, Ausi would take the tin of coconut oil that had been warmed in the sun and sit beside her. She would then gently massage and stroke the distended belly with the warmed oil as though she was a loving mother herself. At the loving touch of those rough hands, the aroma of the oil, the winter sun, the heavily pregnant woman would doze off. Under the ministrations of Ausi's loving care, her discomfort gradually went away.

But one couldn't say that she was completely all right. All kinds of problems kept cropping up. Still, the constant tiredness that she had felt before Ausi's arrival had gone.

Her constant dizziness left her. Nabanita's own mother was unable to come to her as her daughter-in-law was due to deliver at that time. Her elder sister had all kinds of problems in her own home. Nabanita would think of her various aunts from her father's as well as mother's side of the family, her younger sister and her elder brother's wife. She would feel restless, distraught. If only one of them could come and stay with her during the final days of her pregnancy. Her husband's family simply blamed her people. They assumed it was the duty of the girl's family to be with her in a time like that.

The truth was that nobody wished to come to this remote place. One could only reach it after travelling on very bad roads and crossing a rickety bridge. Nabanita's heart was filled with sorrow and her pride was hurt. Even as her heart grew heavier, she began to look for support in the dark-visaged girl, Ausi.

And Ausi? There was only joy in her mind. As soon as she awoke in the morning, her mind was filled with beautiful colours. Such a beautiful house, a loving couple, and hardly any work to be done in this orderly home! She would hop around like a sparrow as she completed her chores. The body of this short, rough-skinned girl changed and filled out. She had herself planted a sacred tuloxi in the courtyard. Every evening, she would light an earthen lamp, a *saki*, and pray that all would be well with Baideo. She was drenched in her Baideo's affection. She had done so much for her. Over and above her salary that was taken by Ausi's father or brothers, Nabanita had begun to set aside a sum for her, especially, every month. She told Ausi not to let her father or brothers know about this. Even though she was unwell, she would always sit with Ausi and make her study. She could already write her own name. These days, she wanted to keep writing her own name. While washing the utensils, she would draw her name on the clean *thaal*: Ausi Bala Das. Sometimes she would write her Baideo's name: Nabanita Barua.

Today, Ausi was happier than usual. Today, Baideo would paint a picture. That too, Ausi's picture. These days, Baideo found it uncomfortable to lie in bed for too long, and so she would lounge on a chair outside. Sometimes, Baideo would paint a picture. Ausi would be very busy on the days she painted. She would run around and finish her chores, then sit near her Baideo. She would hand Baideo the colours and brushes that she asked for. She was always wonderstruck. It was as though a magical country was being created before her. The world of detergents, of Surf and soap, of oil and spices, of dusting cloths and brooms gradually fell away. Dancing like a *bulbuli* bird, she would enter another world.

A brush held between long, smooth fingers. The brush would move around a bare space, its bristles laden with colour. She would stare unblinkingly at it. She would breathe faster; beads of sweat would dot her nose. Even her Baideo, who was always physically uncomfortable these days, had a glow on her face. Baideo looked like a Goddess, as though she was not of this earth, but an otherworldly being at these times. So many different objects emerged from the brush, and the colours! Ausi was never tired of looking at them.

Gourob would leave for his workplace in the morning. Ausi would rise early and complete the domestic chores. Nabanita would sit on a chair outside, with her feet up on a cane stool. The coconut oil in the bottle would melt in the warmth of the sun. Nabanita's feet had started to swell, Ausi would massage her feet with the oil. The constant tingling of her feet would lessen a bit. For some days now, Nabanita had started to pick up her brush and canvas. As a student, her paintings had garnered a lot of praise, but after her wedding, the paints and canvases were put away on top of the cupboards. Now, with the effort it took to move around, Nabanita turned to her brushes and paints again.

Her first and main viewer was Ausi. Actually, it was mostly because of Ausi's enthusiasm that Nabanita had resumed painting. Whenever the canvases and the paint and brushes were set up, this girl, who spent her days completing her chores, was filled with a kind of joy. Even the rhythm of her steps changed. Her gait was usually slow, and she dragged her feet. But now, it seemed as though she became as fleet footed as a deer. She needed to finish her chores, because now Baideo would start to paint. Her eyes would brighten up with excitement and curiosity. What would she paint? Baideo's fingers would move around, and the blank canvas would fill up with paint and colours. Oblivious to all else, Ausi would slowly enter, step by step, into that festival of colours. She would fetch this and that for Baideo, and Ausi would become happier and happier.

From Ausi, she would move up, step by step and become Hausi. The desired one. Her mother's beloved Hausi, full of joy.

Today, Ausi has really become the Happy One. Today, Baideo would be painting a picture of her. She told everybody she knew here about it. Hasina's mother, Lata's mother, Runu's grandmother, Lata, Kunu, Moni, Junu . . . she told them all about it. Everybody would be arriving later in the afternoon. Ausi had already pounded rice into powder, mixed it with sesame and molasses, and fried up some excellent ghila pithas. She mixed a bit of paan masala and powdered pepper with the sesame and molasses. When she would serve this with tea that would be flavoured with ginger and bay leaves, the aroma would spread all around. Today, she wore a churidar kurta and dupatta of light green, which Baideo had bought for her. She was wearing undergarments of the kind that could be fastened with a hook, a bra. Indeed, the girl who had come with her father, that same skinny girl with the parched skin, was now wearing a bra, a hooked undergarment. She had shampooed her hair in the morning, and now her long, silken strands that fell to her waist shone in the sunlight. She had creamed the skin of her face, put *kajol* on her eyes, and a bit of colour on her lips. She was not in any want now. For some time, she had been going with Kunu, Lata, Hasina's mother to the market to get vegetables. In any case, the women living nearby would go to the market on the bazaar days for different chores.

The place where Nabanita Barua and her husband lived was quite remote. The colleges in the city were quite some distance from this place. There used to be a dense forest. People were afraid to cross it even in daylight. A few shops came up after the college was established. A few workers built their huts along the railway tracks and began to live there. Most of these people had left their homes and fields because of the terrorists' violence and begun to eke out a living in this way here. The house where the Baruas lived was the most well off. Ausi, the domestic help, who now shampooed her hair and put expensive creams on her face, was respected here. This girl had invited them over to watch her picture being painted. Who would not accept that invitation? They would all come.

Towards late afternoon, Ausi's picture had taken shape on Nabanita's canvas. Kunu, Lata, Bina, Hasina's mother and Runu's grandmother all came and sat in Nabanita's courtyard. The canvas was filled with Ausi's laughing face. One side was covered with her long hair flowing in the wind. And on her dark face, Baideo had drawn a red dot, a phot on her forehead, between her brows. Two hands with short, stubby fingers were stretched out towards the sun, as red as the phot on her forehead. The hands were even larger than Ausi's face, larger even than the sun. Sipping their tea and nibbling on the ghila pithas, all the assembled women were discussing the portrait created by Baideo. They were all unanimously of the opinion that the picture was very good. All their discussions were centred around the portrayal of Ausi's hands. They were huge, noticeably so.

The first one to bring this up was Runu's grandmother. She lived by herself. Of her three sons, one lived in Goa, another in Kerala and the last in Guwahati. She was almost completely out of touch with them. Runu's father, Lokkhon, who worked as a painter with a builder in Guwahati sometimes came over to find out how she was doing. He and his fashionable wife were eyeing the hut that the old woman had built, bit by bit, on half a kotha of land. Along with sweet gojas and singaras, he brought over Runu at times. Her daughter-in-law would just about step into the old woman's house, and then would go off to her mother's house, two kilometres away. She would take some more expensive snacks, borfis and rosogollas, secretly to her mother's home in a separate bundle. But the old lady was satisfied with this. When the boys were just small infants, their father had vanished. Turning her two hands into ten, she had survived. Just like the picture that Baideo had painted, Runu's grandmother, too, lifted her hands towards the sun as it hung above the clump of bamboos. Her hands, like Ausi's, were rough, their joints were prominent, their nails had worn down to the skin of the fingers—the skin was coarsened. Runu's grandmother sighed and said, 'These hands are life.'

Nabanita was startled. Forgetting her bodily aches and pains as well as the world around her for a while, she stared at the hands that Runu's grandmother had stretched out to the sun. Actually, while painting Ausi's hands, Nabanita Barua had in mind Van Gogh's picture of the peasant woman. A hint of that picture was in the depiction of Ausi's hands. Nabanita Barua had moved away from her relatives, her friends, her colleagues and was now spending her days with these hardworking women who brought in the aromas of different aspects of life. These women would come to visit her regularly, and Nabanita would look forward to their visits. Today, Nabanita wished to speak to them about painting.

Leaning on Ausi, she brought down a volume of Van Gogh's paintings from a shelf. She opened its pages to Van Gogh's painting of the peasant woman. All the women gathered eagerly around the picture. They began to speak excitedly in their rough, earthy dialects.

'Ahaha! So much sorrow in the girl's eyes!' said one in a dialect of Bangla.

'She's a mem after all, so she's wearing a frock.'

'Just look at her hands, they're like Ausi's hands painted by Baideo.'

'The girl works hard to make a living . . .'

'Her fingers have become crooked.'

'Maybe she's started to have joint pain, who knows . . .'

'Just look at her face . . .'

'Her skin is burnt by the sun.'

'What's she wearing on her head?'

'This is a japi worn by mems,' said another woman, referring to the Oxomiya headgear.

'True, they wear it while working in the fields.'

'There's no smile on the mem's face at all.'

'Such heaviness in the eyes.'

'She has many sorrows buried in her heart,' said another, in a dialect of Bangla.

'Her man must have left her.'

'There's no *xendur* in her hair.'

'Mems are Christians.'

'Christians don't wear xendur?'

'Maybe her son or daughter died.'

'Women only have their men and their children?'

'Maybe her mother has died.'

'Maybe her father has died.'

'A woman has so many sorrows.'

'So many. Not just one.'

In the meantime, on another canvas, Nabanita captured a crowd of faces of weather-beaten women lit up by the light of the setting sun, gazing at a peasant woman's picture. In this picture, the hands were the most important features. Rough hands, with fingers made crooked through hard work was what caught the eye at first.

After they had gazed at the picture of the peasant woman, the women rushed back to the picture that Baideo had painted. Ausi had served them another round of pithas and tea. She had also cooked a dail soup for her Baideo, which she now served her.

Nabanita was admitted to hospital that very night. The labour pains had arrived early. Taking Ausi with him, Barua left for Guwahati in the evening. All the arrangements had been made and their friends and relatives rallied around. Towards the afternoon, Nabanita gave birth to a pair of healthy twin boys.

After that came the routine of every middle-class family. Raising the two boys, completing her own research, taking on the growing responsibilities at work. In between all this, Ausi was married off. After he returned from Kerala, Ausi's father came to the Baruas and told them about the marriage he had arranged for Ausi. The boy stayed in Arunachal, though he was actually from Rangiya in Assam. He worked as an electrician. The boy's father had met up with Ausi's father in Kerala. Nabanita's sons were ready to start school, and the family did not feel the inconvenience too much after she left. The money that had been set aside every month for Ausi, along with some more that was added to it, made up quite a tidy sum. Taking the gifts that Nabanita's family gave her, Ausi left, weeping.

There was no news of her after she was gone. Gradually, her memory also faded from people's minds. Nabanita would sometimes see Ausi in her dreams. Perhaps Ausi, too, saw Nabanita in her dreams, wherever she was. There was a thick fog between the two of them now, through which no light could penetrate.

Life picked up pace and whirled Nabanita around, dropping her in the dark fog of loneliness. The twins settling abroad and her husband's death occurred one after the other. Both occurrences transformed Nabanita's life. Her successful sons carved out their own lives in a foreign country. There was no place for Nabanita there. The news of her sons getting their Green Cards and purchasing houses there reached Nabanita almost simultaneously. It was at that time that Nabanita's husband passed away. A massive heart attack took him away within an hour. He died without saying anything.

And the respected, retired professor Nabanita lay by the wayside, surrounded by an impenetrable fog. She could not move forward, could see nothing. The darkness of the approaching night mingled with the fog all around. She saw only darkness before her eyes. There were no voices of people, no birdsong, no flowers, no forests. There was only the fog, engulfed by darkness. Her world was bereft of sound. Only the sound of the trains, tearing everything apart, would enter her silent world at intervals,

The courtyard that Ausi would sweep to clean every day was now overrun with weeds. What was the point of cleaning it up? Nobody came here to sit any more. The small huts in which had lived Runu's grandmother, Hasina's mother did not exist anymore. They had illegally encroached on railway land. Who knew where they had gone? The fog had engulfed them all. A large railway station had come up in place of those huts. A couple of trains would tear apart the silence of Nabanita's world, as they shrieked through the days and nights.

The afternoon train would pause a little quite near the lane leading to Nabanita's home before reaching the station. A few people alighted here. The train would continue on its way, and the people, too, would go in different directions. Nabanita would wrap herself in a shawl and watch the people coming her way. Who knew, maybe somebody would alight from the train, and crossing into the lane, open her gate and come in. Perhaps they would say, 'Baideo, I thought I would drop by to see how you're doing.'

Many people crossed her line of vision and then vanished into the thick fog beyond.

One day, the train had come in the evening; perhaps it was running late. From the direction of the halted train flew an owl, a large owl with round eyes. The owl flew to a branch on the mango tree in front of Nabanita's verandah. Nabanita always felt very cold, especially in winter, and now she felt shivers go through her body. It was just a bird after all, she said to herself. It came and nested in the fog-encircled darkness of her heart.

The owl would often come to the tree in front of the house, and call out, hooting. Nabanita remembered her grandmother, who would say that when an owl called out in this way, it was calling out to death. She began to look out for the bird. One day, she noticed that a pair of them had built a nest in the mango tree. The trees of the compound had not been trimmed for a long time, and now her house was darkened by their deep shadows. These thick-leafed branches attracted not just the owls, but quite a few other species of birds as well. Nabanita began to sit on her verandah when the owls came out at night, till quite late.

The train was late that day. The pair of owls had emerged from their nest on to the mango tree and had begun their ululation. They were giving notice of the approaching spring. Nabanita smiled to herself as she listened to the auspicious call of the owls, and as the train stopped on the other side of the lane, she looked out with restless eyes at the shadows of the passengers alighting.

One of the shadows did not merge with the others. It crossed the lane to the train lines, and then it crossed the road. Nabanita tried to get up from where she was sitting but couldn't do so at one go. For some time now, Nabanita's legs would tremble if she got up abruptly, or if she walked fast. She kept a walking stick nearby. She knew very well that this was not an illness. She would eat a frugal meal that she cooked once a day, and then sit sluggishly around the house. Her body was getting rusty. Her life was lethargic, and she lived in anticipation of her grandmother's premonitions coming true; of evenings filled with fog indicating imminent death. Indeed, she had nothing else.

The shadow was not continuing down the road. It continued towards her. It had now placed a hand on the gate. The hand was trying to reach in and unfasten the latch that was inside. It was unable to do so. How could it? Nabanita had not unlocked the gate at all. The woman who came to sweep and swab the house had not come over for three days now, and so she had not unlocked her gate. Nobody else came here, after all. The boy who delivered the paper flung it into her compound from outside.

From inside came the sound of her phone ringing. One or the other of her sons would call at this time. But these days, their calls came much less frequently. The phone was ringing today after a long time.

Nabanita did not or could not accept these calls. The call would fall silent after ringing for a while. By the time she got up from where she was sitting and went to pick up the phone, it would fall silent. In any case, Nabanita was increasingly reluctant to receive meaningless calls. They were like festering sores. She kept the numbers of her sons written down where she could easily access them, so they could be informed of her death quickly. She had already made arrangements to donate her eyes and the rest of her body to those in need and had kept the documents ready. She had also kept aside a sum of money, in case somebody wished to do the formal obsequies after her death. She had arranged to donate her house, too, to a school after her death. Now there was only the waiting.

Throughout the day, Nabanita would look at the paper that lay under the weight of the phone. Was it there in the proper place? She did not have the courage to move the phone from its place there. What if people could not find the numbers when they came here? All the numbers were on her contact list. The papers contained all the relevant matters.

The shadow remained waiting near the gate. Nabanita went down slowly and placed her hand on the lock. A woman was waiting on the other side of the gate. Nabanita hesitated to open the gate. So many elderly women had been . . . She swallowed. Her throat was dry.

'Who is that? Whom do you want?'

'Baideo, it's me, Ausi.'

Two voices floated out from two bodies that had been ravaged by time. Both voices recognized each other, but that was all. The sky was filled with two familiar voices.

In the dying light of the evening sun, the owners of the two voices were astonished to see each other. Nabanita said to Ausi:

'You've become an old woman now.'

'Your hair is white.'

'Have your teeth fallen out?'

'You've become so thin!'

And Ausi exclaimed to Nabanita:

'Baideo, you've become really old . . .'

'Eh, Baideo walks with a stick.'

'Who comes to do the housework now?'

'Who cooks your meals?'

'How are the boys?'

'Where is Dada?' she asked, referring to Nabanita's husband.

'Why is everything overgrown with plants and weeds?'

'Why is everything so dirty?'

The laughing young girl known as Ausi had morphed into a hoarse voice and was moving around Nabanita. The clumps of silence and loneliness came crashing down. Annoyed and exasperated, sad and happy at the same time, astonishingly, the woman with the broken health became vibrant and alive again. Ausi's gleaming mane of hair had changed to a rough clump that revealed her temples. Her skin colour resembled that of a burnt brinjal, the joints of her fingers had become even more prominent, her teeth had become long and loose, her back was bent, her feet were badly chapped, her lips dry and dark. This woman had silently borne all the many storms that had come her way. An amazing liveliness and power, however, still remained in her voice, which had become loaded with emotions.

When she heard that Runu's grandmother and the others had left after the railway station had come up here, Ausi wept. She cried when she heard of Nabanita's husband's passing. She smiled when she heard that the two boys were now married. When she came to know that they each had a son and a daughter, her joy knew no bounds. But she was astonished when she heard that they had bought homes there, in the place where they now lived. She sobbed, saying that her Baideo had become very weak, and was angry at the shabby and unkempt condition of the house.

And Nabanita's condition was the same when she heard Ausi's story. She was angered when she came to know of the beatings that she received from her drunkard husband, and when she learnt that Ausi's brothers had taken away every single rupee that she and her husband had given Ausi. Her eyes became damp when she heard of Ausi's several miscarriages. She wept when she heard of how her alcoholic husband had kicked her in the stomach while she was pregnant. She felt a sense of relief when she learnt Ausi's husband had finally died. His body had swelled, and he couldn't handle the water retention. She shivered when she heard of Ausi's experiences in the so-called hotel in which she worked, which was actually a liquor den. And then she smiled when she heard how Ausi had escaped, got on the train and reached her home.

The untainted voices that came from two broken bodies played like the melodies from a stringed musical instrument, a tokari, as they sat through the night.

Surrounded by towering trees and a rampant undergrowth, they sat in that untidy, uncared-for home, talking. The pair of owls continued their ululations, the *dauk* birds from the pond purred, the aroma from the overgrown kodom plant came floating in from the open window. Towards dawn, Nabanita went to sleep on her bed, while Ausi spread a sheet on the carpet and slept there.

The next morning, after a long time, Nabanita called her two sons. With great enthusiasm, she gave them the news, 'Ausi has returned!' Naturally, her sons did not ask anything. When the call had come from her phone, both sons had thought that something had happened to the old woman. How could they go for the obsequies now? When she spoke in her excited voice, they could not understand the name Ausi too well. It was only later that they remembered that there had been a help in the house by that name when they were little. Well, whatever. They both heaved sighs of relief—that nothing had happened which would necessitate them having to travel.

Ausi returned to Nabanita's home. She wore Nabanita's old clothes, as she dashed about the house, garden and backyard.

Bedsheets, curtains, cushion covers were washed.

The toilets and bathrooms became clean.

The floor of the house began to shine.

The utensils began to gleam in the light.

The trees were trimmed.

The puni plants growing over the water in the pond were removed.

The front yard was cleaned of its weeds, and the undergrowth was removed.

The damp mossy growth on the steps disappeared.

Seeds of ridge-gourd and white-gourd were planted in the backyard.

The parasitic dodder vine was removed from the gardenia shrub.

Nabanita looked on in astonishment. What was the source of the lifeforce within the broken body of this woman, to whom life had dealt only blows? These days, unlike in the past, there were no daily wagers nearby who would come and clean up the compound. Ausi would wake up at dawn and go to the crossroads some distance away to hire the labourers who had come there looking for work. In the afternoon, after wrapping up her chores in the house, she would go to the village behind the station looking for the upper portions of bamboo. These would be used to support the ridge-gourd and white pumpkin vines that put out their tendrils to clamber up. She would return from the village, with a smile, on an e-ricksha, that ran on batteries, bringing with her the bamboo and a sack of cow dung to use as fertilizer. She went to the shops on market day and brought back a new net in which she caught the mature fishes in the pond. She would cook them in a nourishing skunk vine curry and feed it to Nabanita. She would bring a few flowers from the gardenia plant, which was now free of the dodder vines that had once smothered it and place them on Nabanita's table. Nabanita only looked on in astonishment.

One day, Ausi placed a cane murha on top of a chair and brought down Nabanita's paintings that were piled on top of the cupboard. As she was spreading out these dusty, cobwebby canvases on a bamboo mat in the sun to air them, she became as agitated as a freshly caught fish from the pond. They looked quite all right. But when she took them out, they crumbled. All the canvases had been attacked in places by termites. Ausi alternately wept and grew angry. In between, she would spread out these termite-ridden canvases on the split bamboo mats and wipe them.

The blue body of the picture of the kingfisher as it sat on the branch of the kodom tree which came curving out from the shore towards the water was undamaged. Its beak and head had vanished. One side of the vermilion puthi fish that had been put in the bamboo colander, each with a vermilion stripe was not to be seen. The black-hooded oriole bird had lost its yellow stomach as it sat on the flower of the ridge-gourd plant. Only the stems of the bunch of red lychees remained. Nabanita had painted these pictures on Ausi's request. Nabanita had been heavy with her twins at that time. The middle portion of the picture, which had her children when they were babies, was nowhere to be seen. Only the feet were visible. She wept as she placed the picture of Barua on her chest, the picture that had lost its head. Wiping the tears from her eyes, she took the termite-infested canvases to the bank of the pond and set them on fire. Nabanita kept watching her. She felt no regret, no sorrow. Ausi sobbed aloud as she looked at Nabanita's expressionless face.

After this, Ausi would constantly nag Nabanita. At times, Nabanita would get fed up. It would anger her. This girl, she really could keep on about it. She herself had been fine when she was surrounded by the wild, untrimmed trees, termites, cockroaches, moles and rodents, and other pests. The time she had been waiting for would have come in due course. What was the need for so much light and air?

Every day, Ausi's nagging grew stronger. As she went about her work, she would mutter loud enough for Nabanita to hear,

'There's no illness, no disease, but this woman can't get up.'

'Her arms and legs are fine, they aren't fractured or anything, but she can't walk.'

'She eats like a bird; can a person survive like this?'

'She used to drive smartly to college while she was working. Now the car just sits in the garage. When she was asked to paint a picture, she said she couldn't.'

Ausi did not stop just at nagging. She set about to work.

She called the mechanics from the garage, and had the car repaired. She had the tyres and battery repaired for which Nabanita spent quite a large amount of money. Ausi washed the car herself. She rinsed the paintbrushes with kerosene and after drying them, put them in a bag she had stitched from old clothes, and placed them on Nabanita's table. She took the help of a college-going girl from the neighbourhood and gathered canvases and paints. And yet the lady wouldn't get up from her chair. She would lean on Ausi and go to the verandah. Once she sat on the chair there, she remained there awhile.

One day, Ausi brought in a *bez*, a traditional healer from the village where she had bought the bamboo. As directed by the bez, she gathered xendur, duck's eggs and bihlongoni ferns. At that point, Nabanita's anger, irritation and impatience peaked. She said in a loud voice, 'It's good that you have come back, you can keep doing the work, but what's all this?' she scolded and grumbled at Ausi.

'I'm paying you; I'm giving you food and shelter. Stay here, but what kind of bullying is this? Who told you that I've been possessed by spirits? You've brought a bez, a shaman, he will start his mumbo-jumbo with these objects, these ferns. Who taught you all this.'

To herself, she added, 'She wanders all around, where did she learn all this? Who knows?'

When she heard her Baideo scolding her in a loud voice, a stream of black pearls came flowing down Ausi's rough cheeks, the colour of roasted brinjals. The tears glistened in the sunlight. Sniffing loudly, she began to sob. For a while, she rested her face on her hands and sat by the pond. It was possible to see the back verandah clearly from this spot. Baideo, too, was sitting there with her face in her hands, just as she herself was. The paperboy came and left the paper there. She didn't even glance at it. Previously, she would sit around waiting for the paper.

Ausi got tired of sitting there. How could anyone sit around like Baideo? She looked again at Nabanita. She was sitting in the same way. After a while, she would go to bed.

It wasn't as though she went to sleep once she was in bed. She kept lying there, staring at the ceiling. She looked like a lifeless corpse.

Ausi rose and went to the kitchen. She dragged the heavy gas stove out to the courtyard. The three burners were made of thick steel, and there was an oven too below them. The colour of the steel wasn't visible. Grease and other foodstuffs had blackened it over time. Who knew how long it had not been cleaned up? But who would have done it? This half-dead woman had nobody. Ausi gathered some detergent, kerosene, steel wool, some coconut husk and a rough stone, and sat at the water tap outside. She began to clean up the burners and the oven, creating a medley of different sounds as she did so. Nabanita's backyard filled with sounds of scrubbing and cleaning.

After her outburst against Ausi, Nabanita grew tired. She went and lay down on her bed. But here, too, she could not escape the sounds. Even so, she fell into a light doze.

She got up from bed after a while. Everything was quiet. But there was always a lot of sound around Ausi. There was silence everywhere now. What had happened? Nabanita's heart started to pound. Where had she gone? She got up and went to the backyard. Had she scolded her too much? But why wouldn't she be angry? She had called a bez, a traditional healer, who chanted mantras and suchlike. Once more, Nabanita's anger boiled over.

Of course, Ausi went to fetch the milk at this time. She would buy a few things from the market as well. But why did she bring the bez? For whom? Her heart cried out. In agitation, she went down to the yard. Were Ausi's things still here? But what were her things, anyway? Only Nabanita's old clothes.

On a cane *murha* in the backyard was the gas stove. Ausi had placed it there. That same stove which had become black with dirt, now shone like silver. It reflected the bright sunshine like a mirror. Rays of light sparkled out from it.

Nabanita kept looking towards it. After this, she took out the canvas, brushes and paint that Ausi had kept carefully on her table. Slowly, the blank canvas filled up with a gas stove that gleamed in the light, and by its side, a woman. The picture was like the woman's skin that resembled roasted brinjals, rough and dry. Her hair was scanty at the temples. Her salt-and-pepper hair had been oiled and tamed into a small bun at the back of her head. Two dark, knotty hands were placed on the shining gas stove. It seemed they were holding a ray of light. The rays of light that scattered and bounced out from the stove had fallen on the woman's face and body. With great love, Nabanita filled up the woman's bun with a bunch of soft, white kothona flowers.

The sun would set soon and Nabanita felt tired. She had been playing with the rays of light since afternoon. There was a sound of the gate being opened. There, Ausi had returned. In one hand was the bottle of milk, in the other the bag of groceries.

In a bright voice, Nabanita called out aloud, 'Hausi, Hausi, come, just come and see this!'

THE AFTERNOON
GRANDMOTHER

(Originally published as 'Bhorduporor Aita')

She would come quite often to meet me and always call out, 'Baideo!' in her nasal voice. She would appear when I was extremely busy, rushing around to complete all the chores as though I was the Goddess Durga with her ten arms. From seven to eight in the morning, there would be seven or eight chores dancing on my hands. And at that time would come the nasal voice, 'Baideo, will you buy some homemade lentil balls? Have enough newspapers been collected, are there enough for me to buy?'

'I've brought some elephant, boris and dhekia,' she would say, referring to dried lentil dumplings and fiddlehead ferns she had brought to sell. 'Do you have an old cotton sari for me, Baideo, I will stitch a *kantha* with it.' She would layer the soft material and stitch them together with artistic designs as coverings during winter.

Her words would change every day, but the essence would remain the same.

She would stretch out her legs and sit on the verandah as soon as she came. She knew that she would get a cup of tea. She would often enquire about old newspapers. We subscribed to several Assamese as well as English dailies and journals, and the pile of old newspapers grew quickly. With these, she would make paper bags and would sell them to some shops. She had done this job since her childhood along with her mother. She would place a piece of cardboard from a shoebox and create an excellent paper bag. Some time ago, the popularity of plastic bags had snatched this occupation from her. But now plastic bags had been banned and once more, she had taken up her occupation. Her means of feeding herself were as numerous as the legs of a centipede. It kept moving ahead, but the number of its legs could not be counted.

Who knows what her name was? Everybody called her Manobor Ma, Manob's mother. I would call her Manobor Ma as well. Manob was her only child. I had met Manob as a child, when he used to accompany his mother. He was rather naughty. These days though, he did not come with her. He had been working in a garage for a few years. She had wanted a good education for her son, but her husband's sudden and violent death changed her life forever.

Manob's father had been a small-time vendor of vegetables and leafy greens. He had a tiny hut on the banks of the river, as an illegal squatter. That hut, that bit of land, was her paradise. Her elder brother's wife's angry eyes did not exist here, there was nobody to nag her, and she lived without fear. She had lost her parents and was with her elder brother, a carpenter and his family. In their home, she would always feel apprehensive. She would be extremely fearful about such things as pouring a bit of milk in her tea, frying an egg for herself, taking a piece of fish and asking for a new blouse. She felt like an empress when she entered the hut by the river. She wiped the mud floors with a mixture of cow dung and earth. Right next to the verandah, she grew a brinjal plant which resembled goat's horns, but it yielded an abundance of brinjals. She would put the pot of dail on the fire, and while these lentils cooked, she would get the tender fronds of pumpkin to cook as greens. She planted some chilli plants that a crunchy purple, almost black variety of fruit that she could reach out to and pluck even when her husband had sat down for his meal. There was an ever-laughing toddler who chased the ducks and hens in the courtyard. What else did she need? These people lived a precarious existence. She felt like an empress, but that hut could be washed away by the river at any moment. They were in as perilous a position as the six senior wives of the merchant in the folk story, who sold their husband's favourite eighth wife, the daughter of the legendary kite bird, to a roving vendor while their husband was away. On his return, on coming to know of what they had done, the merchant, to ascertain their guilt, made them all walk across a magical cord which was stretched across a dry well filled with thorns and stones. This cord had the power to separate the truth from lies. Six of them crashed down and died in the well. Only the innocent seventh wife who had had nothing to do with it all, remained alive.

These people who lived on the riverbank did not think of guilt or innocence even though they were illegal squatters. The cord could snap at any moment, and they could fall into the well and die. Their position was as precarious as that of the guilty wives in the fairytale.

Manob's mother, too, fell into the well when the cord snapped. She fell so badly that she could not get up. On that fateful day, she had just spread her wares of vegetables and greens in the marketplace. The Sunday crowd of shoppers was increasing quickly. Manob's father had arrived late because the bus in which he had been travelling had burst a tyre. Not just Manob's father, almost all the vendors who were coming from that direction were setting out their wares a bit late. From the north came a large, jet black car with huge tyres and stopped. In those days, even in small rural marketplaces, one could see these youths. Clad in knee-length shorts that exposed their calves, with modern guns which they did not hesitate to carry openly in broad daylight slung across their shoulders; these young men could often be seen now in rural marketplaces. They were feared more than wild animals, because they had limitless and unrestricted power, and the vendors handed over whatever they were asked for with or without payment.

A couple of these boys, who alighted from the vehicle, had masked their faces with black cloth. From the small guns slung across their shoulders that shone in the sunlight, came the flash of fire. Everything was destroyed. In the blink of an eye, the marketplace was awash with blood. The blood-soaked, fragile cord on which Manob's small family balanced themselves broke. The empress was flung on to the streets. And it was after this that thousands of centipede feet grew on her body. Trying to make ends meet, she would do whatever came to hand. She would spend her nights gathering, with her centipede legs, grain by grain, a fistful of rice.

It was she who would come to my verandah and ask, 'Baideo, do you have newspapers for me? A cotton sari? An old petticoat, maybe? A couple of rupees in exchange for a few *boris*?' The veins in her neck and hands had become very prominent. The white clothes that she wore were getting threadbare with every passing day.

This woman was now many things. On some days, she was possessed by the Goddess Kali. She became a Debi, a deity. On other days, she was a woman whom the rays of the sun could not touch. At midnight, she became a mother of flesh and blood, a mother-in-law, and a grandmother with a heart drenched in love. By daylight, she became a Debi, a deity who could not be touched by the seductions of this illusory world. She had the power to chase away evil spirits and erase ill fortune that lurked in the destinies of people. As time passed, she became the Noon Grandmother.

This story unfolded in front of my eyes. It is not easy to understand the meaning, the significance of this astonishing story. Can one become the teller of this tale if one understands its meaning?

The newspapers grew to become a huge pile. A foul smell came out of the storeroom. Lokhmi investigated the matter and saw that the entire lot had been shredded to pieces by rats. Only a huge heap of shreds was now left. Five or six mice had died and rotted. As she laboriously cleaned up the space, Lokhmi began to mutter, 'I've told you this so many times. Manob's mother will not come for these. She became a Goddess yesterday. These papers could have been sold to the peddler who comes for bits and pieces of old and broken utensils and stuff. But will Baideo listen to me?' she continued, referring to me, her employer.

Manob's mother had become the Goddess Kali?

The woman known as Manob's mother had indeed turned into the Goddess Kali. The Goddess, Ma Kali, roamed among these people in a living form. Nobody could say when and whom she would possess. And now Manob's mother was possessed by the Goddess Kali as well. Perhaps it was not that strange that she turned into the Goddess. What was indeed strange was that she also turned into the Afternoon Grandmother within the short span of a single story.

Within this seemingly straightforward story lie many knots, many twists and turns, many spaces that need to be filled up. Before telling this story, one has to tell the story of the river on the shores of which people such as Manob's mother built their huts. The story of the trees that were cut down also needs to be told. The story of how the heart of the river was dug up needs to be told. Although they have been heard many times before, these stories still have to be told. Otherwise, how can one relate the story of the transformation of the woman possessed by the Goddess Kali into the Afternoon Grandmother?

The slender, graceful river, which bore within itself fish of many colours and jewel-like pebbles, overflowed in a frenzy. There was no tree left on the shore which she could grab as she flowed past. Which way could she flow, she with her dug up, wounded body? The beautiful river flowed this way and that. In her anger, she became as damaging as the Goddess of Destruction, Ma Kali herself. The river eroded a graveyard. Carrying skulls and skeletons with her, she became the Goddess of Destruction. It seemed somebody had opened the floodgates of a dam somewhere upstream, in the hills. It was the same story always; people were tired of listening to this being repeated all the time. Perhaps a temple, too, had been washed away somewhere. It was a temple dedicated to the Goddess Kali. The river brought this image of the Goddess, about four feet tall, and deposited it along with a lot of debris in the neighbourhood where Manob's mother and others lived.

The water receded. It was Manob's mother who first saw the image. It wasn't made of clay, but carved out of stone, as a result of which it had remained relatively undamaged. Actually, Manob's mother had got up very early to see if she could gather some driftwood left on the shore by the river. The image was revealed when she pulled out a branch. As happens after the floods, the sun was very strong. It had become humid and steamy because of the water that surrounded the area. Besides, Manob's mother had hardly eaten anything, and she was on a half-empty stomach. And on top of all this, was the sight of the Kali image that had risen from below the branch. Her head began to spin, she felt dizzy, and fell on the ground.

There was a huge commotion. Certainly, there would be a commotion, why not, for there was Manob's mother, lying unconscious at the feet of Ma Kali. In the ensuing confusion, it was unclear exactly who lifted her up, who sprinkled water on her head, who brought her home and fanned her brow and, with great deference, offered her a glass of milk. Nobody could say exactly who the people were, who with great respect and shouting hosannas rescued the statue of Ma Kali, established the temple and began to offer prayers and invocations. Though the walls were of woven bamboo strips and the roof was of corrugated iron sheets, still, it was undeniably a temple. It was nothing less than a temple dedicated to Ma Kali. And to top it all, Ma had come of her own will and shown herself to them. The news spread quickly, and money began to come in. Several workmen took the responsibility of building the place without remuneration. From oil lamps of brass, containers to burn incense, bells of different sizes and articles for worship, to fans—many things came in as donations. After all, who does not wish to earn merit? And along with all this, a helpless, needy woman attained divinity.

Lokhmi was right in saying that Manob's mother had become Ma Kali. She was now surrounded by all kinds of gossip.

It was said that towards dawn, Manob's mother had had a dream. It was well known that early morning dreams always came true. Ma Kali herself had appeared in that dream. Ma, it was rumoured, had told her that she was buried in the mud and the branches of trees. She was unable to breathe. As soon as Manob's mother woke up, she found a stick in the water by the shore. Yes, of course, otherwise why would somebody go to the riverside even before sunrise? And then, even if she did, why would she keep digging till the sun rose in the sky? Yes of course, there had to be some divine directive.

Ma Kali, it seemed, had looked at her face. There was the aroma of incense, of *dhup*, *dhuna* and lotuses all around. Unable to bear the sight of Ma's radiance, Manob's mother had fallen into a dead faint. When people came to investigate, they saw that she was lying unconscious, while holding on to Ma's feet. It was at that time that Ma Kali entered her body. Yes, certainly, Ma Kali was dwelling in her body. Otherwise, how could Romen's mother become with child after eating a fruit given to her by Manob's mother? Romen's mother was known to be barren. Her mother-in-law had already fixed another girl for her son.

And did you hear of Piku's grandmother? You haven't? What, you haven't heard till this day? Well then, listen. Piku's grandmother had a very bad chronic backache. Yes indeed, everyone knew this lady who, with hands on her back, walked unsteadily, swaying from side to side. She was given a bottle of oil. Manob's mother had chanted some mantras over it. The lady who was bent over in pain now walks straight.

All these different stories made a Debi, a Goddess out of Manob's mother. This woman who had grown thousands of limbs on her own two arms as she tried to gather, grain by grain, a fistful of rice; this dark-skinned woman with large, grief-filled eyes, was now invested with divinity. Her dark colouring, the hue of ripe jamun fruits, also became significant because it was the Goddess's skin colour, too.

In this way, Manob's mother became an extraordinary
person, in whom Ma Kali resided, and who possessed
supernatural powers. But what about the Afternoon
Grandmother? Is it possible for a woman possessed by
Ma Kali to become a grandmother, an Aita, that too an
Afternoon Aita? But it did happen. It happened right in
front of my eyes.

Usually, this woman never entered the homes of
other people. The dust from her holy feet did not grace
the thresholds of others. But she did come one day to our
home. Earlier, our Lokhmi would be unwilling to give this
woman who came looking for old newspapers even a cane
stool, a murha to sit on. And if she was told to give her a
cup of tea, Lokhmi would grow quite angry. Today, the
woman had brought fruits and sweets as *prasad*, blessings
from the Goddess, tied up in a bundle. Lokhmi fell in
reverence at the feet of the same woman. Even before I
could tell her anything, she had a cup of tea ready for her.
But the Debi did not touch the tea, or any food or water.
She was after all a Goddess, a Debi. She did not have any
food or water in the homes of others.

The woman looked in much better health than before.
Her clothes, too, were clean, new. On her forehead were
lines drawn from sandalwood paste. She had called me
once to the temple. When I asked about her son, she told
me that the owner of the garage had made him a permanent
employee. He was married. She had a grandson now. They
stayed in the hut that Manob's father had built. They had
made some improvements. Everything is by the grace

of Ma, she said and smiled. In her smile was the joy of fulfilment and the taste of success and satisfaction. It was obvious that she was happy.

Pushed by Lokhmi's nagging and my own curiosity, one day, at about three in the afternoon, I set out for the Kali temple on the bank of the river. I really wanted to see Manob's mother up close, she who had been possessed by Ma Kali. On the way, Lokhmi regaled me with all kinds of stories about Manob's mother . . . no, about this woman who was now Ma Kali.

The girl who worked as a domestic help in the house of the owner of the garage where Manob worked, hung herself from a fan in her room. She had just returned from a trip to her village for her mother's shraddha, the death rituals and obsequies. Just a few days after she returned, she hung herself. The whole matter was quite simple. She had lost her father early, and now her mother too had died. She could not bear it anymore. What was not simple was the arithmetic regarding the sum of money that the girl's brother and sister-in-law had received from the garage owner. Anyway, what had happened, had happened. But her soul did not leave the house. The garage owner tried to flee the house at night, but she would come after him with the rope which she had used to hang herself, to throttle him. Manob's mother, with the power of Kali within her, went to the house. With sacred chants, incantations and mantras and by sprinkling holy water and rice, she contained the spirit that inhabited the house.

In gratitude, the owner of the garage built a beautiful space, covered with marble near the river for the devotees of the Kali temple. The devotees would flock there in the evenings to sing beautiful songs in praise of Ma Kali. After that, there was no sign of the ghost. Manob, too, was no longer a contractual worker at the garage and was instead elevated to a more permanent position as member of staff, on a payroll.

Lokhmi continued to tell me stories of Kali and the woman she had possessed. We reached Manob's house. The temple was at some distance from there. Once, when Manob's mother had fallen ill, I had come, accompanied by Lokhmi, with medicines and some nutritious food meant for invalids. That wretched-looking hut was no longer to be seen. In its place was a two-room concrete house. Lokhmi had told me that Manob had got building materials for the house, a decent toilet, a gas connection and a Ration Card from the Government.

Manob had just returned from the garage. He, along with his wife and son, came out of the house when they saw us.

'Is Ma at home?'

All three of them hung their heads and remained silent. What could have happened to the woman who had been transformed from Manob's mother to a Goddess— possessed by Ma Kali! This woman, Manob's mother, had just got a bit of security after being possessed by Ma Kali. She was slowly building a better life for herself, and her family. What could have happened? Did she have to walk on that cord stretched across the well once more?

'What happened?' my voice sounded agitated to my own ears.

'She,' I was told, 'I mean Ma Thakuroni is at the temple.' They used the formal form of 'she' for her now, even though she was their own mother.

Manob's wife laid out cane murhas in the courtyard for us to sit on. She brought puffed rice and biscuits along with black tea. While sipping on it, I heard another tale, a story about a woman who was Ma in the mornings and evenings. There was envy in the air. Many hearts burned with resentment on seeing a woman who had been living on the edge, now able to establish a footing at last. Just before Kali Puja, during the meeting of the Temple Committee, a question had come up. How could a woman in a domestic setup become a Thakuroni, a Goddess? Thakuroni was a widow, she did not sleep on a mat with a man. The son had a family. What was she doing there?

Somebody put forward the view that Thakuroni could only have anything to do with her own family before sunrise and after sundown. If, in between, she was shackled by the bonds of domesticity, the Kali temple would become impure, people would be consumed by Ma Kali's fury. The Goddess was fearsome, she would annihilate everything in sight.

This was the final decision.

Manob's mother would take her grandson in her lap before sunrise and feed him. She would then take off her white clothes and wear the red garments that made her the Thukuroni, the Goddess of the temple. It was only at midnight that she could come out of the earthly bonds

of the temple. She would finish the work at the temple.
She would have a bath and put on her white clothes and
go home to her sleeping grandson. She would wake him
and place him on her lap. The grandson, too, became
accustomed to snuggling in his grandmother's arms
before dawn, and at night, sleeping in them as she told
him stories. He would place his mouth on her cheeks
and say, 'Aita, tell me the story of the jackal and the
monkey.' Only when it was time for the owl to return
to its nest to roost that the grandmother and grandson
separated.

What an astonishing story!

Lokhmi went to the temple. I was engrossed in the
story of the Night Grandmother. I remembered another
Thakuroni. That Thakuroni sported dreadlocks, Joti. Joti
Thakuroni was the Mother of Morning and Night. She was
the dimwit Sadhon's mother.

It had happened so many times. So many known
characters merged with people in books. The people in
a book and living, flesh and blood people who could be
touched, and were living real lives. So many times, both
had merged. I found Dickens' Miss Havisham in the
character of Borma in Panbazar, and I discovered Howard
Fast's Miss Mary in the Wednesday Haat market. In
the arrangement of Albert Maltz's chairs in the circus I
found the children who fell asleep while watching the real
circus at the religious event held in father-in-law's home.
Mahashweta Devi's characters were amid people who
lived on the riverbanks behind my house. In fact, the talk

of the people whom I met and saw, the flesh and blood people, melded with the characters that were created a century ago.

The grandmother who was possessed by Ma Kali took her grandson at midnight and showed him a sky full of stars. This woman now became the cherished wife of a loving man who had been snatched by a horrific death, the mother of a quiet young man who had wanted to study, but could not, the affectionate and caring mother-in-law to her son's wife. Here, she was not the Goddess, the Debi Thakuroni, who, with her presence and speech, made the whole environment misty with a supernatural aura. This dark-hued woman would wear a tattered mekhela sador. Her daughter-in-law would clean it with washing soda and keep it between two sheets of old newspaper. The Midnight Grandmother would come home and wear these widow's white clothes. The daughter-in-law, too, would look forward to midnight. Her mother-in-law would come home and comb out her hair; she would fry a trayful of sweet, melt-in-the-mouth pithas, with the rice powder that she, the daughter-in-law had pounded during the day. The grandmother would cook a gravy of fish fingerlings with ginger paste. She would finish knitting the fancy muffler with complicated designs for her son to wrap around his neck in the winter and start on a sweater with soft wool with a red rabbit on the chest for her grandson. If there was no other work for her to do, she would make piles of paper bags with the newspapers she had collected and brought back from the temple.

The daughter-in-law wished that this mother-in-law would stay at home during the day, too. The grandson would insist on going to the temple. He would call out to his grandmother, and say, 'Aita, come home and feed me my lunch.' He knew, even in his childish mind, that this was not possible. As soon as she donned her red clothes, his grandmother would disappear. Her son, Manob, too, would bring fish, ridge-gourd, and pluck the edible potherb, the modhuxolleng or knotweed greens and herbs as he waited for his mother to return and change her red clothes before having her bath. She would cook a curry of fish, with steaming hot rice. In a trice, she would fry dumpling balls of rice powder with cilantro. She would grind sesame seeds with ginger and garlic and place the dish on the side of the *thaal*. She herself would only have a little milk and rice. A devotee had donated a cow, and it had calved. She fastened a tiny bell around the neck of the calf. The mute, innocent calf would jump around, its bell tinkling. As the dauk birds called out through the night, that melody from the bell would reverberate in the hearts of those who heard it. At sunrise, everything became quiet. The grandson grew silent. Like the night blooming flowers, the entire house remained folded up during the day as it waited for nightfall again.

It was midnight. Elsewhere, everyone was asleep. But like a flower that bloomed at night, the house too had blossomed; the tinkling sound of the bell was heard everywhere.

'Look, look there, do you see the red star? That's your grandfather, he's looking at you.'

The grandmother took her grandson in her arms. She looks at the star, the child looks at her face.

'Ma, that sweetmeat that Deuta used to bring from the market every day,' said the son, referring to his father, 'it was part white, part yellow.'

'You used to say, "*Onga boga mithai*",' his mother said and smiled. Red-and-white sweetmeat. As a child, her son had not been able to pronounce the 'r' in *ronga*, red. So '*Onga boga mithai*'. To her daughter-in-law she would say, 'You know, *bowari*, you should have met your father-in-law. He was a really affectionate man.'

Gradually, the child fell asleep on his grandmother's chest.

Handing over the sleeping child to his father, the Midnight Mother-in-Law took up a bottle of coconut oil and unfastened her daughter-in-law's hair from its bindings. She was heavy with another child and the oil soothed her restlessness.

'You know, bowari,' she would tell her daughter-in-law, 'your father-in-law was very keen on educating his son properly, get him married with much fanfare, bring home a daughter-in-law and give her a chain of gold . . .'

The Midnight Mother-in-law picked up a small bundle tied with cloth that was lying nearby. A pair of silver bangles gleamed in the moonlight. In that silver light, a bright smile lit up the younger woman's face, half hidden as it was by her unfastened hair. The two heavy *balas* with ornate elephant heads at the two ends gleamed even whiter in the light of the moonbeams.

The dauk birds continued to call out. The sky would soon be filled with light. Like a night fruiting plant, the home, too, was beginning to wilt. The Midnight Grandmother, too, would soon vanish. Snapping all her worldly ties, Aita would don red robes and become a Debi.

She was under scrutiny. People were observing, watching with eagle eyes. Did something happen that could offend Ma Kali? At the slightest hint of such an occurrence, another Kali-worshipper, a Kali devotee, man or woman, would replace her. The glory of the temple was growing by the day. Devotees were gifting ornaments of gold and silver, too. The Temple Committee had also bought a strongbox. Before the elections this year, representatives of political parties would arrive. Meetings would be held in front of the temple. There were many assurances about donations regarding twenty-four-hour running water, toilets, new kitchens fitted with tiles for preparing the offering of cooked food. This woman, who had shouldered the burden of being possessed by Ma Kali, had not broken any of the rules. She had continued to carry out her duties flawlessly towards the temple. She relinquished her domestic existence and came to the temple before dawn. She would clean up the temple, and only after the singing of devotional songs at night, would she return home. She was bound to do it. Sometime later, she also received a monthly wage. There were many eyes on her, but nobody had found any flaw.

So how did she become the Afternoon Aita? She had cut all worldly ties during that slot of time. What had happened? How did she become a grandmother with the grandson in her arms in the afternoon? Ignoring all strictures, did the child call out to her? 'Aita, is that red star Koka?' In the light of the afternoon sun, did she become a woman, then?

Yes, it did happen. She became the Afternoon Aita.

Therein lies another story.

The little grandson was unwell. He had a fever. His mother, too, was unable to pay much attention to him. She was seven months pregnant. There was much work around the house, there were cattle too to be cared for. He was being given his medicines, too. Who knows what happened? His teeth clenched, his eyes rolled up to his forehead, his limbs began to shake uncontrollably. The neighbours dropped everything and rushed to Manob's home.

She was arranging the platter of offerings before the image of Ma Kali when one of the neighbours rushed to her and told her about the little boy. The woman's limbs began to tremble, not because she was possessed, but out of fear and worry. One of the neighbors, probably Roop's mother, yelled, 'His condition is really bad.' She clenched her jaws and became immobile. She could hear wails coming from the direction of her home. She shed the sacred clothes and recused herself of her Goddess-hood. Instead, she wrapped a gamosa, the cotton cloth around her petticoat, held her breath and ran.

She became the Afternoon Aita. She picked up her grandchild, who was burning with fever. He was unconscious. She poured water on his head. His stomach was distended. He had not urinated since the previous day. She went to the pond and brought duckweed. She crushed it on the mortar and applied the paste on his navel. Taking up a hand fan, the grandmother blew air at her grandchild. After a while, the child peed out a copious amount of urine. His fever, too, came down. He opened his eyes, and putting his arms around his grandmother's neck, said, 'Aita.'

With sunshine all around, in the blinding light, she became Aita. The Grandmother. She became the Afternoon Aita.

She resumed coming to our house in a pair of white cotton mekhela sador. She often brought her grandson and sat on the verandah with her legs spread out in front of her. She would ask, 'Baideo, do you have old newspapers?' Lokhmi did not fetch a cane murha for her to sit on. When requested to bring a cup of tea, she flounced out, saying, 'There's that huge pile of clothes to be washed, I shan't be able to make tea for her.'

True, only the grandchild would love this Afternoon Aita. Why would anyone give her any importance? What was there for people to accord her any? There was nothing. She was a very ordinary being, like a grasshopper in the forest.

THE WOMAN WHO BECAME AN OWL

(Originally published as 'Manuhjoni Phesa Hol')

It wasn't a very big river. It came down from the hill and merged with the large one, which, in turn, flowed into the Brahmaputra. This small river looped downstream. It was fringed with bamboo. Indeed, the river looked like a tunnel through the bamboo. Up until the point it reached the larger river downstream, it also acted as a boundary: this side of the river, or that side. The two sides were connected by the bamboo bridges that spanned the breadth of the river, and the footbridges that tried to connect the two banks. This side of the river was bustling, the paths and roads were smooth and easy to access. There was vehicular traffic too—trains and buses plied along its banks. There were main roads and highways; there were schools and colleges; and there were wealthy people living in fancy houses that dotted the banks of the river. There were markets selling tasty fish and vegetables. The price of land on this side of the river was rising by the day. There was a huge difference in the land prices on this shore and the other one.

Who would want to live with the fragile swaying bamboo bridges connecting them to the outside world? The land on the other side of the river was marshy. When it rained heavily in the hills, the marshlands would fill up and create great inconvenience. For various reasons, the other bank of the river stopped developing. A few families with low incomes lived there. The land was inexpensive, rents were cheap. It was convenient for them. Nobody owned a car. There were a few two-wheelers. They would cross over by the wooden bridge in the extreme north. The wooden bridge was full of gaps. Even a little carelessness would result in a leg going through it. A couple of bamboos or leafy twigs would be inserted into the gaps. Things would continue as usual . . .

But the place on the other side of the fragile, swaying bamboo bridge was magical. Astonishing things, which brought shock into people's conversations, happened in this area. When people heard about these events, they would touch the ground and bring their hands to their ears out of respect.

What were these strange happenings? Who could believe them? With the great strides made by human civilization, it seemed impossible that such events could continue to occur. But they happened. In the dark of night, in the light of day, at dusk, in the dry season, during the rains . . . these things happened all the time. Simply hearing about them was a hair-raising experience. Listeners' throats grew dry, their limbs began to tremble, and their vision grew hazy as they heard about these unbelievable, horrific events that were taking place there one after the other. Who was there to obstruct it? Who could stop it?

A woman became a tree.

A man became a bull.

A woman who was standing in the field became an owl.

The teacher found a six-year-old boy.

The fish in the bamboo containers became human skulls and bones.

What nonsense! It was all made up, all stories. How could a human become an owl, a tree or a bull? And another woman find a six-year-old boy? How could fish turn into human skulls and bones? Who would believe any of this? But it was all true. In the marshy land, among the impoverished people who lived in the darkness of the other bank—without lights—all these happenings really did occur.

Let me narrate to you the story of Sita, the woman who turned into an owl.

Sita was the fourth daughter of an impoverished family living on the other bank of the river. She grew up unloved, neglected. At a very young age, she was sent across the river to a rich household to work as a domestic help. She grew up there until she reached the marriageable age. Then, she was sent home, because 'a young woman could not remain in the house'. There, she remained amidst great hardship for a couple of years, after which she eloped with Suren, the local vendor of beads and bangles who peddled his wares at the weekly fairs.

Suren gradually found it difficult to support Sita, who had grown up in a rich household on the other side of the river. On the one hand, he had to support his parents and his siblings, on the other, there was a deeply disappointed, perpetually discontented woman with two children. How could he do all this?

Suren went off to Gujarat. Up until then, Sita was still a living human being. At first, Suren would send a bit of money. Later, it stopped. But it wasn't just the money. The news about his whereabouts stopped too. Some people said that Suren had died there. There had been an accident in the mill where he worked, and he had been trapped under a machine. The owner of the mill hid the death to escape from the legal and financial obligations.

With her two children, Sita fell into a sea of misery. It was from this time that she gradually started to become an owl. While she was searching for jobs or money, she met the proprietor of a mid-sized clothes shop. The middle-aged man was married, had a home and children. At first, he placed her in the shop. It was Durga Puja season. Crowds thronged the shop, and this was the reason he hired her. She was a good salesperson, able to entice customers through body language, smiles and speech.

But once the Puja season ended, the crowd of customers reduced. The proprietor felt emptiness in the shop without Sita. Many of her needs, and requirements, too, were met. A couple of times, she even went with the proprietor to Kolkata to pick up goods at the wholesale markets. He could not control his desire for Sita who had been with him in the hotel rooms even after his return.

After Suren's disappearance, Sita had lived with her two children under the roof of her mother's verandah. The proprietor of the shop made arrangements on a plot of land on the other side of the river, that too, right in the middle near the fields. Everything on that side was government land. Even though many poor people had cleared the land and settled there, they did not have legal documents. A barbed wire fence came up on about three *kothas* of land beyond the field, at the edge of the marsh. A two-roomed house came up there. A tubewell was installed, as well as a bathroom and toilet area.

Sita went and settled in her new house. People commented, of course. How could a young woman with two children stay by themselves on the edge of this lonely swamp? Sita had a straightforward answer. She was a woman without a man or a guardian to provide shelter over her head; it was more than enough that she got a house and toilet given to her by the government. This happened only because the proprietor of the shop helped her by taking care of the paperwork. How would she survive if she lived in fear?

The gossipmongers talked about Sita's new house. The mother lived in one room by herself, and the children lived in the other. Her room was locked. Indeed, why would it not be locked? What a room! Lokhmi's mother had seen it one day when she had gone to wash the clothes and swab the floor. Was that a widow's room? It was a bridal boudoir! There was a huge bed, and what could one say about the bedsheet? There were multi-colored flowers on it. There was a large, mirrored dressing table, a steel almirah, a small fridge, and inside the fridge . . .! Inside were bottles of liquor. The eyes of the gossipmongers, who were listening to Lokhmi, grew wide. Was this true? They spoke in whispers.

What did Saraswati's mother see on the dressing table? Pills, long sheets of them. While in her mother's home, Sita suffered from low blood pressure. She would feel so dizzy at times that she would have to stay in bed. Maybe they were pills for blood pressure. But when Moni's mother went to air out the mattress outside, she saw a plastic bag full of that stuff.

The chatter continued. How could one get a house built by the government unless it was a *myadi* land, with a periodic *patta*? Which government, which *sorkar*, built this house for her? Well, who else would give this? It must have been the actual sorkar, the master, who gave her this. Who was it that came on a bike at night to her house across the broken wooden bridge, wearing a balaclava? These days, he could no longer bring the bike. Several planks had been stolen from the bridge. Even the bamboo that had been placed on it had been taken. And the bike remained behind Madhu's paan shop. He would arrive at night and depart at night, too. At home was the formidable lady, his wife. She was like the *raikkhox*, the demoness who had tried to kill the baby Krishna. And her brothers, what could one say about them! They seemed to be descendants of the evil Kauravs. All of them lounged around in the home of the proprietor of the cloth store. There was a fish dish at every meal, and meat on market days. Certainly, they would lounge around, why not? The proprietor of the clothes shop returned home late at night. He left for the shop late in the morning. If questioned, he would say that he could return home only after giving the keys of the shop to Sita.

He was getting older; it was difficult for him to rise early as before and open the shop. It was only because he had a trustworthy employee that he was able to get this bit of rest. Irrefutable logic.

People on the other side of the river saw Sita getting her children ready for school, and then leaving them at her mother's home. She would then go at this early hour to open the shop. She would sweep and swab and clean up the shop and offer prayers and incense sticks to the image of Ganesh. The owner would arrive in the afternoon.

Leaving aside their fear and nervousness, Saraswati's mother, Moni's mother and several other women gathered behind Sita's house. Sita and the owner of the clothes shop got to know of this. Madhu, the paan shop owner would not betray them. Sita was prepared for this. In a sweet voice, she invited the women into the house. Hospitably, she offered them tea and sweets. After a while, the proprietor arrived, gave her the keys and went back without setting foot inside the house. Sita wept a bit before the women and said that for her, the proprietor was God. She showed them the locked room as well. She told them how she had collected the items, one by one. She would rent out a part of the house to some poorly paid woman teacher. If this house had been located on the other side of the river, the rent would have covered her children's school expenses.

The women left. People only saw the bad, they said among themselves now. Here was this woman who worked so hard to educate her children. She had built a house and was living so courageously in this lonely place.

Now, Sita arranged for the women to buy saris during the Durga Puja celebrations, paying back in instalments. She also mentioned that the proprietor was a compassionate person who understood the misery of the poor.

Suddenly, a pair of owls hooted from the side where her children slept. The girl hugged her mother tightly. Her mother would discipline her by saying that if she did not go to sleep on time, the owl would take her mother away. The two of them would have to go to bed right after dinner. They would sleep, for they feared that otherwise, the owls would take their mother away. What would happen if their mother became an owl? They were terrified, and this terror made them gullible.

That night, the proprietor had to endure mosquito-bites and stay under the tree for a long time. The time to return home had come too. Sita would be bathing with sandal soap, she would perfume herself with *kamini*, orange jasmine body spray. She would probably wear that red silk outfit that had come in the latest consignment of clothes to the shop, that red garment that revealed even while it feigned to cover. The image of Sita's body draped in a red silk garment made him pause and change his plans about going home. Paan shop owner Madhu went to the home of the clothes store's proprietor with the news that he had gone to Rangiya to fetch a consignment of clothes that had come by train. He would only reach home at about two at night.

Sita no longer had to worry about where the next meal would come from. Her body had responded, and now, in that red silk nightie, she looked like a ripe pomegranate, split open. That night, the proprietor of the clothes shop had not wished to leave her and come away at all. By the time he reached Madhu's shop, the sky was getting lighter. For some time now, the owner, the Malik, had only been able to leave Sita at this time. He was completely under Sita's spell and intoxicated by her charms. He planned to marry Sita. Who could do anything to stop him? His wife, who now looked like a huge sack weighing two maunds, what could she do? Her aches and pains wouldn't let her leave the bed at all. Since Sita had arrived, the shop, too, was doing well. She would accompany the Malik, the proprietor to the big cities and choose clothes there that women would like. Each time, they would go for a couple of days, but it would take them a week or more to return. Now, the Malik wanted to have Sita by his side constantly, day and night, just like those times in the big cities. But there were hurdles, such as bad weather, guests at home, and so on and it was becoming difficult to carry on like this. The income was his; it was his to spend as he liked. What could anybody do? He would take Sita to a temple and put xendur in her hair. He would build a house on this side and take Sita there. He was past caring about anything. Without giving any explanation to anybody, on the days when the shop was closed, he had begun to spend whole days with Sita in her house on the other side. People were becoming aware of this.

It was a day like any other. As always, Sita left her children at her mother's and went very early in the morning to open the shop. On her return, she had her food at her mother's home. She had cooked mutton curry that day. Seeing that her children had fallen asleep after dinner, Sita went back alone to her home by the marsh. On those days, she had felt uncomfortable to close the door to her children's room before entering her own bedroom with the proprietor of the clothes shop. Her son was growing up, and she felt awkward before him. She knew this could not continue for very long now. The Malik was talking about putting xendur on her head, and she had agreed. He had bought a plot of land on the other side and was now thinking of building a house there. She had gone and checked out a couple of plots herself as well. She quite liked the plot in front of the high school. It stood by itself beside the large field. At times, Sita would put xendur in her hair and wearing a beautiful pair of mekhela sador, would come and go to the house that was being planned. She would quit her job at the shop. She would become a simple homemaker. She would educate her children and look after her man.

But that day, Sita did not come over at any point in the day. Her mother assumed that she would come at night and take her children back. But she did not come at night, either. The next day, the children were sent to school from their grandmother's house itself. After school, they returned to their grandmother's house. They were not in the habit of going to the house by the side of the marsh by themselves.

Sita's mother had knee pain. She found it difficult to walk. She spoke to her son and her daughter-in-law about finding Sita. The son snapped back rudely to her. Sita's mother understood the meaning of this. She kept quiet. Earlier, too, Sita would leave her children here and go away for a few days. If it was a place from where she could not phone up, she did not call.

Three nights and two days passed. The girl was beginning to cry. The old lady took some women along and limped to Sita's home by the marsh. The children needed fresh clothes and books. The old lady had a key to the place. The other women walked six paces when the old lady walked one. They had set out in the afternoon, but by the time they reached, it was evening.

The house was in darkness. The old lady told the others that Sita had gone to get a consignment of clothes from a place with no phone connectivity. Why would this woman who would otherwise call three or four times a day not ring up even once? Sita's phone, too, was not connecting. Sita had bought a phone for her mother so that she could keep in touch about her children. Sita's house was in a lonely spot beside the swamp. Nobody came or went that way. Sita herself had wished to live away from the prying eyes of other people.

The gate to Sita's house was open. So were the doors and windows. There was no sound anywhere. Only the owl was hooting as it sat in the hollow of the pakori tree, the wavy-leaved ficus touching the rooftop of the house. The old lady along with the other women went through the open gate. Several bikes had muddied Sita's otherwise clean courtyard. The verandah was always wiped clean, but

now there were shoe prints on it. The floor was full of clods
of mud fallen from the shoes. The door to the children's
room was closed. But the one to Sita's room was open.
The house and the courtyard were pervaded with such a
horrible stench that none of the other women wanted to
enter Sita's house. The old lady, too, paused. The hooting
of the owl had stopped. There was only the soughing of the
wind, amidst the stillness. Even the leaves of the trees did
not stir.

The old woman collected herself. Clapping her hand
to her breast, she rushed towards Sita's open room. In the
descending gloom of evening, the sight of the old lady
dragging one foot and trying to run appeared very strange.
A little while later, a fearful cry was heard from inside the
room. The women who had been waiting near the open
gate reached the spot. The lonely silence that had gathered
in that area was shattered in the ensuing commotion of
screams and cries.

Sita was lying on the floor of her room. She could not
even be called a human anymore. Her body had swollen to
a gigantic size. The blood and froth that had come out of
her nose and mouth had clotted up. Her eyes were bulging
out. Sita's body, from which a foul smell was coming out,
was grotesquely stretched out on the floor.

People were beginning to gather around. They came
from the other side of the river; even the police arrived. In
the middle of all this came the news that the home of the
clothes shop proprietor was locked up. Accompanied by the
clan of Kauravs, the wife had gone somewhere to attend a

wedding or was it to consult a doctor about her ailments? It was the people on this side, those impoverished souls without food or clothes, who cremated Sita. They did not allow the two children to see the mother's dead body. The funeral pyre was lit by Sita's elder brother. Her son shaved his head.

One day, the grandmother took the two children to the house. They would have to go. There were books and clothes that had to be brought back. The old woman was very worried. Who would look after them, who would educate them, who would pay their expenses? Sita had been paying for it all. Since Sita had taken up the work in the shop, her entire household was well stocked with clothes, blankets, sheets and everything else. And yet her son and daughter-in-law had not ceased to say all kinds of things to her. Now she was afraid that she, along with the two orphaned children, would be thrown out of the house. Where could she go, what would they eat? The old woman was perplexed. The old woman had come to see what Sita had left behind, and where. If her son and daughter-in-law threw her out of the house, would she be able to stay in this lonely house beside the marsh? With each step that brought her closer to the house, the old woman's throat got drier. Her daughter's beautiful face floated in front of her eyes, the daughter about whom so many things were being said. But immediately, that dreadful image got superimposed on this. The eyes were bulging out—her face and eyes were full of dried blood clots; there was froth in her mouth and a stench was coming out from her swollen body.

Sita had been wearing her newly bought thick gold bangles, her balas, her gold chain and ring. Those gleaming ornaments had been buried in her swollen flesh. She had been cremated while wearing those. There was no question of taking them off. Remembering those ornaments, the old woman grew distressed. They could have been kept for the daughter. The Malik had already given her jewellery and clothes; in a few days he would have put xendur on the parting of her hair and taken her away. Tears rolled down from the old woman's eyes. The grandson and granddaughter gazed at their grandmother's distressed face. Their eyes, too, grew damp. They had not seen their mother for such a long time. Their childish hearts were filled with sorrow.

By the time the old woman limped to the abandoned house by the marsh, it was evening. She had started out in the afternoon after washing the utensils, cleaning the rice and chopping the vegetables for the evening meal. She was always afraid that her daughter-in-law would be dissatisfied by something she did or did not do.

The house was still open. Nobody came this way, now that there were so many rumours floating around. Seeing the familiar house, the children ran forward. The pair of owls sitting on the pakori tree were constantly hooting. The girl clasped a pair of mekhela sador belonging to her mother that was hanging on the clothes rack and began to weep. The boy asked his grandmother, 'Where has our mother gone?' The girl, too, looked at her grandmother's face.

'Your mother has become an owl.'

On hearing their grandmother's words, the innocent children were frantic. They hadn't done anything bad. Why did the mother become an owl then? The old woman looked around in the cupboards and under the mattress and pillows to see if there was anything worth taking.

The owl was hooting constantly. '*Ji uth, po uth*!' Get up, daughter, get up son! Their mother had told the children that the owl woke up her children at dusk, '*Po uth, ji uth*!' After sleeping through the day, it was only at night that the owls came out of their nest. And so, the mother would wake up her children as night approached. '*Po uth, ji uth*!'

The children looked towards the tree, now enveloped in darkness. Maybe their mother was telling them to get up. Sita's mother had gathered a few things into her bag and had locked up the house. But the old woman too, felt an eerie pair of eyes gazing at her from the corpse that had lain there. She screamed, 'Come on, come on, let's go! Fast!' and hurriedly dragged the children away from there. The eyes that had popped out from the putrefying corpse seemed to chase her.

This is the story of Sita. She was a girl who had grown up neglected and unloved and became a domestic help in a rich person's home. She became the wife of the roving vendor of bangles and beads, and the mother of two children. After she was widowed, she became a burden on her elder brother and his wife. She became the mistress of the proprietor of the clothes shop, a man who was her father's age. She died and became a putrefying corpse.

Her two children thought that she had turned into an owl and flown away. People, too, began to say that Sita's soul could not leave her body after she was assaulted, and had turned into an owl that was imprisoned in the house. As the evening fell, the owl began to hoot, '*Po uth, ji uth.*'

Yes, in a lonely house beside a marsh, it was entirely possible for a woman to become an owl.

ANITA'S JOURNEY THROUGH LIFE

(Originally published as 'Xonxar Jatrat Anita')

Anita was to get married. Whoever heard this was astonished. Nobody had expected the girl would get married. She was getting older and was now almost forty— two or three years were left for her to reach that age. Who was the bridegroom, where was he from, what did he do . . . all of this was irrelevant. The main thing was that Anita would be sitting by the sacred fire and getting married.

Anita was going to marry a widower who had a pair of grown-up children. They stayed with their mother's brother, in their maternal uncle's home. Some people said that Anita's to-be husband was an alcoholic. He would often be found on the streets or even in the ditches, overpowered by alcohol. His income came from a grocery shop that had been established by his father. At that time, it had run quite well it seemed, but now it was very much in the red. His brothers lived elsewhere, and so the man lived in the house his father had built. It was to this person that Anita was getting married. Her eldest brother had arranged this wedding.

The wedding celebration was magnificent. Anita's elder sister and brother, and her two younger brothers had been making arrangements for the wedding for the last six months. People were astonished to see the material goods that were being organized for the bride to take with her after her wedding. What had they not got together? Starting from a sofa set to dining table and chairs, to a steel almirah, and there was even a mirrored showcase. Anita's father had been a well-known criminal lawyer and had acquired much wealth and property in his lifetime. He had established his sons as well. The eldest son followed in his father's footsteps and became a well-known lawyer. The middle son was a teacher in the local high school. After acquiring his university degree, the youngest son became a contractor. The eldest son bought land and built a house on it to live in. The teacher and contractor divided the house, which they had inherited from their father, into two. The youngest daughter, Anita, began to live in the room in which her parents had stayed, in the corner of the house. She had been their parents' favourite child. Even though it was considered that she did not have great prospects, she was not somebody to be passed over, either. After her matriculation, she had studied for a couple of years in college, but her mother passed away during her examinations. Without her even being aware of it, she became the sole caregiver to her father, who was bedridden and paralyzed on one side of his body. She took on the full responsibility of nursing him. She was by his side day and night.

In the beginning, several proposals of marriage had come for her. While her parents had been alive, they had been choosy and had refused these offers. Everything changed after her father became bedridden. Imperceptibly, all the caregiving responsibilities for her father fell on her shoulders. Even at that time, marriage proposals had come for her to her elder brother. But then, any thought of marrying her off had been considered inappropriate.

While confined to his bed, Anita's father had divided his assets equally among his sons and daughter and had also ensured that they were able to live comfortably on the rent from the two shops located in the heart of town. One-third of the main house, too, was given to her. When he could sit up for a bit in bed and swallow some food and talk in a way that was intelligible to his daughter, he spoke about building a small house for her. He called his sons and told them of his decision. They all knew that after the division of property, their father had no money left to build a house. They understood that their father wished that they would all make a collective effort to put up a small house for their sister.

Anita would bathe her father, sweep and swab the floors with phenyl, light an incense stick and put it in a gap in the wall. At this time, her brothers usually looked in before leaving for work to enquire about his health. After the matter of building a house for Anita came up, their visits were reduced before they stopped coming entirely. A few days later, her father died in Anita's presence.

How old was this girl at the time? She was at most twenty-five going on twenty-six. Everybody felt sad when they saw her. Indeed, her parents should have got this girl married before they departed. If they had settled her in marriage, her father would not have died under so many inauspicious stars, bringing ill fortune to the family. They flung these words: marriage, domesticity, bridegroom at her and left, and these words whirled in her head like broken pieces of the dodder vine.

While her father had been alive, her sister-in-law took it in turn to bring nourishing semi-solid food for the invalid and some food for her into the room. One day, she suddenly realized that she had not had any lunch. Hungry, she stepped into her brother, the contractor's room. Her sister-in-law made some rutis and a stir-fry of vegetables for her with a grumpy face, on which irritation and dissatisfaction were clearly written. The contractor was getting less work these days. He had been thinking of setting up a shop in one of their houses in the town, but the plan had fallen through.

Anita hesitated to eat in the home of the teacher. Her father had willed two large rooms to her, but they were on their side of the house. It was becoming increasingly difficult to cater to the growing needs of his family. He had thought of renting out those two rooms, but that plan did not materialize either. The daughter, Anita, somehow had managed to get into those rooms. Nobody seemed to notice when she began to cook her meals on a stove there. Later, to save the costs of cooking gas, she created a small space outside with a roof but no walls and began to cook her meals there with firewood and twigs foraged from the compound. She managed on the rent she received from the shops that her father had left her, even though it had not been increased since he had been alive.

In the meantime, the dodder vines that people had flung at her were now tangled up in her head. She was fiercely protective of the objects that she owned. One day, when a nephew took a tumbler from her to have a drink of water, she grew as ferocious as Kali in her anger. There were squabbles and fights in the house. Her sister-in-law flung the lidded tumbler of bell metal on to the floor. She picked it up, and muttering invectives all the while, cleaned it with ash and sour tengesi leaves.

It was this Anita who was now getting ready to get married.

One day, the doctor brother of her eldest sister-in-law mentioned that Anita could train to be a nurse. He would be able to arrange everything. She would feel so much better if, instead of sitting around in the house like this, she went out. She would also have some income. Anita did not take well to this suggestion. As fiery as the Goddess, she could not be appeased till late into the night. She knew exactly what they were hoping for; to get rid of her from her house and seize the property.

So angry was she that it was as though a fiery king chilli had been smashed within her mouth.

Everything stopped at the same point. Was anybody actually thinking about her? She was a young woman sitting at home, shouldn't the family have been thinking of getting her married? There was no worry about finances. Their father had left them everything. Didn't she deserve a home of her own? And a family?

For a few years now, every time she stepped out of the house, or if somebody came to meet her, or even if she met somebody briefly, she had to listen to these words until they came to roost in her mind, growing thickets of dodder vines in her brains. Shame, hesitation, a sense of what was proper, were all stuffed in that thicket and were all rotting there.

Finally, her wedding had been fixed, and her family really went all out to celebrate it extravagantly. Pujas to propitiate the deities before the ceremony, amulets and charms to ward off the evil eye—what had they not done? Her brothers and sisters-in-law, her sister, her aunts had all approached so many people with a proposal earlier. Now the veins were standing out clearly in her dry skin, which had taken on an ashy hue. This girl had withered up like a sheaf of dry straw. And her glance, the way she looked at people! One could not meet that gaze without trembling. Her sunken, hollow eyes were becoming more and more bewildered by the day. But nobody had noticed. All they could see in her were her belligerent traits. Only her sharp, bitter words rang in their ears. A young unmarried woman in the house . . . didn't she need a companion?

One day, the teacher had stood on the verandah and shouted, 'When I get up tomorrow, I shall marry her off to the first person that I see in front on our gate.' His wife had cut in, saying, 'If that person is willing to take her, let him.'

It was at that time that this marriage had been fixed.

Everybody was astonished. The girl was the butt of much merriment. People were informed. Lists were made of what needed to be bought. There were no quarrels, no anger or irritation, only the expression of affection and love. Tears would be shed seemingly for no reason.

The family was, of course, keenly aware of the amount of work she did around the house and the degree of inconvenience it would cause them after she left.

Yes, it was true, that they got irritated with her at times, but only when she flew into a temper. At other times they thought, how many girls were as hard working and affectionate as she was? The whole family came to a decision even while partaking of the puffy lusis, the pithas, larus and pickles prepared by her. Her share of the property would be sold off. Let the ownership remain within the family. The contractor would buy the two shops. The value of the two rooms would be given by the teacher and the lawyer would give the value of the land to the north where their father had wished to build a house for Anita. Their mother's jewellery was still there, wasn't it? But her brothers' wives were vocal in their disagreement. Would they send off their only *nonod*, their sister-in-law, with just that old jewellery? They would also give some precious ornaments of the latest designs. She had said that she didn't need them, but it was decided upon nonetheless.

Why did she need to know how much her properties were bought for? It was enough if the necessary items could be provided. Anita wiped her tears. She felt a great attachment to her home, her brothers and sisters-in-law. She signed the legal documents. Her father had left her a considerable sum of money in the bank. She signed the papers authorizing them access to the money. They took out all of it.

Besides the expenses for the wedding, there was also another expense. When the marriage had been fixed, a promise had been made that a sum of money would be given to the bridegroom in order to expand his shop. When the groom was mentioned in her presence, she lowered her head shyly like a bride.

The rooms in the house gradually filled up with the gifts that were to be sent to her marital home with her after the wedding. Her elder sister, who lived in Mumbai, brought along a record player and a large bedcover. When it was spread out, the image of a colorful peacock with its tail unfurled in varied hues, lay on the bed. It was impossible for anyone to pass by without admiring its neat handwork, its beautiful patterns and colours. A sewing machine was bought as well. Clothes were bought for different occasions . . . for home wear and to wear outside. There were clothes to be given as tokens of respect to the seniors of the bridegroom's family. Two large suitcases filled up. There was a dressing table, a dining table set, a steel almirah, a large double bed with a luxurious foam mattress. A pressure cooker and a full set of dinnerware crockery were purchased, as well. In short, there was no miserliness when it came to furnishing her with a dower.

She would get up at night and stroke these items slowly, gaze at them lovingly and sigh deeply. The special aroma of newly bought items would enter her as she breathed. She would open every bundle and then knot them up again.

Everything was so beautiful. The red-and-yellow prints on the dinner set felt like freshly fallen blossoms from a tree. She would be drenched in their aroma. She would be soaked by the colours and fragrances. People would no longer be able to wound her with the same words, repeated over and over again. She would have a home of her own, surrounded by these objects. A life of her own. Yes, it would really happen. She would stroke these objects. Yes, it was all real, just as these objects were real. She would really be a bride. A man, a bridegroom, would arrive at her gate to take her home with him. There would be wedding songs, there would be feasting, the tumult around a house of celebration, many guests . . . yes indeed, her wedding would happen.

Anita's wedding finally took place. Her contractor brother turned the old tenants out of the two shops in town. In one of them, he started an outlet for steel furniture which he planned to run himself. He let out the other one after taking a fat advance from the prospective tenant. The teacher had the huge rooms in the house repaired and painted and built a kitchen adjacent to the set. He renovated the old washroom, which now gleamed with new tiles and marble. He got a tenant who paid a good rent. The lawyer put up a building in the corner of their large compound, intending to start a printing press there. His eldest son was sitting idle at home after clearing his master's. Everything was completed in a very short time.

And Anita? With her truckful of goods wrapped in hessian, she landed up in a place completely alien to her.

She had come in search of a home of her own, in search of domesticity. But the three-room house she arrived in had almost rotted away. She was startled, as she came in to fill it with the shiny new goods she had brought with her. Things were not what they were meant to be. There must have been some mix-up. The people around her had always talked about getting a companion for her. They had said that it was necessary to have a person to call one's own on the journey through life. Her bones would not have peace without such a man in her life. If this man had brought her home earlier, her father would not have died under so many inauspicious stars. This man, whom she saw only now, frightened her. She had had no idea that such a man could even exist. She had never seen this appearance in all the men she had met and known—her father, her uncles from her father's as well as her mother's side or her brothers.

The man could not put his mind to anything. He was unwilling to do any work. She was stunned to see the shop she had heard about. The house was infested with termites and anthills. Propped up in various places, it would not last another rainy season. The man's mouth always reeked of alcohol. She was as out of place in this rotting house with its invalid mother and strange man as were the shiny new objects that were now placed there. It did not take long for her to understand where the money that he was spending so freely had come from. Her brothers had withdrawn the money that her father had left her in the bank and given part of it to this man to repair and renovate his shop. In the meantime, more than half the money had been spent. At this rate, it would be finished up within a month.

On the flowered bedsheets spread over the foam mattresses on the double bed, she saw another side of this man. Was this the companion that people talked about, was this the mate they said she needed? People had created that tangled web of dodder vines in her mind just so that she could get a companion like this? So much hate and disgust had been waiting for her. Just because he wanted a full-bodied young woman, how could she transform herself into one? She could not eat her meals, drink her tea, sleep, she could not bathe with the putrid water from the handpump. She could not be free with the neighbours.

And yet, she tried. She tried to accustom herself to eating plain rice with a chilli. She learnt to eat puffed rice with her black tea, she tried to filter the muddy water with layers of stones and sand. She planned to sell off her jewellery and repair the shop. She looked after the aged mother. She never complained about anyone. She did try.

But after that night, she just could not try any more.

It was drizzling. The man had come home heavily drunk. It was already quite cold and now with the rain, it was even chillier. She had been washing up with cold water and was shivering in the cold. He looked at her for a bit, and then tore the clothes away from her body. A violent kick landed on her, and she fell to the floor. He began to yell at her. She did not remember all that he said, but she understood that huge waves of revulsion and loathing were washing over her. He switched on the fan that he had bought with money taken from her. She had stepped into this house when the weather called for a fan. And now it was time to use quilts. She was lying on the cold mud floor in her nakedness. The breeze coming from the fan going at full speed made her shiver uncontrollably.

The man began to kick her shuddering body. With cruel precision, he aimed two kicks at her. The first kick he aimed at her breasts, and the second at the place where her thighs joined.

Between clenched teeth, he said, 'What do you have? Nothing on top, nothing below.'

She fainted.

When she came to her senses, she found that a bedcover had been thrown over her. That beautiful, embroidered bedcover with its design of a peacock with its tail unfurled. She was running a high fever. With an unsteady gait, in her fevered condition, she put on some clothes and tottered to the nearby Public Call Office. She telephoned all three of her brothers and told them that if they did not come to fetch her back by the next day, they would find her corpse here after that. If she had to stay one more night here, she would either poison herself or pour kerosene on herself and set herself on fire.

All three brothers came early the next morning. She herself supervised the loading of the truck with the things she had brought with her. The packages with the dinner set and the tea set had not even been opened. There was no difficulty in loading her things on to the truck. The man was not at home. When she was ready to leave, she went to his ailing mother and paid obeisance to her by touching her feet. Tears ran down the old woman's wrinkled cheeks.

She was still shaking with fever. Holding on to her eldest brother, she walked slowly to the car. On seeing the new vehicle, she tried to smile. 'Dada,' she said addressing her elder brother, 'You bought a new car?'

Sending off the truck to their home, the brothers took her first to a pharmacy to get some medicines for her fever. She began to sweat profusely after having them. Nobody, neither she nor her brothers, spoke a single word during the journey home.

As she stepped into the house she had been born in, things seemed out of place. When did all these changes happen? She had left only a few months ago. She stood at the gate for a while. Where was the entrance, which way would she go in? The two rooms where she had stayed in, had become very different. There was a grilled verandah in front, new curtains at the windows. A woman came out in kurta churidar, carrying a baby in her arms.

The wives of the contractor and teacher, her sisters-in-law, supported her and took her inside. Her fever, which had momentarily subsided, came galloping back.

For a few days, she hovered between consciousness and semi-consciousness. She was unaware of who gave her medicines, or who cooled her burning fever with cold compresses on her forehead. All she was aware of was that somebody was beside her at all times, protecting her, sheltering her.

When she recovered, she realized what had taken place. She was not annoyed or upset with anyone. It had all happened with her consent. When she was a little stronger, she dragged herself to the verandah and looked at her scattered possessions. At the boundary of the house near the road was a kind of waiting room for his clients that her father had built while he was a practising lawyer. She herself proposed to her brothers that this place should be renovated, so that she could stay there. This place with its double sloped battened corrugated iron roof became quite livable after just a few repairs. Nobody disagreed. The place got an electrical connection.

Bending down in obeisance at the threshold, she entered the house. It was right next to the road. A few people said, 'Will this woman stay in this place that is open to the road just beyond? Is it proper?'

She herself gave a reply. 'But that's a good thing. I'll be able to look at passersby throughout the day.' She engaged a couple of daily wagers and brought in the stuff she had got as dowry to the house. For a whole week, she opened the packages. The next week, she arranged them around her house. Spread over the double bed was the bedcover with the embroidered peacock, with its tail unfurled. The red-and-gold sofa set, the glass-topped dining table, all found their places in her home. On her dressing table were arranged bottles of perfume, a pretty beauty box and several expensive jars of face creams. Along with the perfumed mothballs on the shelves of her steel cupboard were arranged neatly folded sets of mekhela sadors, in *paat* and *muga* silks. Her jewellery sets were in the cupboard's locker. The dinner set, the tea set, and the oven were arranged in the glass-fronted cabinet, while the HMV record player was displayed on the top of the cabinet. On the last rung of the clothes rack, the alna, a pair of golden high-heeled shoes was carefully placed. Everything gleamed, everything was spick and span, there was not a spot of dust anywhere. She got the bathroom and the toilet near the well that had been used by the domestic helpers during her father's time cleaned up. After all her possessions were arranged in the room meant for her father's clients. There was not an inch of space left to put her cooking stove. She put up a shed adjacent to the room and fashioned a *souka*, a fireplace out of a round-bottomed cooking utensil, a kerahi. If she wished, she could cook something in that kitchen for herself. Mostly, though, the curries and fries that her sisters-in-law sent would be enough.

She would dust and clean her possessions till noon. She would repeatedly wipe and shake out the covers and arrange and re-arrange the objects beautifully. She never actually used anything. Not once did she have tea in golden teacups with floral designs, never did she put her feet into the golden high-heeled shoes. Those silken garments never touched her body. One day, her contractor brother came and gave her a record. 'Listen to it sometimes. Your sister-in-law says you keep doing housework throughout the day.'

Anita would simply smile. Her behavior became synonymous with this tranquil smile, this soft-spoken persona, a heart full of love for all. Really, the things that had happened to this girl ever since her father passed away! From the day of his shraddha ceremony after his death, till the time her marriage had been arranged, she had been quite unrecognizable. When they remembered that fearsome aspect which she had displayed at times, all of them still felt scared. She never once said, referring to her parents, 'Deuta has left so much money, Ma has left such a large amount of jewellery, why does one need to sell off one's land, and property? Let my property remain in my name. I shan't let anybody take away this from me, just because I'm getting married.' This girl was so completely taken in by the idea of marriage that she did whatever they asked of her. After she had signed the documents, the Goddess of Wealth, Lokhimi Debi showered her blessings on the teacher, the contractor and the lawyer.

Anita did not play the record. Not even once. It was just one more object to be kept clean. She kept the cotton maxis and sari that her sisters-in-law had given her for Bihu on the alna to wear. She did wear the maxis, but the sari was never worn. Along with her silk mekhela sador, this too was aired in the sunlight every week, then kept away. She opened the box that had belonged to her mother and took out her old cotton mekhela sadors. She went around wearing those.

At first, she was very nervous when she went out with her sisters-in-law to Rupa's son's birthday. But nobody came rushing up to her, nobody looked at her and then stroking her face said, 'Oh dear, her friends have two or three children each now, why has she been left behind like this . . . if her parents had married her off before they died . . . this girl's bones will remain unpurified.' Nobody lowered their voices to badmouth her brothers and sisters-in-law. 'Actually, they were scared that they would have to nurse the invalid. We had taken a proposal for her, for marriage to Bolin. The way her sister-in-law spoke to us . . . 'Our father,' she had said to us at that time, 'his condition is such now, how can we even think of a wedding?' As though she was so attached to her father-in-law. Actually . . . we know otherwise, don't we?'

No, nobody came rushing up to her. Putting red xendur in the parting of her hair, a phot on her forehead, wearing her mother's cotton mekhela sador, she became one with the crowd of people there—a bird, unnoticed in the flock, a fish that was part of the shoal. Only Jumi's mother, Jinu's aunt, asked, 'When did you arrive? Will you be here for a bit, or will you be going back?'

Anita smiled back tranquilly at her in reply.

One day, her brother, the lawyer came over. She had just had a bath after dusting and wiping the objects in the house. She put the xendur in her hair, and then lit a joss stick before the photographs of her parents. Her brother had brought some documents. 'Sign on these. We'll cut off all ties.'

She knew that a short while ago, the man she was still married to had brought home the widow from the place where he habitually went to drink. She now made this liquor at home and sold it from there. His old mother had died shortly after she had left. Her brothers had been making enquiries. She heard all about it from her sisters-in-law. Softly, she said now, 'Why go into all that now, what's the need? Let things remain as they are.'

She brought up something else with her brother, instead. The roofing of CI sheets was old, dating back to her father's time, and had developed holes here and there. It leaked water when it rained. All her stuff would get spoilt. She showed him the large stain that had been made on her sofa by the dripping water.

Though they intended to change the CI sheets, they had not actually been changed for one reason or another. The leaks had become much more bothersome. Also, she had become even busier, with even less time to even eat or sleep. She would drag the objects out into the sun to dry them, and then bring them back again. The road was being broadened and tarred. Truckloads of earth had been brought here, which, in that windy weather of Phagun, February, turned to dust and spread over everything. Through the chinks in her old house, the dust came and settled everywhere. She would clean the place thoroughly, but in no time at all it would become dusty again. The pods of the silk cotton tree had burst, and the feathery filaments floated down and settled in this house that had no ceiling. Just after she shook them out and cleaned out the place, they came and settled on everything again. Termites had infested several places.

One day, she saw that one side of her double bed was covered with termites. She created an uproar. Everybody came rushing in. They examined the place. Yes indeed, termites had made their way up from the earth and were now infesting the place—its corners and walls. They all agreed that things could not continue like this. Something needed to be done. And what else was it that could be done but rebuild the whole place. The teacher immediately called in the mason, Badol. It was an old house; it would tumble down if hammers and mallets were wielded.

Gifting a record, some maxis, a bowl of mutton curry did not pinch. But to build a new house and erect it with their combined resources was a different thing altogether.

Naturally, the subject was discussed for a time. But matters came to a halt.

Anita got even busier now. She had to protect her possessions from so many different enemies. Rain, water, the covering of the silk cotton filaments that had spread everywhere, dust, termites, cockroaches, rats, ants . . . they were all around her. The house was by the roadside. There was the threat of thieves, beggars. She seemed to be the ten-armed Debi Durga. If one hand clutched a bottle of phenyl, another had a broom; if one held a trowel, the other grasped a mousetrap. Cleaning rags, mopping cloths, medicines to exterminate the termites, Lakshman Rekha herbal chalks to kill cockroaches, the ant nests full of eggs . . . all these things constantly appeared and reappeared in her home. And yet, even with all these things, her possessions looked brand new. Her hands grew coarse and chapped, her nails were broken, revealing the nailbeds. Shaking out the cotton mixed with the dust, she would sneeze uncontrollably.

One day, she mixed the anti-termite medicine without covering her nose and mouth. This resulted in her feeling so unwell and dizzy that for a full twenty-four hours she lay in her sister-in-law's bed. That day, the topic of rebuilding the house came up again. Once more, accounts and finances were tallied. They also agreed on the amount that each one of them would contribute. It was decided that after this rainy season ended, they would erect the house in the beginning of the dry winter months itself. The mason Badal came once more. Measurements too were taken.

In this month of Bohag, which went from mid-April to mid-May, there was less rain than usual. However, there were many storms that seemed to crush everything around them. As soon as the sky darkened, somebody or the other would ask Anita to come and shelter in the main house. There were so many empty beds around. She should just come there. They all knew that she would never leave her home and go there. She would always say, 'It's okay, I will stay here, I am not afraid of the storm and the rain.'

For some time now, she had stopped going anywhere, leaving her possessions behind. It was as though her belongings were a suckling baby that she could not abandon. What would happen? She would become agitated when there was a storm coming, when the surroundings became dusty, or when she discovered fresh attacks of termites, or deluges of rainwater. She would gather together tarpaulin sheets and plastic covers, and sit, waiting. When it rained at night, people saw light coming through the chinks in the walls of the old house. If there was electricity, it would be the light from the electric bulbs. If the electricity went off, the light from candles or a kerosene lamp would be seen. She owned not one but two hurricane lamps. One of her sisters-in-law had bought them for her. There would be sounds coming from her house throughout the night. For some time now, even if it was not raining, there would be light coming out from the house. The knocking sounds would continue. Passersby on the road in front of the house would notice that a shrunken woman with a blaze of bright xendur on the parting of her hair was hurriedly spreading silk clothes with dazzling motifs on the clothes lines outside. There was also a warm Kashmiri shawl with floral embroidery all over its body. They would see her dragging out a red velvet sofa that she would brush down, or carefully wiping down a pair of golden sandals with a soft cloth. She would repeatedly shake out the clothes she had put out to air, drag back the sofa that she had taken out earlier, carefully fold up the warm shawl with its embroidered flowers.

Her elder sister who lived in Bombay wished to take her back with her for a month or so. Her eldest brother's wife and her family were planning to go to Allahabad to immerse her father's ashes in the holy Ganga. They invited her to accompany them as well. Her elder sister-in-law's brother was getting married. Her sister-in-law insisted that Anita should go with them. Her contractor brother's wife was going to a temple with ritual offerings. It was not going to be a long trip, but couldn't Anita accompany her for a single day? Exactly what was the work that bound her to her home? Did she have babies, or a household full of people who had to be looked after? But Anita would not go anywhere. She would not budge. It was with the same tranquil smile that she responded to everybody's pleas and requests.

The storm started at midnight. The clump of thorny bamboos became the Bordoisila. This was when the myth of the Bordoisila, the kite's daughter came to life. The howling wind, the pre-monsoon storms were Bordoisila herself, so intent on reaching her mother's home that she was quite unaware of the trail of destruction she left in her wake. With hair streaming behind her, Bordoisila, the mythical kite rushed onwards, wreaking havoc. The tall betel nut trees began to sway. Branches were wrenched off trees and flung at a distance. Roofs of houses were yanked up and thrown elsewhere. Even in the middle of this furious storm, somehow the teacher and the contractor managed to reach her home. By the light of the lamp, they saw her sitting among her possessions. Rainwater had entered her house. Her brothers wanted to take her to the main house. But she replied slowly and softly, 'How can I leave these things and go?'

The very next day, the mason Badal plugged up the holes in the CI sheets of the roof with pitch. The leaks diminished appreciably. Her workload lessened a little.

This was the last bit of work that mason Badal came to do for this house. Ultimately, it was not necessary to break down the house and then rebuild it.

It was the teacher who noticed it first. He grew a little concerned. What could have happened to his sister? For some time now, she had been hunched up, just sitting around here and there. She had told her sisters-in-law that her hands and legs tingled, her heart would thump as well. There was talk of going to a doctor. What could have happened? The windows and doors of her house had not been opened. On other days, she would get up even before the children came to her teacher brother for their tuition and start sweeping and cleaning. There was no sign of the door opening even at nine in the morning. Even when they called out, there was no response. Everybody came crowding to the door. When a few of them pushed, the rusted latch gave way.

In one corner of the huge bed lay Anita's shrivelled body, now stiff. A pair of flies were hovering in circles near her face.

THE REINS

(Originally published as 'Baghjori')

The beautiful house that stood on the spacious compound had been built specially by workmen brought in from Calcutta. It was called Jonaki Cottage, or the Moonlit Cottage. Nowadays, it is quite common for a house to have a name. Even the entrepreneur Moti, who had his fingers in all kinds of shady businesses—from *bhang* to many other illegal deals—had a name for his house. It was 'Moti Mention'. He meant 'Moti Mansion', of course. On the blue-tiled pillar was the golden plate with the red letters that spelt out 'Moti Mention'. It announced the wealth and power of the owner proudly to the world.

But at that time, having a name for one's home was similar to tying up a pair of domesticated elephants in front of the house. It was like possessing four full barns of threshed paddy. The letters engraved into wood made people bow their heads in respect.

The owner of 'Jonaki Cottage' was Arabinda Nath Barua. His father had been a bench clerk, a Peshkar. Arabinda Barua was in any case born into means. Besides, the man was intelligent and hard-working. The first printing press in town was Barua's. The first tea garden in town that he bought from the British, too, was his. The people of the town got their paddy milled first in Barua's rice mill.

They first saw electric lights produced by a generator in the house that the workmen from Calcutta had built. They saw the ricksha that he bought to ferry his daughter to and from school, they saw the marble-topped dining table, they saw diverse flowers—none of which were of the local variety. Arabinda Barua was an intensely powerful and influential person. His anger, compassion, kindness, hobbies and interests were legendary. There was always a goad, a cane crop stuffed into one corner of the ceiling in the verandah. He would bring it down at times and thwack it around in the air. The cane would slash the air, creating a sharp whizzing sound. He lived his life with this power.

Arabinda Barua's cane remained in its allotted place. His only son Madhurjya Barua was one of five siblings, four of whom were girls. He looked after, with care, the wealth and property that he inherited from his father and grandfather's estate. A highly placed government official, under Madhurjya Barua's guardianship Jonaki Cottage developed even more. He used the cane to train his dogs every morning. He was extremely fond of his dogs. There was no question of using the cane on them. He only kept it in his hand to maintain discipline. He loved showing off to other people the tricks that the dogs had learnt. When he raised his cane, the black Doberman would sit upright on its hind legs. When the cane was whirled around in a particular manner, the white Dalmatian with black spots would take a ball from its master's hands and begin to play with it. The furry Bhutanese dog with light brown eyes could bring out the keys from their hidden place. The little doggie that resembled a clockwork doll would twirl around to the whirling of the cane. He loved showing off his dogs as they danced to the rhythm of his cane. The dogs, too, adored him, and obeyed only him. They simply ignored the others' commands. Everybody else in the house feared the dogs.

Like everyone else, Madhurjya Barua's wife Renuka Barua too was afraid of them. She was in any case of a fearful disposition. She was primarily suited to entering 'Jonaki Cottage' because of her bright and beautiful looks which lit up the dark house. Arabinda Barua's wife Jonaki Barua, too, had been beautiful, but even her looks were nothing compared to Renuka's.

She had been chosen by Barua himself. It was like a romantic story written in old books, or the film script of a popular movie. Barua's car had developed a flat tyre near the large pond in Renuka's village. Renuka had gone to fetch water from there. When he saw her, Barua couldn't take his eyes off her. At that point of time, a bull appeared and Renuka screamed in fear.

And so, the beloved daughter of Ramakanta Mastor, she of the delicate, vine-like mesmerizing beauty entered Jonaki Cottage.

Renuka was always fearful. She was afraid of her mother-in-law, the domestic help and she was terrified of the dogs. She was even afraid of her husband and the government official, Hakim Madhurjya Barua. In this constant state of fear, though, she became the mother of three boys and four girls. By the time her youngest son was born, her fears had abated somewhat. Her mother-in-law had also passed away. She had never met her father-in-law who had died before her entry to this house. Gradually, as her sons grew older, her fear lessened a bit a little more.

Arabinda Barua's word had been the law in Jonaki Cottage. And after his death, it was Madhurjya Barua's. People would gossip that had his father been alive, Madhurjya Barua would never have married according to his own wishes. When he got to know of this, Madhurjya Barua, along with a dog trainer, started to work on his dogs with great fervour. As more such gossip reached his ears, his dog training sessions grew longer. With her heart thumping fearfully in her chest, Renuka Barua would only look at the energetic, vigorous man with his dogs from a hiding place.

One day, Madhurjya Barua came to know that his eldest son, a pilot, had decided to marry a girl from another community. He was extremely angry. The eldest son was his banner of success, his pride. With just one blow, this banner fell to the ground and rolled about in the dust. A strange agitation shook him to the core. He got to hear all the gossip, all that the people were saying about this happening. He himself had got married to a girl of his own choice, what could he say to his son? The more he came to know of such talk, the more agitated he became. His eldest son wished to bring Sunita of Chandigarh to Jonaki Cottage. They had been pilots together. His son's father-in-law, his relative by marriage would be his *biyoi*—a person from another community, another religion who could not speak or understand a word of his language. The daughter of that person would now kneel in front of the ancient deity dating right back to Noni Peshkar's days, which his grandmother Jonaki Barua would bathe every day with her own hands and worship. People would come to Jonaki Cottage to attend the wedding ceremonies but would whisper throughout. These whispers would turn into a hurricane and spread all over the town. How could he himself have married Renuka all those years ago? She was not of the same caste. Just because she was fair, she had gained entry into Jonaki Cottage. Only if his father had been alive!

It all grew quite intolerable for Madhurjya Barua. He made some calculations and realized that his son's monthly salary was about the same as the amount that he spent weekly on his personal expenses. His middle son had cleared his MBA examinations and had started a business. His younger son was a doctor.

Madhurjya Barua made it public that he had disinherited his eldest son, and henceforth would have nothing to do with him.

Renuka Barua was distraught. She lost track of what she was eating, what she was doing, or where and when she was sleeping. She only saw her eldest son's face before her eyes. That little baby who had been placed in her lap by the lady doctor attending to her at childbirth—that chubby little boy who would toddle unsteadily towards her and settle with a thump on her lap, the boy who returned home after being bullied by his schoolmates and sobbed before her, the boy with the new moustache who came and hugged her after the good results in his examinations, the handsome young man in his pilot's uniform, the face of the boy who blushed as he showed his mother the picture of a girl who looked like an angel. She would never see that face again. She would never be able to serve him food. She secretly took out a few items from her box and gazed at them furtively once more. A red bag that was as soft as a kitten's fur, two bottles of perfume, a set of handkerchiefs. When her son had come home for the holidays, he had brought these with him secretly for his mother. She understood immediately who had sent them for her. When she was alone, she often communed in silence with a girl who looked like an angel. She had badly wanted to send something for her through her son. She would give gifts to people, no doubt. Behind each one was the sanction of Madhurjya Barua. Once, she had taken two gold bangles with *meenakari* work from the large amount of jewellery that she had and sent them to the girl. These bangles had been gifted to her by her mother-in-law's sister when she had paid obeisance to her after the wedding ceremony.

Renuka Barua had been unable to even weep. A powerful and vigorous person repeatedly crushed her. Once, he had dragged out a suitcase of hers and flung it outside. The soft, kitten-like bag and the silk, lace-edged handkerchiefs scattered all around. The bottle of perfume shattered. Once, with his cane in his hand, he asked where the meenakari bangles were that his aunt, Meena Mahi had given. Another time, shaking his finger at her, he had asked why she had hidden the matter from him, and if she knew, why did she keep it from him. In his anger, he had lost his wits. With inflamed eyes, he had asked why she had kept it a secret. He told her that she had no pride in ancestry; after all, what could be expected of her who had not much of an ancestry herself.

The man, in all his power, was belligerent before Renuka Barua. She was cowering in fear. The son told his father that his mother knew everything. He had told her everything. Everything, from the bag that looked like a kitten to everything else. What had happened to Renuka Barua? The dogs jumped on to her. In the dead of night, she was cowering fearfully near the gate of Jonaki Cottage. The man was standing near the gate. She was really beginning to cringe and sit around here and there.

One day, the eldest son came to Madhurjya Barua's Jonaki Cottage. With him was the angel-like girl, who had descended from the skies. Madhurjya Barua was waiting near the gate. Everyone in the house left what they were doing and waited with curiosity and fear. At that time, Renuka Barua was making the bed in her room. From the window, she saw her son and a tall girl in a *mekhela sador*. With the bed still half made, she fell. The room was filled with her muffled cries. As she lay on the floor, another woman rose from within her. This other woman ran downstairs with a brass platter containing clay lamps and welcomed the boy and girl into the house with auspicious ululations. As Renuka Barua lay on the floor, this other woman took off the necklace that her mother-in-law had given her, and put it on the girl's pale, swan-like neck. With her head bowed, the girl touched the woman's feet. There were reverberations everywhere as the auspicious ululations were sounded; there was laughter, there was light.

When Renuka Barua got up from the floor, Madhurjya Barua had, as always, started to play cards with his companions on the covered verandah. That day, nobody called Renuka Barua to cater to the requirements of food and drink for the card players.

Suddenly, one day, Madhurjya Barua succumbed to a stroke. After the tumult of the obsequies was over and the visitors had left, Renuka Barua saw that everything had changed in Jonaki Cottage. Madhurjya Barua had made a comprehensive will regarding his properties. Madhurjya Barua had not willed anything to his eldest son. Two parts out of four were willed to his middle and youngest sons, the other two were left to his wife. The majority of the estate was to go to Renuka Barua—the income from the tea estate, the rental properties, trucks and buses, all of it. The biscuit factory and the hosiery mill that the middle son had started with his father's money remained with him.

The middle son was barely ever home. He was always travelling, here today, there tomorrow. Everything changed for Renuka Barua after her husband's death. She noticed that the people she used to meet constantly also seemed to have changed. The domestic help, too, had changed. The place where she would sit also changed. Usually, while Madhurjya Barua had been alive, she herself did not go into the covered passageway which served as a kind of verandah.

Most of her time was spent upstairs in the bedroom, the kitchen or the prayer room. These days though, she had to spend most of her time on the verandah, something she had never done before. She did other things too, such as signing papers. But she had been good at her studies. She was intelligent and grasped everything quite fast. And in all this change, her behaviour, her way of speaking, her very walk itself had also changed.

She came to realize that her middle son had begun to stay at home all huddled up and dejected. He would remain sitting outdoors late into the night as well. She had come to know that her son had incurred heavy losses in the hosiery mill.

One day, he was sitting on a chair and puffing at a cigarette. Silently, she went and stood near him. In the past, too, Madhurjya Barua had remained sitting in this manner late into the night. Whenever he sat in that corner chair, puffing at a cigarette, Renuka knew that something was worrying him. Sometimes, when she went to stand near him, Barua would wave her to a chair, indicating that she should sit. Sometimes, he indicated that she should move away immediately. Sometimes, he would get up to go to sleep. He would not speak at these times. He communicated through gestures.

Renuka came and stood near her son. She was actually waiting for a signal from him. Suddenly, her son hugged his mother tightly and began to sob out loud. Renuka was astounded. She could not imagine that somebody could sob in this manner in this house.

'What's the matter, Baba?' she said, addressing him with affection. Her voice seemed to have become hoarse.

'A huge problem, Ma. It's a loss of several lakhs. People will say that I've run through my father's money. I've made a mistake.'

'Don't worry so much about money,' Renuka's said in a steady voice. It held no trace of fear or hesitation, nor was there a any kind of emotion.

'Ma, will you be able to give me a bit of money? A loan. I shall return it as soon as the work is done.' Her son stared at her face.

Renuka remained standing. All this time, she had been dependent on others, she had looked to others for her needs. Nobody had ever asked her for anything. Today, when her son asked her for a loan, she became silent. She placed her hand on her son's back as he sat with a bowed head.

'Don't worry Baba, tomorrow I'll write you a cheque for the amount you need.' When she uttered these words, particularly the word 'cheque', she broke out into a sweat. Even in her wildest dreams, she had not thought that she would have to use this word that had been so frequently on Madhurjya Barua's tongue.

Later, after her son had gone to bed, Renuka Barua abruptly sat in the easy chair in her room. She began to doze. She always woke up at dawn, at the first cawing of the crows. But on that day, she awoke quite late. When she went out of her room, she saw that there was quite a commotion in the house. The coal black Doberman had got loose from its chain and was now rushing about the house. This black dog was temperamental, stubborn and prone to anger. It would bare its teeth and approach people without any provocation. The doll-like little puppy would play with the others throughout the day. It would nip at one's ear, tumble around with another and ride on the back of a third. But whenever this playful puppy saw the black Doberman, it lowered its tail and slunk away.

The help came rushing up to Renuka Barua as soon as they saw her.

'Aideo,' they said, addressing as 'Mother' respectfully, 'nobody can go out of the house because of the dog . . . it's scaring us all.'

'Aideo, he tried to jump up on Kanai!'

'There are people who have come from the tea estate to meet you. They are still outside; they can't enter the compound.'

'Aideu, there are visitors. The dog has become angrier after seeing these strangers.'

Previously, the help would address her as 'Aideu' only when conveying some request or demand from Madhurjya Barua or her sons.

'Aideu, Deuta is asking for a *tamol* . . .' they would say earlier, referring to Madurjya Barua's request for an areca nut to chew. Or 'Adieu, elder Baba is asking for a cup of tea . . .'

She was used to complying with these requests by doing what was required. But she felt that this address was different today. Nobody had come to her earlier, asking her to solve problems.

Renuka Barua got up and took Madhurjya Barua's cane in her hand. With the same familiar gesture of her husband's, she slashed the cane through the air. There was a whipping sound. Everybody looked at her, astonished. The black dog, which had terrorized everybody with its teeth bared, was now sitting on its haunches. It was soon tied up by one of the helpers.

Meanwhile, her middle son had woken up. With a firm hand, Renuka Barua wrote out a cheque and signed it for him.

Gradually, Renuka Barua sorted out a few things. She repaired her mother's house and opened a shop for her unemployed brother and welcomed her eldest son, and his family back. She also visited her daughter-in-law's natal home. She proudly told the others in Madhurjya Barua's family about her daughter-in-law's Chandigarh home, her family and their wealth. She started giving small and large gifts to relatives on various occasions. She felt very happy when she did this. Otherwise, the family had only distributed gifts during major festivals like Bohag Bihu or the Assamese New Year in earlier times. But Renuka gave gifts to the domestic helpers and employees even on the death anniversary of her husband, or the birthdays of her children. Gradually she began to run Madhurjya Barua's business affairs efficiently.

She also derived a lot of pleasure from yet another activity. She began using Madhurjya Barua's cane to play with the dogs. When Renuka Barua made the dogs prance around and play, all the other people in the house stopped whatever they were doing and watched with great pleasure.

Renuka Barua got her middle son married to Madhuri, the daughter of a lawyer called Gagan, who was a friend of Madhurjya Barua's. She was well-suited to the Barua family. She had heard rumours that her son was going around with some girl. Renuka Barua called her son before her, and simply said one thing. Since he was going to stay at home, he would be receiving fifty per cent of the property that Madhurjya Barua had willed to his sons. The other two would only get twenty-five per cent each. After this, she told him about the marriage proposal brought by the laywer, Gagan. Her son agreed immediately to the match.

Things were going well. Her youngest son had passed his medical examinations and qualified as a doctor. Renuka Barua had not been at all worried about him. But now, here he was. She had never thought that he would do such a thing. Actually, it was not really something out of the ordinary. A young man had fallen in love with a young woman. It had happened to Madhurjya Barua, it had happened to her elder son, and, in a small way, it had happened to her middle son too. But this ordinary thing loomed over Renuka Barua in all its seriousness. The girl that her youngest son wished to marry was of their caste. She was from Renuka Barua's own village and was a nurse in the same hospital in which her son was a doctor. She was a quiet girl. Even though she was not exactly like Sunita, or the lawyer Gagan's daughter, she was not to be scorned, either.

Renuka Barua brooded and fretted. That girl could never be allowed to set foot in their house. Impossible that

Madhurjya Barua's son should set foot in the ploughman Rongai's home and bring his daughter home. Accepting Sunita of Chandigarh was totally different from accepting ploughman Rongai's daughter. Madhuryja Barua had always placed great importance on considerations of caste and social status. However, according to Renuka Barua, these things were now obsolete and quite meaningless. Let her doctor son bring home a girl like Sunita. She would raise no objections about language, caste or creed. How many marriages such as these were there in the Barua family? But how could Renuka Barua go to the ploughman Rongai's home and ritually put the vermilion powder, xendur, in the girl's hair at the Joron ceremony? This was when the mother of the bridegroom went with other women with gifts of clothes and jewellery for the bride. It was the prerogative of the bridegroom's mother in these parts, not the bridegroom himself, to put xendur in the parting of the bride's hair. How could Renuka Barua do this? When Rongai went to Renuka Barua's mother's home, he was given a mat to sit on the ground. Her brothers, too, voiced their strong objections. They would never be able to accept that household as their relatives by marriage. Renuka Barua would have to hang her head in shame before her own relatives, in her own village. She told her doctor-son that she would give him land and money to set up a nursing home. She told him about his share in the family property. She told him about the doctor daughter of a relative of Gagan, the lawyer. In a quiet voice, the youngest son refused it all.

On the day that her doctor son got married in the Kamakhya temple and then came and stood at the entrance of Jonaki Cottage, it was Renuka Barua herself who was standing on this side of the gate. Her younger son returned as he had come. On seeing their much-loved youngest *bopa* return in this way, everybody else in the house stood, transfixed. Nobody could open their mouths to say anything.

After her doctor son left with the ploughman Rongai's daughter, Renuka Barua unchained the newly acquired golden Alsatian dog. It was as large as a pony. The dog was in the process of being trained. It was a very intelligent dog. Renuka Barua had bought him from a Dog Training Centre. It knew all kinds of tricks, such as playing with a ball, jumping through a ring, walking with its weight on its hind legs and so on. But all this did not make him special. The dog also knew how to take the receiver in its mouth when the phone rang, how to open the swing doors with its paws, and, if necessary, ring the call bell that had been specially placed at a low height.

As Renuka Barua played with her dog, a woman sat on the ground and wept on the upper floor of the house. It was Monobai, the middle-aged widow whom Renuka Barua had brought home from the village as a domestic helper for her personal chores. Monobai and Renuka Barua were from the same village. She knew the girl, Rongai's daughter, whom the doctor son had married. It was she who had nursed her, Monobai, when she was bedridden, till she was able to walk again. If, today, she was able to earn her living at Jonaki Cottage, it was only because of Rongai's daughter. And yes, the youngest son, Xoru Bopa as she called him affectionately. He had done so much for her! She kept imagining their two young faces which kept floating before her eyes. How the two young people had come right up to the gate, and then gone away.

Monobai could not cry openly. She was sitting on the floor of Renuka Barua's bedroom before the half-made bed. Only her silent tears coursed down her face, wetting it. In fear and with sadness, she groaned like an animal.

THE WATER IS
WITH CHILD

(Originally published as 'Pani Ghabini Hol')

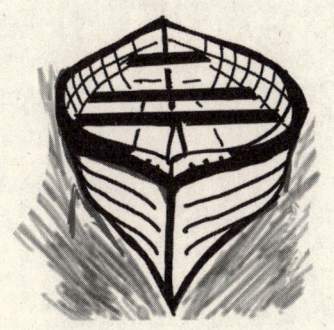

Noir nijorao nijora
The stream of the river is a stream, too.
The stream from the eyes is a stream, too.
Even if the stream of the river dries
The stream from the eyes never dries.'

It was one o'clock at night. In the winter darkness, a thick mist had smothered the riverside. The roaring of the mighty-armed Brahmaputra was punctuated repeatedly by the hoots of two or three owls, and a pair of *jom dakini* birds which are considered an evil omen. The owls and the reeds were whistling near the river's landing stage. Continuous rain had made the place very muddy.

It was only tonight that the experienced boatman had brought out the boat from the pond and set it on the river. The people waiting near the shore had held up hurricane lamps. A couple of them even lit their electric torches. The season of water was beginning. The boat entered the water for the first time as winter ended, when the rains began. All this time, in the rainless months, the rooftop of the boat had peeped out from the half-dried pond in front of the boatman's house. If this wasn't done, this sturdy boat that had been with them for two generations would dry up and die. If it was coated with the mud from the murky water, the boat would be fine. And where else could it be kept if not in the pond in front of the house?

Why was this boat, which was such a precious piece of heritage, left outside in the fields and ditches? During the season of rain and flood, the entire earth was covered with water here. The chief boatman who used this boat had another vessel as well. At this time, it was smeared with tar and placed on a bamboo platform.

The boatman was also a potter. His family had been making clay pots for two generations. It was with these two boats that he had carried out his business. This heavy, eye-catching boat would be moored at one river ghat after another with its load of earthenware. It was from the money earned from this business that some land had been bought—land so fertile that any twig stuck into its soil would sprout and grow. But those days were now over. Still, the boats had not abandoned the family, even now they brought prosperity to the homes and kept them afloat. The river had clawed away much of the land that had been bought with business profits. The family was surviving because of the remaining land and the two boats. It was said that Baba Brahmaputra recognized this boat of this boatman, Ghatoi Krishna. The river's waters would gently touch the boatman's oars. Large whirlpools remained at a distance. Different stories, various myths were related about the life of boatman Krishna. His sons had grown up and did not allow their father to ply the boats on the water anymore. He had gone back to his grandfather's profession

and begun to love this play between clay and water. Praise
about boatman Krishna's handicrafts floated all around.
Several white people had come to try and learn the craft
from him.

Leaving all this aside, here was Krishna Ghatoi, the
boatman Krishna trying to get his boat safely on the misty,
mighty-armed river. At one point in time, this landing
stage, this ghat, had been in a very good condition. But
heavy erosion had leached away its conveniences some time
ago. The riverbank sloped down to the water earlier, but
now was almost perpendicular. The boatman's sturdy boat,
made of saam wood, went and hit the riverbank. At this
point, though, the riverbank was somewhat sloping. The
boat was caught next to the riverbank, its length jammed
against the shore. The ground had become muddy. This bit
would become slippery after even a brief shower so that it
was difficult to get a foothold there. A couple of days of
sunshine would harden it up again.

This soil would certainly be unlike others. Where else
could one find soil that was as moist as the breasts of a
nursing mother? The flowers of the mustard plants would
tumble like the waves of the rising river, the paddy fields
would flow in a golden spate right up to the sandbanks, the
trees and shrubs were of such a dark green that the leaves
would glisten in the sunlight like silver, the vegetables
would be so succulent that if they were put in a kerahi
over a fire, they would soften like ghee. This island was
hugged by the arms of the river. It was a part of the kernel
of the Mahabahu's heart, the heart of the mighty armed

river Brahmaputra. This bit of land was made fecund every year by the fertile silt deposited there. During the months when the fields were not flooded, the homes and yards of the farmers would be filled with sacks of potatoes and other vegetables. The legend had it that a certain king, after committing patricide, had come with a treasure of gold and silver, pearls and jewels to this river. The waters had parted into two arms and flowed around a beautiful land created in the middle. It did not accept the evil king's gift.

The vehicle came down to the river shore, till the spot where its wheels would take it. From there, one needed to walk to the ghat. The silty land was very slippery, it was difficult to get a foothold. The boat was standing at the edge of the steep shore as though it was a baby stuck to its mother. Krishna Ghatoi was waiting with the oar that was used as a rudder. Several people could be seen getting down from the vehicle and coming through the mist.

Two men and three women. The rain, which had stopped for a moment, came down once more in a light drizzle. Many umbrellas opened briskly. Under one of them was a young woman held up by two other women from both sides. She was standing, rather strangely, on one leg like the large, long-legged adjutant storks that filled the fields in winter. Her other leg was slanted out at an angle. The mekhela she was wearing had been cut with scissors. Her leg, bare and bent, could be seen through the slit. It was as though some sorcerer had broken this tender female body and twisted it. It seemed like her heart was a fluttering *mynah* bird imprisoned by this sorcerer. This wizard had twisted the bird's leg. One limb was misshapen. Unable to breathe, she fluttered helplessly as he throttled her neck. This young girl had a swollen belly. The pregnant girl's distended stomach hung low as she cried out in agony. This was her first pregnancy. Her time had come a little earlier than expected. Her pains had started the previous morning after she had lit the oil lamp in the prayer room. Her water broke after a little while.

Immediately, there was a commotion. Arrangements were made. Another clay lamp was lit under the sacred tuloxi plant. A silver flower was pledged to the Xattra, the place of worship, for the safe delivery. Her mother and grandmother came running. She was the first daughter of the family. Her grandmother, in particular, wished to keep her where she could see her. Her husband was a schoolteacher. They possessed fertile fields, and there was abundance in their home. They had all celebrated the wedding with great joy.

As soon as her grandmother came, she sat down and placed the girl's head on her lap. She had brought some water over which some mantras and spells had been chanted. She bared the swollen stomach and began to lightly massage it with water. The experienced midwife, old Miliki arrived. Two ASHA personnel, social health workers who looked after basic health requirements, arrived as well. The doctor of the local hospital was not available, but a nurse arrived. Her maternal and paternal aunts, who had crossed many hurdles in their lives, came, too. And the lame grandmother was already there.

A middle-aged woman was by the side of the girl who was walking carefully in the mud with one leg stretched out. The middle-aged woman was walking with her weight pressed down heavily on the ground. But even then, there was no sign of weakness in her walk, no unsteadiness in her gait. With her left leg she pressed down, and, taking the weight of the pregnant girl on her body, she walked ahead with firm steps. In the light of the lanterns and the chargeable torches, these two women with their twisted gait looked like two supernatural beings who had risen from the shadowy, mist-filled night. The girl was hopping on one leg, while the other was pushed forward. Her mekhela which had been scissored from the side was red in colour. It was covered with black and yellow flowers. In the half-light, this tattered mekhela looked like the colour of clotted blood.

The two of them were grandmother and granddaughter. This was the first granddaughter from the lame grandmother's son's side. The girl who was limping and hopping with one leg outstretched cried out at times. Even though she gritted her teeth and tried not to make a sound, sometimes she failed. At these times, her grandmother hugged her even closer. Two women were approaching the boat rather crookedly. Even the two sturdy men, burdened with bundles and packages were finding it difficult to walk down the muddy slope to the boat.

The young woman cried out once more. She tried to stretch out her leg even further. It seemed, if she brought her legs together, the life between them would get injured.

If required, she would suffer pain, but the being enclosed within her legs should not get hurt at all. She was unable to climb down the muddy slope.

Her cries could be heard over the hoots of the owl, the roaring of the river and the chatter of men assembled near the boat. With her leg outstretched, she was standing erect. Her beautiful face was wet with tears. After all, she was not a crane or a stork that she would be able to stand on one leg and then smoothly fly off. She was of the earth; she would have to walk on this earth. This crane that was unable to fly had now turned completely stiff.

In a sonorous voice, the boatman called out, 'Why are you standing there, why aren't you moving? Bring the girl to the boat. Don't delay.'

The boatman started chanting a devotional verse, calling out the different names of Lord Vishnu.

Jadobo Mukundon, Madhobo Madhusudan,
You are Nitya Niranjan,
You are Narayan.

Over the chants in the baritone voice, it seemed as though there was a hint of poignancy. 'Narayan, Narayan' . . . it seemed as though the air resonated from all sides with the sounds of the cymbals and drums of the evening prayers. The blue image of Narayan in the sanctum of the Xattra's shrine, redolent with the fragrance of incense and perfumed oils with its tranquil, soundless otherworldly smile seemed to hang in the mist. The reverberation from the large bells, the Gojoghonta and Moyurghonta, resonated through the air. The great bird, Garuda, unfurled its wings and surrounded and sheltered that voice filled with entreaty. The oil from the lamp lit in the sanctum of the shrine trickled down the face of the image. The aroma of the offerings of prasad that the devotees were distributing was everywhere. Automatically, the heads bowed.

'Hold her, hold her up!' the lame old woman shouted. The young man, who had been standing by the girl's side very dejectedly, immediately hugged her. The old lady lifted the leg that was spread out. Another young man, who was accompanying the first youth, lifted her up. With both legs spread out, she became an egret on a buffalo's back. Her private parts could be seen through the gap in her mekhela that had been cut almost to the top. This was now stretched out, and a tiny foot, like a gardenia, was sticking out from it. This was the first pregnancy of this recently married young girl. Men fight, they go to war, women give birth. But giving birth was a battle in itself. She was in the battlefield now. She tried to cover herself with the ends of her sador. She was embarrassed to be exposed to so many people around her.

The lame grandmother sat down with her legs straight. She was unable to bend her knee. After that accident, her right knee would not bend. It had happened when she was still a new bride. She had lived her whole life with her knee like that and was now an old woman. She was Lengeri Aita, the Lame Grandmother. Her son's daughter, her granddaughter, had placed her head on the old woman's lap. She had fallen on this battlefield. The dejected-looking youth sat down near her feet. Her legs were spread out, between them was a delicate foot, its toes revealed. The sad-faced young man tried to cover her legs. The old woman thundered, 'What are you doing? Leave all this useless shame now.' She started a prayer, an ancient devotional hymn:

> *Muktito nispriho jitu*
> *Xehi bhokotoko nomo*
> *Roxomoyi magoho bhokoti*

The boat rode on the waves of the water and moved away from the shore. The boatman Krishna raised his oar, and bending over, took a palmful of water from the river and placed it on his head.

'The water is pregnant.' Saying this, he took up his oars and manoeuvred the boat further out. The river started to swell. After a few days, the river would be full. Once more, the drizzle started. A dense mist canopied the area. It was as though this vast covering had covered the earth just so that the young girl—this pregnant woman who had fallen in the battle—could be sheltered from the eyes of the world.

'Take out a bit of xandoh,' the grandmother commanded the girl's mother curtly, telling her to take out roasted rice powder.

That day, the mother had wished to take some curd and liquid molasses with the special soft rice, komol saul, in a steel tiffin carrier. The old woman thundered at her.

It was going to be a difficult journey. She dispatched somebody to bring the container of spiny bamboo that had been there since her own mother-in-law's days. This container was an inch or so in depth but as wide as an elephant's trunk. It looked as though an elephant's trunk had been cut off, and the container was made from it. The old lady filled up the container with xandoh, with her own hands. She poured in some liquid molasses made from the juice of sugarcane that grew in her son-in-law's fields. She poured some curd from the pot. There was abundance everywhere in her grandson-in-law's home. It was as though the Goddess of Prosperity, Lokkhi herself had made her home there. The sight of it brought contentment to the heart. If this girl had to leave this abundance and go away with the being in her stomach! The old woman's heart heaved with dread. There was no mother-in-law in this house. It was this girl who had brought this abundance to this house.

The old lady called out impatiently, 'Come on let's go. Hold on to her. Take her to the boat. Krishna Ghatoi is waiting.'

The girl's mother took a bit of xandoh to the girl's mouth. She turned her face away.

The old woman said loudly, 'Eat! Otherwise, you will have the same fate as your mother-in- law!'

She swallowed the xandoh.

A whirlpool began to spin near the boat. The vessel rocked to-and-fro before it steadied. The silence all around was broken only by the sounds of water as it lapped against the shores. The mist seemed to grow thicker as the boat moved ahead.

The old woman took out some pre-heated mustard oil from a bottle. Inside were some cloves of garlic. She took out some oil and began to massage the soles of the feet of girl fallen on the battlefield. Her face contorted in pain. Lengeri Burhi told the girl's mother to feed her some milk, a bit at a time.

'Keep giving her some milk . . . make her sip some. Otherwise, the girl will be become even more weak.'

Her husband, the young man standing by, had tears coursing down from his eyes. Despite all the planning, this had to happen. Every arrangement had been made to admit her to the Jorhat Mission Hospital where she was to go in a day or two by the ferry. The doctors had assured him they had a few weeks ahead of them until the delivery, but she had accidentally fallen after her bath. She was putting her sador out to dry when the heavy fall caused her water to break.

It was the hour of the Narasingha Avatar. It was evening, the time when Lord Vishnu had smashed his way out of the pillar of the palace to show Himself to His devotee, Prahlad, as half man, half lion. Even fit people are warned to take care at this twilight hour, and here she was, pregnant. Why did she have to have a bath at that time? Which mother-in-law would show her displeasure and glare at her with red eyes, then? All right, even if she had a bath, could she not have simply shed her clothes and left them there? There was nobody else at home. Her father-in-law had gone to the Xattra, and her husband had gone to buy essentials from the market. Jogen Kai, the live-in help was in the house. Indeed, he was like a member of the family, what else? He had been with them, keeping an eye on the house for a long time. The word 'servant' did not exist on this river-island. Every person who helped out in others' homes was known as 'belonging to the family'. They would be introduced to visitors: 'This is Jogen Kai, or Elder Brother Jogen. He is a member of our family.'

This member of the family, Jogen Kai, lifted her up and put her on her bed. By the time the others returned, it was night. Her water broke, and she had fainted with pain. And yet the baby did not emerge. Just as the midwife old Miliki, and the ASHA workers were giving up hope, a tiny foot was seen between her legs. Everything turned upside down. In this place surrounded by water, there was no arrangement for instruments to bring the baby out— through a forceps delivery. Between her home and the place where such arrangements were available was the huge Brahmaputra thundering all around.

Krishna Ghatoi had put his boat on the water so that she could cross this Brahmaputra. Everybody was startled by a huge roaring sound. The boat had started to rock. Krishna Ghatoi cautioned them to be careful. A huge column of water had burst out on the Brahmaputra's breast. With expert hands, the boatman manoeuvered the boat at an angle, and then straightened it again. All the people there, including the girl who had collapsed, saw an exceptional sight through the veil of mist in the light of the moonbeams. The water was whirling around in circles. The column of water was created in the copious ring of water. Taking the mist and the moonlight to itself, this column of water gushed up with a roaring sound. Without them being aware of it themselves, everybody's hands moved up. Their heads were bowed.

Now, the Ghatoi started on stories of gushing columns of water, the *doka*, in the river.

What kind of a doka is this? There is no wind, no storm. In this weather, this can hardly be called a doka. Let me tell you about a real doka that roared up one day. It was raining heavily. A storm began in the middle of the river, Baba Brahmaputra began his *tandav*, his dance of destruction. Huge waves came up on the water. The Ghatoi was then a young man. He had strength in his arms and courage in his heart. Nobody from the other boats dared to get near the boat to help. At that time, Ghatoi's boat had an outboard motor. Time, Death had called out the Ghatoi that day. Fate was calling out to the souls in the boat. Putting their faith on the Ghatoi, they had all prayed to their own personal gods.

That day, in the middle of the river, suddenly it seemed as though a demon from the underworld was pulling down the boat. The water of the river took on a horrifying aspect. A whirlpool emerged and soon after, a column of water rose up in the air. That day, the doka had burst out with a tremendous roar. Even the heart of a person such as the Ghatoi quaked when he saw the soaring column of water. The other people in the boat were terrified. They were never tired of recounting to their grandchildren and great-grandchildren, the sport, the activities of the great River Brahmaputra. The whirlpool, the vortex tugged at the boat. The machine was crippled.

There was a sick person on the boat that day. Bhudhor Goswami was lying helplessly with chest pain. It was his eldest son's wedding, and the pain had started just before the bride and groom arrived home. And after that, the journey on the Ghatoi's boat. The Ghatoi had grasped the oar that dated back to his father's days. Though it was badly battered, it was still intact. Ghatoi crossed that supernatural doka, the vortex in the river. Within the night, he had taken the passengers to shore. On his return, Goswami had accepted the ritual obeisance of his new daughter-in-law.

Nobody was aware that when he beheld the ferocity of that supernatural column of water, Ghatoi had pledged a many-tiered stand for earthen lamps to the Xattra. Later, he went to give the *gosa*, the stand, at the Xattra, and paid his respects to the deity there. Once more, he became very fearful as he remembered the ferocity and power of that doka on the storm-swept Brahmaputra.

What was this doka before that one?

The boat went forward through the mist. The pregnant girl was groaning. The baby she was carrying between her thighs had a foot in the outside world, while the rest of the body was inside the mother's womb. The boatman's story seemed to pull her away from her immediate pains. Her heart-rending cries seemed to diminish somewhat. The mother and grandmother were, by turns, lightly massaging and stroking her pain-wracked body. They kept feeding her milk sweetened with liquid molasses, its top layered with thick cream.

The Ghatoi's story had ended. There seemed to be magic in his baritone voice. Everybody who listened felt their hearts lighten. Some of their anxieties abated. The girl, Moni's mother, silently pledged a gosa to the prayer house, the Xattra's inner sanctum, just as the Ghatoi had done earlier. The vision of the lamp stand, with its earthen oil lamps surrounded by the smoke from the fragrant dhoop sticks and the burning incense calmed her somewhat.

The rain paused. The canopy of mist became denser. Through this canopy the moon was visible. Its light seemed to be almost like the waters of the Brahmaputra. It scattered here and there from the gaps in the mist. The boat was now going past a sandbar. It was not inhabited. People only farmed this bit of land. This year, they had planted a crop of melons. It was yet to fruit. The green creepers had completely covered the sandbar.

The young man was running his fingers tenderly through his beloved wife's hair as she lay with a leg raised in a very arduous position on the boat. In a low voice, he said, 'Moni, be patient, be strong. The Ghatoi will surely take us to the shore. All arrangements have been made on the other side. Your uncle, your grandfather are waiting, they will do everything. They are all coming to meet this boat.'

'Courage, my girl,' said the grandmother as she put another bit of roasted rice powder, xandoh, which had been moistened with curd and molasses into her mouth. She had straightened her bent leg and was massaging her calves.

'Aita,' said the girl, addressing her grandmother. 'Is your leg aching?' Panting, the distressed girl, Monimala asked.

'These pains will go with me only when I leave this world. Why are you worrying?' Moni's grandmother's leg was swelling up. She would have felt better if she could walk around a bit. If she had been home, by now there would have been a warm poultice of heated salt tied up in a cloth bundle. A couple of the old woman's groans mingled with Moni's gasps and whimpers.

'How did your leg get twisted, Ai?' asked the Ghatoi, addressing the old woman as Mother.

Moni's grandmother took a deep breath. Her long sigh held the story of how the prefix 'Lengeri' came to this young and beautiful married girl. Today, as she took her half-dead granddaughter in the darkness of midnight across the Brahmaputra, her heart was breaking. Only the person who carried its weight tied up to her body knew what it was to bear the burden of the word 'Lengeri' before her name. Today, Moni's grandmother was tired of carrying that burden around. The words came tumbling out of the old woman's mouth, as though an embankment on the river had burst, and drenched the people in the boat as they sat there shrouded in fear and anxiety.

This happened many years ago. Rongdoi was an old village near Jorhat. It was just beyond the Nimati Ghat, a prosperous, progressive village. The roads were good, the fields yielded abundant crops. It was progressive in its educational facilities, too. Within the deep green environment of this village, not just people, but even animals lived peacefully.

In the traditional lullaby, a stork had been chased by a mad dog. But now, even the stork from the lullaby who was chased by a mad dog as she tried to enter a home was also pecking peacefully at worms and grains in the courtyard before the barns of the villagers. The village of Rongdoi was full of joy, of colour . . . *rong*. Indeed, what was it if not Rongdoi?

Moni's grandmother, Kiron was a cheery, laughing girl from Rongdoi. This serious and grave name was her formal appellation, Kiron. It was her other name, Hanhisompa, that suited her. The laughing frangipani. Kiron's grandfather had bestowed this name on this girl, who laughed constantly.

This Hanhisompa's marriage was arranged with her grandfather's friend's son. In her grandmother's words, the boy was just like the flower of the mustard plant. Her parents went to visit his home. On their return, they couldn't stop talking about their fields of lentils, mustard, their barns, their many sacks of potatoes, the pitchers full of molasses, borali catfish and elephant apple and the sweet bao rice. Even with all this abundance, the family was hesitant. How could they send their daughter to a far-off place across the mighty Brahmaptura? It could only be accessed by boat. And who knew what hardship this girl would face in this place which was frequently flooded and awash with water? And then there was erosion. There was no saying when a house would collapse, when fields and cultivated land would be completely washed away, leaving no trace behind. How could they send Hanhisompa to live in that kind of place after her marriage. But the boy, the one who looked as radiant as the mustard flower, won them all over. Even Hanhisompa. Her grandfather, getting an inkling of Hanhisompa's feelings, quickly began preparations for the wedding.

It was that same Hanhisompa who had morphed into Lengeri Aita, the Lame Grandmother, who was crossing the river at midnight in the Ghatoi's boat with her fallen granddaughter, groaning in pain. She was now telling them the story of her own lame foot.

The laughing Hanhisompa of Rongdoi, as tender as the frangipani flowers, became the mother to a beautiful girl. But her laughter went away, dropped like dew on the leaves of the frangipani. After just a month, the baby contracted a high fever. The local doctor advised them to take the baby to the big hospital across the river. This otherwise happy girl's tears that day were like the rain that fell on the bosom of the river. Just as the shore came into view, the baby grew stiff in her mother's lap. Crying and weeping wildly, the mother had jumped into the river. Who knew what happened then. The bones of her foot were broken in three places. Ultimately, the passengers of the ferry she had been travelling on brought her up. She survived but was maimed for life. Perhaps she had fallen on some undergrowth below the water.

That beautiful, firm body was mangled and did not recover. Rongdoi's laughing Hanhisompa became Lengeri Aita. Dragging her crippled foot through three-quarters of her life, here she was, spooning a bit of milk with great love into her granddaughter's mouth.

'Aita, throw me into the river also. Don't' bring me up.'

'Keep quiet. Don't talk of such inauspicious matters like this, in the middle of the night, on the deep waters of Baba Borhomputtor.'

'I've seen him several times in my dreams,' said the girl in between her moans. Her cheeks were wet with tears.

'What was he like when you saw him, Ai?' asked the old lady, addressing her affectionately as Mother.

'He always drags himself around the yard. He wears a peacock feather on his head.' She seemed to be whispering in a dream. Her grandmother could only hear her when she bent her own head to the girl's mouth.

'Don't you worry, Ai. The child in your womb is a saint. Be strong.'

A streak of lightning branched through the skies. In the waters, another creeper of lightning reflected. It suddenly startled the people on the boat with its brightness, and then merged into the silent darkness of the night. The entire surroundings resounded with the growl of thunder. Her anguished groans were dimmed by it. Spreading her legs constantly for such a long time was becoming unendurable for her, but she bore it with fortitude. The pains were wracking through her in unbearable spasms. She was wavering in and out of consciousness, everything was grey.

Like the column of water that had risen from within the river between light and shadow, an image came constantly. A plump child, playing in the dust and earth of the yard. On his head was a peacock feather. On his waist was a girdle—the silver girdle that Moni's grandfather had given her was lying in a corner of a box. A soft tinkling sound came repeatedly to her ears.

For a while, everybody was silent on the boat. The Ghatoi's helper, as was his habit, began to hum a melody. He could not stay without laughing, smiling, talking, singing. How could one keep one's mouth shut. Certainly, he could not, even if the whole world sank into the water. The Ghatoi said to him, 'Sing it out loud.'

To the others, he said, 'He has a very melodious voice. He's learnt the river songs from his grandfather.'

The face of the boy called Numol Noroh glowed with shyness and a little bit of pride. He loved to sing these songs, whether in the mustard fields, or the banks of the river, or while sitting in the paddy field. He was happiest when sitting on a boat in the middle of the river. He glanced sideways at the groaning girl who had a baby between her thighs. A mother's love came alive through his voice.

> *The little one's cries*
> *Are like a pipe of straw.*
> *Listening, I forget myself*
> *Oh my little one,*
> *I'll weave a fine sador*
> *To carry you around near my heart.*

'Sing another one!' The melodies that danced around fields of mustard, along the shores of the river, through the paddy fields echoed in Lengeri Buri's heart, too: 'Sing a song, do, Little Mother here will like it.' With infinite compassion, the old woman asked her granddaughter who was trying to hold back her anguished groans, 'What do you say, Ai?'

She tried, feebly, to smile. The little smile settled on her face like a cry.

> *My precious little one,*
> *Hush your cries,*
> *The kopou bird has not yet flown,*
> *Cry only when it flies.*

It seemed that at the sound of Numol's melodious voice, the baby that had got stuck upside down between the mother's legs was now freed and began to play.

> *Hush your cries,*
> *At the bottom of the huge silk cotton tree*
> *A huge python sits,*
> *Looking this way and that.*

Numol paused. The soft melodies of the riverside seemed to be choking his voice.

'The river washed away Numol's home five times. They rebuilt their home five times. This time, they will build their house right near the road . . . it's at quite a height.' In the boatman's voice was a world full of sorrow.

The Ghatoi's voice hit him hard. Since his birth, he had seen that a house had barely been built, a home just established before the river washed it away. In front of his eyes, the river gathered to itself their homes, fields, ponds and pools. There would be commotion, a huge uproar, but the land would fall into the river in huge chunks. The dreams of the people and their deep-seated desires would be washed away. From Numol's throat came the echo of an uproar, like the strong river currents that washed everything away when the embankments crashed down.

> *The cormorant calls,*
> *Ko Lo Pi*
> *Ko Lo Pi.*
> *Piteously, it calls,*
> *Ko Lo Pi,*
> *Ko Lo Pi*
> *O Great Spirit,*
> *You've raised your head*
> *You have covered*
> *The very road that we*
> *Who live on this land, travel,*
> *Ko Lo Pi*
> *Ko Lo Pi*

At that point, a cormorant really did call out, 'Did it cry Ko Lo Pi, Ko Lo Pi?' The moon hid behind the clouds. The rain had not abated yet; it was still drizzling. It was very cold. This unseasonal cold was as frightening as the Great

Spirit of the river. The cold entered the body just like the water that smashed into the earth. It would cause fever and colds and weaken the people. Numol's voice trembled on the waves as they moved on.

In a loud voice, the husband of the girl, who lay groaning, almost shouted, 'The herd of wild elephants that were once domesticated completely destroyed the sugarcane fields.' Had the call of the cormorant frightened the boy? The song describing how the River God snatched away the very path on which Numol walked could make even a strong man's heart quake. Why did he bring up the topic of those wild elephants that were once domesticated out of nowhere in the middle of the night? The Ghatoi, Numol, the girl's mother, grandmother, husband fell into the herd of wild elephants as though they were spiraling down into a whirlpool.

Lengeri Burhi was warming the medicinal oil by putting some drops of it on Moni's palms and rubbing them together. She applied it to the hands and soles of her granddaughter. The girl's mother was giving her some milk to sip, little by little. Her groans and cries had dried her throat, and she drank the milk without protest. Her husband fixed her clothes and using that as an excuse, stroked her face and head. He imagined and dreamed of so many things. Her pain was gradually becoming more intense. Would she not, then, set eyes on the divine child who, with a peacock feather in his hair, would jump into her lap? Would her husband's dreams come to naught? Into her fevered consciousness, thumped the memories of his much-loved sugarcane field. The money from that crop was supposed to be kept aside separately. She had seen how he had returned from surveying the sugarcane field destroyed by elephants and had remained sitting dejectedly by himself. Even when the broad swathe of land on which he had cultivated turmeric had been flooded, and the crop had subsequently rotted, he had not been this sad.

Actually, all of this was probably a sign, an omen, that the divine child, who was happily playing in her dusty courtyard, would no longer come to their home. Actually, she had sinned. She had said that this holy land was cursed, a place of exile. She had thrashed her hands and feet around, saying she wouldn't stay in this place. She had not agreed to this marriage happily. And now it had come to roost. Along with the being within her body, who had put out a foot to enter the world, she too would rot in the Ghatoi's boat. She would, she certainly would; nobody had the power to save her. A huge sense of hopelessness and sadness clotted her feeble body. It became a whirlpool, and began to pull her down, deep into the waters of the river. There was nothing else, just the cool darkness. Her groans were becoming softer. She fell into a light doze.

The other people in the boat were still being trampled on by the herd of wild elephants. There was a strict law that elephants could not be used for transporting logs cut from the forests. After this, the owners of the elephants in places such as Arunachal Pradesh, Dhemaji and Lakhimpur freed their elephants into the forests. They would fall foul of the law if they used them for work, and they could not sell them either. Was it so easy to keep elephants? The herds of domestic elephants who had been freed into the forest grew in number. At present, they were on the fertile island of Majuli. These cunning elephants, having lived in proximity to humans, understood the ways of people completely. They knew when the sugarcanes were most juicy, when the paddy ripened, how and where people laid traps for them, what instruments they used to make a huge commotion to frighten them and chase them away. People on the island were in great misery due to the depredations of these cunning elephants.

The conversation came to rest on the person who roamed around the jungle with a camera, in the ditches and water bodies, in the fields and rivers. He was making a film on the once domesticated, now wild elephants. Using some foreign-made liquor as bribe he would try to find out from people the whereabouts of the herds. Once, it seemed, he found some boys hanging upside down from the branch of a banyan tree on the broken embankment. The sight terrified him. How would he know the fearlessness in the hearts of these boys, raised amid the vastness of nature? Even in play, they were daring. It was no mean feat to hang upside down like that from a tree. It could be achieved only through lots of practice and exercise. How could this city-bred filmmaker have any inkling about these things? He had smeared his body with mosquito repellent, and wearing clothes that smelled strongly of his body odour—unwashed, smelly clothes—had moved around in the jungle. People laughed heartily when they heard about his fear.

Monimala's brother-in-law had worked with him for a few days. He could not have a bath before going to the jungle. It was necessary for him to wear his sweaty, dirty clothes. Otherwise, how could he mingle with the smells of the forest? The once domesticated, now wild animals vanished as soon as they got a whiff of an unfamiliar odour. He did get some money, but he could not tolerate these restrictions. After this, he made a house on stilts with a platform and began to run it as a resort. Several kinds of people came to stay in his platform house on stilts, his Sang Ghor. Just like Numol whose voice was full of songs, he too, was a storehouse of stories. Both storyteller and listeners would be engrossed in his tales. Indeed, there were so many different kinds of people on this earth!

The young man felt a deep attachment to his beautiful birthplace. These birds, fields of mustard, the fragrance of incense, the sound of the cymbals and drums, the mystery of the masks, the beautiful Raax festival during the full moon in November . . . which other place had these? No wonder so many people came here from all corners of the world. There was much to see, much to learn, much to love.

During this midnight ride across the mist-covered river, the young man felt great love for his land. He had never felt this way before. All this time, he had been planning to move across the river to the mainland as soon as he collected some money. He would not have to be at the mercy of the river all the time. But today he decided that he would remain in this place, among the paddy and mustard fields. He would not shift anywhere else.

Softly, he called out to his elder brother. 'Kokaideu,' he said, using the respectful term for elder brother, 'I shall name the resort after my new nephew or niece.'

'I shall build another platform house on stilts. It will have the same name. The land under the tamarind tree is just lying there. I shall enlarge the pond and make arrangements for boating. I shall serve the guests meals made from the milk of cows from our own shed, fish from our pond, vegetables and greens from our own yard. I shall send my nephew abroad to study management in tourism. What do you think of it, Nabou?' he turned to his sister-in-law and asked as she lay in a fitful doze.

At the sound of her brother-in-law's voice, she slowly arose from the sugarcane field, which the once-domesticated wild elephants had destroyed. This boy, who would always say that he would leave this place, this land at the first opportunity, was now speaking of new dreams. He was even thinking of the child in her womb. She who had been constantly saying she would not eat or drink what her grandmother was giving her, now said softly, 'Give me a bit of that roasted ground rice, I'm losing my strength.' She asked her mother, 'Will I be able to do this?' Her voice was indeed very weak.

The grandmother placed her hand on Moni's stomach. 'Be strong, Ai. The little divine boy inside you is fine.'

The elder brother looked at his younger sibling as though he was a stranger. 'What, will you keep the party of cyclists in your new place? Or won't you?'

'What are you two brothers talking about among yourselves? Tell us, let us hear it.' In the old woman's voice was a suppressed joy. The living being inside, whom they had given up for dead, was moving inside the mother's womb. The grandmother pledged a flower made of silver to the Xattra. She had a couple of silver coins among the things she had brought with her after her marriage. A magnificent flower could be created out of one of those silver coins.

'How much longer, Ghatoi?' There was anxiety in her mother's voice.

'We'll be reaching the ghat at sunrise. The weather is improving. The wind has come down, the rain too has lessened.' The Ghatoi's baritone voice was reassuring. It was as though he would make sure everything would be fine, just as he would make sure that the boat would go in the right direction. The voice brought some light, even if briefly, to the gloominess that had engulfed the minds of the others.

'Aita, I had asked if he would keep the white mems who come cycling in his resort.'

'Did any incident happen between him and white mems?' There was curiosity in the old woman's voice.

'Yes, there was, Aita. But it's not what you're thinking.'

A bamboo cylinder full of stories that were bottled in her brother-in-law's throat came rushing out. What were they if not fairy tales? These stories were gathered from the guests who came from all corners of the globe for a few days. How could one say they were not stories?

The white lady cyclist had come from distant Germany. She had packed with her a collapsible cycle that could be folded and put into a bag. As soon as she set foot on Majuli, she fitted the cycle together. It was as though it was not a cycle, but a pair of wings. She went all around the place, taking photographs.

One day, as she roamed around the island, the cycle got stuck in the mud and broke. It broke so badly that it could not be put together again. The white mem, stuck in the mud, began to cry loudly.

Time passed. It was almost midnight. In the meantime, Komol Barua, the owner of the resort she was staying in, was searching all around the island on his motorbike. The white woman was young. If anything happened to her, he would surely be having his meals in jail in the future. A herder of buffaloes from the Xattra's cow pen said that a white woman was lying in the mud and crying. Komol speeded up on his bike. It was midnight. He brought back the white woman, now covered in mud, on the back of the bike, and reached the resort at one at night. As he was putting the white woman on the ferry to the mainland the next day, he swore that he would never again take white people, who come as guests, on bicycles. All the people at home, and others too, had been very anxious that night. His father had paced round the front yard, saying, 'There's no need to make money by taking on guests from another country.' Let him, Komol, catch hold of a plough, there would be golden returns.

It wasn't just the story about the white woman who got lost. The one about the wealthy old white sahab was quite a story, too. This rich man who had crossed the age of eighty arrived at Komol's resort along with helpers and servants. A guest had posted on social media about the resort in Majuli. He was not just any old sahab, but a demon of a sahib. As soon as he arrived, he cut off all contact with the outside world and went off to sleep. He slept on and on. The sahib showed no signs of waking up. He was dying; he would die in Komol's house, at his resort on stilts. Monimala was, at that time, a very new bride who had just come into the house. She, too, was petrified. The white sahab would wake up every four to five hours and drink from bottles he had brought along, and with it, he ate something. Komol and a few of his friends began to keep a vigil on this sahab who slept, dead to the world, for long periods of time. After sleeping for a full three days and three nights, the sahab arose. It seemed he had not slept well for a very long time. All around were the calls of the birds, the cool breeze, the tranquility, the night sky full of stars that was visible through the door that was always left open. There were the sounds of the *oinitom* song of the Mising community, and the flute. The rhythms of the khol drums that the boy in the next room played at times, the aroma of incense and the oil lamp that was lit at dawn on the altar below the sacred tuloxi plant soothed him. There was the cooing of the pair of turtle doves, the *kopou*, from the window near his head, and also the sound of the flock of water birds near the bamboo stand.

Every now and again, the aroma of the sap from the paddy in the fields in front of the house on stilts would waft in. The sahab, who had throughout his life worked extremely hard, took to all this like a fish to water. And then, he descended into Kumbhokorno-like sleep, the brother of Ravan, who slept for six months of the year. When he left, the sahab gave Komol a hefty tip, enough to gladden his heart. It was on the strength of that money that he could now plan to build another house on stilts, a resort, in the name of the nephew or niece who would be arriving soon.

That millionaire couple from America who had wanted to buy up the whole of the island of Majuli, the young women from France who had wanted to learn the art of mask-making, those students from London who had come to give aid to the flood-affected people living on the island, those two stunningly beautiful actresses from Russia who had come to dance at the Raax festival . . . everybody on the boat listened avidly to the stories that came out from Komol's storehouse of memories.

Monimala's eyes were closed, but she was muttering inaudibly. Her mother and grandmother, who had been stroking her body and head, looked at each other. Moni's body seemed to be on fire. Her grandmother soaked a thin cotton towel, a gamosa, with water, squeezed it out, and applied it as a poultice on her head. Her forehead was hot, her feet were as cold as stones. These were not good signs. Even with the cold wind coming in from the river, the grandmother began to sweat. Moni's mother-in-law too had passed over in the same way on the ferry. Her forehead too had been hot with fever, her feet had been stone cold. Moni's grandmother had been on the same ferry going to the mainland. She had been going for her brother's son's first rice ceremony to Rongdoi. Her mind at that time had been full of joyous colours, she had been able to leave behind her domestic responsibilities after a long time. She wished to stay for a few days if possible. Moni's mother-in-law had been lying in one corner of the ferry. At that time, Moni's would-be husband had been studying in a college in Jorhat. It was he who had insisted that his mother should be seen by a doctor in the city. He had rented a car and was waiting on the other shore. Even though, at that time, they had not been close, Moni's grandmother knew the people of that house. In her delirium, the fevered woman had babbled and raved. Several times, her teeth had clenched together. Her brow had been fiery, her legs were icy till her knees.

Moni's grandmother shivered. Hadn't she said angrily with her own cursed mouth as they had come onto the boat that Moni would meet the same fate as her mother-in-law? The old woman recollected her grandson-in-law's sad face and tearful eyes. Superimposed on that came the memory of this boy's face, the face of her grandson-in-law, who at that time had just stepped out of boyhood, rolling on the sands and howling in anguish. Cursing herself, Moni's grandmother looked at her grandson-in-law. The sad-faced boy was wiping his eyes with the palms of his hands. Would he lose his wife on the river, just as he had lost his mother? Had destiny really written such a tragic fate for this sad-faced boy? Moni's feet were slowly beginning to get colder; the cooling poultice was drying up very fast and it had to be dampened again. Tears flowed from both the mother's and grandmother's eyes now.

'Ghatoi, how long now? Shall we reach at all?' Moni's grandmother's panicky voice alarmed everybody on the boat. What had happened to this stout-hearted woman? Or had Moni taken a turn for the worse?

Ghatoi did not reply. He was looking towards the east. It was completely dark. Even if there was a ray of light somewhere it was indistinguishable for them on the boat. Moni's brother-in-law Komol looked at his watch. It was three-thirty. A gust of wind came roaring down from the north. The boat began to rock. In the light of the dying moon, they saw a whirlpool. Spinning around furiously, it moved away. Komol shouted, 'How much more misery is there in store for us? The world has progressed so much, but for us getting a bridge to the mainland is a matter of life and death.' The boy cracked his knuckles.

'It's we women who have to bear the burden of the world's troubles. There is no bridge, what does it matter to them? There are so many arrangements for staying for them, on this bank or that. Every arrangement is at hand for them. It's we who suffer. The government wanted to build the bridge, but what possessed the irreligious people to say that they did not want it? Somewhere, someone's milch cow would dry up, someone's power would run out. And the rest of us can just be thrown into the Borhomputtor and left to drown . . .'

'All right, that's enough, keep quiet.' Her mother-in-law, Moni's grandmother, was aware of Moni's mother's nature very well. The quiet woman would hardly speak, but if she felt deeply about something, she would rant till her mouth frothed. Those who listened felt their ears grow hot.

'What's wrong in what I have said. Why should I keep quiet? To speak out is wrong, just tolerating it is good.'

'Ai, my dear, there is a time and place for everything. This is the time to pray to the Almighty, not for anger and resentment. Be strong, be patient.'

'What's the point of praying to the Almighty? You say your God destroys the wicked, supports the virtuous. There was that God-like man, who could very well have lived luxuriously in a big city. He came here for the sake of our place. He gave up his life for this place. Why did they kill him and throw him into the waters of the Tuni River, among the thickly growing water hyacinths?'

'Ai, why are you scratching at those old, rotten sores?'

'I've kept these rotten sores close to my heart for a long time. I can't go on anymore.'

The agitated woman began to sob, 'I've fallen into a very deep ditch, there's no help for me.'

'Ma, why are you carrying on like this? Nothing will happen to me.'

As soon as she said this, Monimala vomited. A sour smell spread around.

'She'll feel a little better now. Keep quiet now and look after the girl. Change her sador.' The old grandmother was relieved that she could put her overwrought daughter-in-law to work. Monimala's mother and grandmother changed her clothes together gently so that she would not be hurt. They wiped her face with a wet gamosa and cleaned the vomit from her hair. Her feet were getting warmer, the temperature of her forehead too had lessened. While her clothes were being changed, she had screamed out once. It was a very sharp and loud scream.

'Prabhu, save this tiny life.' The boatman went to the prow of the boat and prayed. Who was he praying to? Probably to his Baba Borhomputtor. The Ghatoi stuffed a tamol paan into his mouth.

Monimala's eyes drooped. The little being inside her was really fighting. When Monimala fell into a doze, her mother and grandmother gave themselves up to the sleep that comes in the last part of night.

The Ghatoi spoke softly. Moni's husband and brother-in-law came and sat near him. The Ghatoi had suddenly remembered the person that Moni's mother had mentioned. How the body of this God-like man had lain in the water hyacinth near the bridge of the Tuni River. His head was hidden by the thick growth of water hyacinth. The boatman had seen that body with his own eyes. He had also worked with him earlier, labouring through the night. It wasn't just the Ghatoi. Many people, who had lost their land and homes to merciless erosion, and those who had been crushed by floods had come to this man, to help him in his work. Perhaps, who knew, some good would come of it. The sight of one's own home collapsing into the water felt like the tearing away of the flesh over

their hearts, the sight of their fields being washed away by
the river had disheartened them completely. Just leaving
everything behind and fleeing was not the solution. They
did not want to flee, they wanted to fight it, face to face.
They had all wanted to help the man as much as they could.
The Ghatoi, too, had become one of those who helped him
in his plan to stop the erosion. They had gone through thick
undergrowth. The bank of the river had been fashioned
into a slope. In that sloping bank trees and shrubs with
long roots, which would hold the soil together, had been
planted. The people who had come to help had always
seen these plants with long roots which would come to the
shores and germinate. The same thing was now being done
in a planned manner. Sand, mud and other deposits were
placed on the side of the bank that faced the river. This
bank was covered with a jute mesh. The public, the people
of the island had helped him by creating the slope of the
bank, and in planting the trees.

The Ghatoi's heart grew heavy as he remembered all
this.

Monimala's husband remembered the occasion when
the Danish Ambassador had visited their island. The
sahab had come and observed the work being done on the
embankment. He had spoken of monetary aid. That man
whose bullet-ridden body lay among the hyacinth plants
had tried very hard to make Majuli a World Heritage Site.
None of this happened. What happened instead was that
he was shot, and his body was left in the water among the
water hyacinth plants. These plants were not there at that

spot under the bridge across the Tuni River. Even though that patch was surrounded by a thick growth of those plants, that area was clear. Just near that open patch lay his corpse, with his head and body, lying face-down in the thick growth of hyacinth. That water would turn red in the glow of the sunset, like a tank of blood. In that pond of blood, many dreams circled around like fish. They would turn round and round, they would disappear . . . once more they would go around, and then disappear. On the lonely bridge across the Tuni River, at the time when the water turned to blood, people had seemingly heard a dying scream. It was impossible for the people living on Majuli to ever forget this scream. Stories about this man who lay face down in the water, surrounded by thick growths of hyacinths, would continue to be told. They would keep hearing that shout, that scream of death.

And now, today, in the Ghatoi's boat as they went across the river with the pregnant girl hovering between life and death, the past dug deep holes in their hearts. In the quietude of the last phase of night there was only the sound of the boat being paddled, intercepted by intermittent groans. The horrific memories of the past created an unbroken continuity with the present. It all came rushing back and proved impossible to uproot from their memories.

Even today, mothers would hush their wailing and fussing children, 'Wait, the tongue slasher is coming for you.' It seemed that at one time, a demon had roamed around cutting off peoples' tongues. He went around with a weapon in his hand. He did slash off peoples' tongues it seemed. That person who had been gunned down as though he had been an animal in the forest, those youths who openly roamed around carrying weapons, that lot who donned the identities of police and military men when they left the island . . . the inhabitants of the island had been terror struck. All their tongues crumpled and fell in fear. The melodies of the devotional *borgeets* were silent, the reverberations of the khol drums and cymbals were not heard, the strains of the oinitom songs were not carried around in the air anymore. There was only the sound of the groans coming from the mouths with the tongues cut off.

The Ghatoi said with folded hands, 'Prabhu,' entreating his God, 'let those days never return.'

'No, those days will not return,' said Komol. 'They will not, be assured, I'm just about managing to survive by taking on guests from outside. If those days return, I shall have to jump into the river.' There was fear and terror in Komol's voice.

'That's all in the past. Just do your own work. Don't just hold the memory of those awful days so close to your heart. Storms come and go. Do they stay forever?' Moni's husband was afraid. His only brother had been by his side throughout. If he too went off like his friends to Kerala, Gujarat . . .

'Yes, your elder brother is right. Throughout the night there were whirlpools on the river, there were doka, we were in a whirlpool. Just look now.' The Ghatoi pointed a finger at the river, which was now visible in the pale light of early dawn. Still, calm. It was flowing like a soft silk sador. A few boats were also visible.

Moni's grandmother who had fallen into a light doze had a dream. It had a large flowering field of bright yellow mustard. A small child was running around in it, chasing butterflies. The chubby little boy had a peacock feather tucked into his hair. The feather was waving in the breeze like a butterfly's wing. The old woman grabbed hold of the child, but the water came rushing in and drowned the field of mustard. In the area that had been covered by mustard, there were now only paddy fields, submerged in water.

It was the month of Kati—in October. The woman went to the field to place a saki, an earthen oil lamp for Kati Bihu, the occasion between the two harvests when food was scarce in the villages, to pray for a bountiful harvest. But instead of placing the saki, she stood transfixed. The whole field was submerged in water, from one side to the other. She made a raft from the outer sheath of the stem of the banana plant, and placing the saki on it, she set it afloat on the waterlogged field. The flame of the saki trembled on the raft. Would the flame of the saki die out? She wished to go and retrieve the saki on the bamboo stem raft. She gathered up her mekhela in order to bring back the raft that had floated away. She wanted to wade into the water but found that she could not. Her feet had got stuck where she was. She couldn't lift them. The harder she tried, the more firmly they stuck.

Moni's grandmother moaned in her sleep.

'Aita, what's the matter?'

'Ma, are you feeling unwell?'

'Are you dizzy?'

These questions came all together, and the grandmother woke with a start.

'Aita, did your grandchild fall off from your lap?' Her grandmother's eyes grew moist at this question asked by Moni's husband. Teardrops fell from the old woman's eyes.

'Ai, if you've had a bad dream, throw an offering into the water.' The Ghatoi offered a coin to Moni's grandmother.

'Good or bad, I don't know. I had given a saki in the field submerged by water for Kati Bihu. I had floated it on a raft made from the sheath of the stem of the banana plant. I wanted to go and bring it back in case the flame was extinguished. My feet got stuck in the growth of hyacinth.'

Seeing this woman who had been consoling everybody else so far in this agitated state, everybody grew silent.

The Ghatoi replied, 'Ai, this last Kati Bihu, I too lit the saki and placed it on the banana sheath raft. Not in a dream, but in reality. In broad daylight. The fields were full of water, even though it was the season for scattering the seeds of spinach and mustard greens. Yes indeed. There was so much water everywhere. It was poisonous, toxic. Just touching the water made you break out in rashes, as though a caterpillar had crawled over you. The water was full of rubbish and garbage.'

Komol added, 'They blocked up twenty-one streams and rivulets in the name of the embankment. How can the water move out? It's like binding up the veins in a human body.' Anger came into his voice. 'The job of building embankments is a milch cow for them.'

'Earlier, the water used to spread out over the fields, and exit.' Moni's husband, too, had seen that water earlier. 'That used to be a blessing for everybody around, in those days.'

'The silt that the water would leave behind on the land, the fields of mustard . . .' Ghatoi seemed to be weeping, rather than speaking. 'The potter's wheel was there, the occupation from my father and grandfather's days was there. The boat was there . . . our stomachs were full.' The Ghatoi seemed to shrink like putrid paddy in the stagnant waters. He bowed his head.

'I heard that the *bundh* across the Tuni River will soon be sliced open, and the waters will be freed.'

The woman who had not spoken at all now said softly, 'Let Prabhu bless everybody.'

The Ghatoi began to sing a religious song:

Baghbor Abhoy Soroney
Xotye xotye poxilu xoroney?'

Moni's grandmother joined in:

Ram Raghupoti Raghu Nondon,
Tomar soroney Loilu Xoron.'

They prayed to the deity and asked for shelter at His feet.

'Aita, Aita, the khol drums of Lokkhi Puja are being played!' Moni's voice now had a strange strength, her words came out clearly. She was delirious. Like a twisted leaf floating around on the river, she was going this way . . . she was going that way. Perhaps she would keep moving. Perhaps she would drown. In her feverish condition, wracked by pain, she was simply floating. She had lost track of time. She was helpless, she had no control over anything, she was just drifting. It was now the end of the winter month of Magh. And she was hearing the khol drums of Lokkhi Puja, which was always celebrated in autumn.

'Yes, Ai,' said Moni's grandmother, addressing her with affection. 'We can hear the drums. Say a prayer.' Tears flowed from her eyes in a steady stream.

Moni really did join her hands together in prayer. Seeing this, her mother grew even more agitated.

'What's happened, what's happened to my girl? We'll have to sacrifice her to the river.' As the burning words left her mouth, she realized what she was saying. It was considered an ill omen to say such things, and she bit her tongue. Her mouth filled up with blood.

Moni had heard the khol drums. For the people of Majuli, it was a blessed sound like that of sacred conch shell being blown after prayers. The sound of the khol at Lokkhi Puja meant that the festival of Raax was approaching. The water would have receded, and the fields would be abundant with maah lentils and mustard crops. Birds would come down in large flocks, visitors would come from all over the world. The sound of the khol played during Lokkhi Puja was a signal for the people to take out the knives and large, heavy-bladed *daas* that had been set aside for some time and sharpen them again. They began to repair and put up the broken bamboo fences and gates once more. There was so much work to be done in this season. The masks would be needed for Raax. It was not an easy thing at all to make these lifelike masks. And it was not just crafting the masks. The homes that had been damaged by the flood waters would need to be repaired again. It was only those people who had to constantly rebuild their shattered homes who knew the huge amount of labour that went into this task. It was like climbing a steep mountain time after time. Surmounting many hurdles, people would be visiting their island from all over the world. The place would be crowded with visitors duing the Raax festival. They had to be fed; they had to be housed. Everyone who came here wished to take back something, as well—some souvenir or memento. They would have to ready the textiles, as bright as the fields of mustard flowers. At this time, people hired out SUVs, they earned money. The areas where the Raax would be staged would need to be readied. There were no fewer than forty or fifty stages, where the Raax festivities, the songs and dances, the masked presentations would be showcased. Even if just a couple of visitors arrived, the people of the island would have to prepare everything. But, a large number of visitors arrived at this time, crowding the fields, the riverbanks, the edge of the waterbodies, massing on the island. There would be birds all around, and they would fill people's hearts with colour. Forgetting all their sorrows and disappointments, the people would plunge into the rhythms of the khol drums.

Baba Borhomputtor, too, changed his character, his appearance. The water became with child. In time, it swelled to become heavily pregnant, about to give birth. It became so vast that the opposite shore was not visible. The river would be constantly agitated by whirlpools and rising columns of water. And then it would fall quiet again as it calmed down. It would become as slender as a young girl. The khol drums of Lokkhi Puja would be played. The people would become like migratory birds. Even those who had put down roots in a particular place were constantly migrating, moving—from sadness to happiness, from happiness to sadness. Alongside these migrations, like the seeds of mustard, young shoots of stories too grew and flourished in an endless sequence.

Moni had a smile on her face. Under her lids, the pupils of her eyes were moving rapidly around. Her dream had not yet ended. At times, she would move her legs. Had the rhythms of the *gopi* dance of the Raax festival come and settled on her legs? After all she had heard the beat of the khol played during Lokkhi Puja. How could the rhythms of the gopi dance leave her blood?

'My Ai had danced as Radha with Krishna,' said Moni's grandmother. As she gazed at her semi-conscious granddaughter, she was remembering her dance when she had been a young girl.

'People who saw her blessed her . . .' Moni's mother bit the edge of her sador now.

There, in the distance, could be seen lines of trees and plants. The skies were clearing up. The river now had a soft blue hue. Several boats were darting around the water, looking like toy vessels. The Ghatoi started to sing a devotional borgeet in his baritone voice.

Rojoni Bidur Dix Dhowoli Boron . . .

The others hummed along with the boatman.

The boat would dock in the ghat in a little while. Everything around was getting clearer. The boats that were tied up on the shore, the reeds that were growing in the sand, the small teashops were visible, so were the large ferry, the *bhotbhotis*, the boats with outboard motors. The landing stage on which the Ghatoi was going towards was becoming clearer. The ghat, the landing stage, was a steep shore. It was muddy, and its soil was as soft as a field's after it had been ploughed and harrowed. The ghat was as slippery as a slug, and the rain had made it even more slushy and soft. The girl, the one-legged heron, would have to climb up that way.

Komol made a call on his cellphone. The ambulance had reached Nimatighat. Lengeri Aita's relatives from Rongdoi had arrived and were waiting.

'Get up, get up, Ai, we've reached the other shore.'

Monimala opened her eyes. Her mind was still filled with the drumbeats of the khol that she had heard in her dream.

'Look, look there, everybody is waiting.' Seeing her own people from the Rongdoi village, the Hanhisompa within Moni's grandmother's mind came to life again. Sprinkles of colour had dropped into her mind. Her heart grew restless at the memory of her deceased parents.

The boat was about to reach the shore. Two young men were laying logs on the soil. Moni's grandmother realized that they were her brother's twin sons. They were now strong, fit youths. How did they collect all this material this early in the morning? They were young men; they knew how to organize things.

Monimala placed a hand on her stomach and wailed out loud. The living being inside her belly was moving around. Who knew where this half dead woman got the strength from. She became a one-legged stork as she stood up, and supporting herself by placing her hands on the shoulders of her husband and brother-in-law, came down from the boat. The Ghatoi and Numol kept the boat absolutely steady. After this, she somehow went on the wooden logs that had been laid out and hobbled up the steep, slippery bank, hanging on to someone's arms at times, and putting her full weight on another's shoulder. Through Monimala's ripped floral mekhela, a few people noticed the tiny foot sticking out. The nurse who had gone with the ambulance came forward and took charge of Monimala. Her husband, brother-in-law and mother came in the ambulance with her. Moni's grandmother got ready to go along too.

'Bai, come up here.' At the sound of her brother's voice, Moni's mother paused. With his grey hair and beard, the boy had grown into a middle-aged man.

Moni's grandmother looked at her own people. They had come in two vehicles. Her mind was unsettled. Once more, the sun was about to set at the edge of the clouds. Without her being aware of it, time had passed.

'Jethai, come on then,' one of the twins, she couldn't make out if it was the elder or the younger, called out to her, addressing her as his Father's Elder Sister. Moni's grandmother had not yet got up into the vehicle. She kept looking after the white ambulance which had departed noisily. The vehicle vanished in a trice as it drove away at great speed. Moni's grandmother was still waiting.

Now her sister came out from the other car. She too, had gained weight, her midriff was large, her hair had thinned. She looked old. No, she was old. An old woman now.

'Dangor bai,' she said, addressing Moni's grandmother as Elder Sister, 'don't worry. Your granddaughter has reached the hospital.'

'Come, Jethai.' One of the twins supported her, took her to the vehicle and sat her down on the seat.

'You haven't come home for a long time, bai. The boys have remodeled the house, it's changed quite a bit.' Lengeri Aita's brother's voice was heavy with emotion.

'Does the crane come to the house anymore?' Moni's grandmother remembered the crane that roamed beneath the trees in their backyard. Hanhisompa would keep a couple of fish separately for the crane by the side of the tap, without fail every day.

'There are many cranes now. They come to the backyard all the time.'

'They must be the babies of your crane.'

'Bai, your granddaughter has been taken into the Operating Room.'

Stretching out her aching legs, Moni's Lengeri Aita said very softly, 'Keep some fish for the cranes every day near the water tap.'

Seeing their lame Jethai with tears streaming down her eyes, the youthful twins gestured to their father to ask what the matter with her was. Their father signalled to them to be silent. His eyes were damp as he remembered how young his sister had been when their father had married her off. His heart was filled with an odd mix of guilt and affection.

The Ghatoi and Numol bought some buns and tea from the shops near the riverbank. After eating them, they fell asleep on the boat itself. In the meantime, the first ferry of the day left the ghat. Several of the bhotbhotis were preparing to set out for the day. The ghat was now buzzing with people. After a while, Komol came and informed the Ghatoi that his sister-in-law had given birth to a boy.

As soon as he gave them this news, Komol went to meet the couple who had come from France. They were going to stay in Komol's Sang House for some days. This couple had visited the place before. With them were three more people. Jogen Kai, the trusted caretaker of the resort would take care of them. Komol would have returned today itself, but the twin boys had insisted that he stay. He would return by the first ferry the next day.

Meanwhile, the Ghatoi was preparing to leave. He counted the money given to him by Komol. It was quite a large sum. Numol, too, had received more than what he had expected. The Ghatoi opened the small bundle that Komol had given him. It was from Lengeri Aita, a small bundle tied up with a handkerchief.

Inside was a thick bangle, a silver bala embossed with vines and leaves. The ends were fashioned into two elephant heads with their trunks touching each other. The bala gleamed in the light of the rising sun. His granddaughter was growing up, she would soon reach the age of puberty. Before long, she would need to be married and sent off to another home. He would give this to her at her wedding. He carefully stowed it in the cloth bag that was tied to the tin roof of the boat.

The clear weather turned gloomy again. The fine drizzle turned everything misty and hazy. The Ghotoi and Numol set out on the boat again. As usual, the Ghatoi put a palmful of water on his head.

'Numol, the waters are with child, you know . . .' Ghatoi said, as though to himself. 'There's a lot of work to be done. The two boats have to be repaired. The posts of the Sangghor House on stilts have to be changed. A couple of CI sheets over the barn need to be changed. If possible, the yard will need some earth to be spread across it. The verandah around the house . . . the fencing near the kitchen . . . the cowshed . . .'

'Pita is planning to shift our home right below where the embankment starts,' said Numol, referring to his father. 'Many people from our village have already done this.' Once more, Numol touched the money that was tied up in a handkerchief. 'The women have already set up their looms underneath the platforms. Only Nanai, my mother, hasn't yet done it.'

The boat sailed speedily on the waters of the river. The rain had enfolded the surroundings like smoke all around. But the sounds of the woman's groans heard through the night seemed stuck to the boat, unwilling to leave the Ghatoi's ears.

'Numol, sing a song. Sing it in your Mising language.'

Numol seemed to have been waiting for just this. His mind was full of the tangles of his home, almost destroyed by the floods and erosion. Almost destroyed? How could anyone's mind be at peace with a shattered home that had to be relocated elsewhere?

Osi sikur
The stream in the river is a stream, too.
The stream from the eyes is a stream, too
Even if the stream of the river dries
The stream from the eyes never dries.

Numol's sweet voice, drenched with the resonance of youth, became a stream that floated on the vastness of the river whose other shore was not visible.

Scan QR code to access the
Penguin Random House India website